JOURNEY TO THE

CENTRE OF THE EARTH.

JULES VERNE.

Translated by
Laurent Paul Sueur.

Chapter 1.

On the 24th of May 1863 (it was a Sunday), my uncle, Professor Lidenbrock, came rushing back towards his little house, which was located at 19 Königstrasse, one of the oldest streets of Hamburg's historic centre.

Good old Marthe must have thought she was behind schedule since she was just beginning to prepare the dinner.

'Well', I said to myself, 'if my uncle is hungry, he is going to complain, for he is the most impatient of men.'

'Professor Lidenbrock is already here!', exclaimed in amazement good old Marthe as she half-opened the dining-room door.

'Yes, Marthe. But dinner can be uncooked, for it's no two o'clock yet. It has only just struck the half-hour on St Michael's.'

'Then, why has Professor Lidenbrock come back?'

'He may tell us.'

'Here he is: I'm off, Master Axel; you will make him listen to reason.' And good old Marthe went back into her culinary laboratory.

I remained alone. My slightly indecisive character did not allow me to make the most irascible professor listen to reason. Hence, I was about to go back to my little bedroom, at the top of the house, when the front door opened creaking. Big feet made the wooden staircase shiver; the master of the house came through the dining-room and rushed into his office.

On his hurried way through, he had thrown his nutcracker-headed cane in a corner, his broad-rimmed fur hat on the table, and shouted to his nephew: 'Axel, follow me!'

I hadn't had time to move before the professor shouted again, in a most impatient voice: 'Well, are you not here yet?'

I rushed into the office of this strict professor.

I do acknowledge John Lidenbrock was not a bad man. But unless he changes, which is very unlikely, he will remain an eccentric man until he dies.

He was a professor at the Johannaeum, and gave a course on mineralogy, during which he normally got angry, at least once or twice. He did not really care about student attendance, or whether they paid attention, or whether they were successful later; these details did not bother him. He lectured 'subjectively', a German expression used in philosophy, which means he used to teach himself, not students! He was a selfish scholar, a well of science whose handle groaned whenever someone wanted to draw something out of it: in a word, a miser.

In Germany, there are some professors like this.

Unfortunately, my uncle did not speak easily, if not in private, at least when he was in front of an audience. It was really problematic for an orator. Thus, during his demonstrations at the Johannaeum, he used to stop short; he would struggle with a complicated word, which did not want to come out of his mouth, one of these words which resist, inflate, and turn into a swearword: something unscientific, indeed! Then he would have fits of anger.

Unfortunately, in mineralogy there are many words, half-Greek, half-Latin, which are always difficult to pronounce: they would even scorch a poet's lips. I do not want to criticize this science, far from it, but when people must say rhombohedral crystallization, retinasphaltum, gehlenite, fasibitikite, lead molybdate, manganese tungstate, or detrital zircon, the most agile mouths are allowed to make speech errors.

Consequently, the townspeople knew about his pardonable disability, and took unfair advantage. They watched out for the difficult sections; he got furious; they laughed: which is inappropriate, even for Germans. And if there was always a healthy attendance at Lidenbrock's lectures, most people used to come in order to see the professor's terrible outbursts and laugh!

However, I claim that my uncle was an authentic scholar. Although he sometimes broke his samples by handling them too roughly, he combined the geologist's talent with the mineralogist's eye. With his mallet, his steel spike, his magnetic needle, his blowtorch, and his flask of nitric acid, he was highly gifted. From the fracture, appearance, resistance, melting-point, sound, smell, and taste of any given mineral, he could put it without hesitation into any one of the six hundred categories recognised by modern science.

Therefore, Lidenbrock's name was very much honoured in high schools and learned societies. Humphry Davy, Humboldt, Captains Franklin and Sabine meet him when they visited Hamburg. Becquerel, Ebelmen, Brewster, Dumas, Milne-Edwards, and Sainte-Claire-Deville used to consult him on the most thrilling questions in chemistry. This science owed him some important discoveries and, in 1853, he even published, in Leipzig, a *Treatise on Transcendental Crystallography*: a large format book with plates that did not cover its costs.

Moreover, my uncle was the curator of the mineralogical museum of Mr. Struve (the Ambassador of Russia), which was a valuable collection much esteemed throughout Europe.

Such was the character calling for me so impatiently. Imagine a tall, thin man, with a sound constitution and blond hair that made him look a good ten years younger than his fifty. His big eyes darted incessantly around behind thick glasses; his nose, long and thin, was like a sharpened blade; unkind people even claimed that it was magnetized, and picked up iron filings. Absolute slander: it only picked up snuff, but in large quantities to tell the truth.

If I add that my uncle took mathematical strides of exactly 97 cm, and that, while walking, he firmly clenched his fists (the sign of an harsh personality), then you will know him well enough not to wish to spend too much time in his company.

He lived in his little house on the Königstrasse, a half-wood, half-brick construction with a crenelated gable. It faced one of the winding canals that crisscross in the centre of the oldest part of Hamburg, a place the fire of 1842 did not destroy, fortunately.

It is true that the old house leaned a little and also showed its stomach to the passers-by. It wore its roof over one ear, like the cap of a Tugendbund student. The straightness of its lines was not great but, all things considered, it held up well, thanks to an old elm, vigorously embedded in the façade, which, each springtime, would push its flowering blossoms through the latticed windows.

For a German professor, my uncle was wealthy. The house was entirely his, both building and contents. The contents consisted of his god-daughter Gräuben, a seventeen-year-old girl from Vironia, Marthe and me. Since I was an orphan and his nephew, I served as his laboratory assistant during his experiments.

I must confess I loved geology; I had mineralogist's blood in my veins: I never felt bored in the company of my precious pebbles.

Actually, in spite of its owner's impatience, life could be sweet in this miniature house, on the Königstrasse: although he was quite rough, he did not love me any the less. But this man was unable to wait; I would even say he was abnormally impatient.

In April, he planted heads of mignonette or morning glory in the ceramic pots, in his living-room, and, each morning, he used to pull their leaves in order to make them grow faster.

With such an eccentric, the only thing to do was to obey. Hence, I hurried into his study.

Chapter 2.

This study was a real museum. All the mineral specimens that could be found here were labelled in the most perfect order, following the three great divisions (inflammable, metallic, lithoidal).

How well I knew them, these trinkets of mineralogical science! How many times, instead of hanging around with boys of my own age, I had enjoyed dusting these graphites, these anthracites, these coals, these lignites, and these peats. The bitumens, the resins, the organic salts which had to be preserved from the least speck of dust. The metals, from iron to gold, whose relative value vanished in front of the absolute equality of the scientific specimens. And all those stones, which would have been enough to rebuild the whole house on the Königstrasse, even with a beautiful extra room... for me!

But when I went into the study, I was not thinking about these wonders. My uncle formed the sole focus of my thoughts. He was buried in his large armchair covered with Utrecht velvet, holding a book in his hands and looking at it with the deepest admiration.

'What a book, what a book!' he said.

This exclamation reminded me that Professor Lidenbrock was also a book collector in his spare time. But a book had no value in his eyes unless it was unfindable or, at least, unreadable.

'Well', he said, 'Don't you see? It's a priceless treasure I discovered this morning while poking around in the shop of Hevelius, the Jew.'

'Magnificent,' I replied, with forced enthusiasm.

What was the point of making such a fuss about an old quarto book whose spine and covers seemed to be made out of coarse vellum, a yellowish book from which hung a faded bookmark?

However, the professor's exclamations of admiration didn't stop.

'Look', he said, addressing both the questions and the replies to himself, 'is it beautiful enough? Yes, it's great; and what a binding! Does the book open easily? Yes, it stays open at any page whatsoever. But does it close well? Yes, because the cover and leaves form a unified whole, without separating or gaping anywhere. And this spine, which does not have a single break after seven hundred years of existence. Bozérian, Closs, or Purgold would have been proud to have made it!'

While speaking, my uncle was alternately opening and closing the old book. The only thing I could do was ask him about its contents, although they didn't interest me at all.

'And what is the title of this marvelous volume?', I asked with too eager an enthusiasm to be genuine.

'This work', replied my uncle, getting excited, 'is the Heims-kringla by Snorri Sturluson, the famous twelfth-century Icelandic author. It is the chronicle of the Norwegian princes who ruled over Iceland.'

'Really', I exclaimed as well as I could, 'it's presumably a German translation?'

'Well', the professor replied animatedly, 'a translation: what would I do with a translation? It would be useless! This is the original work, in Icelandic, a beautiful language, both simple and rich, that allows the most diverse grammatical combinations, as well as numerous variations in the words.'

'Like German?', I slipped in, fortuitously.

'Yes', replied my uncle shrugging his shoulders, 'not to mention that Icelandic has three genders, like Greek, and declensions of proper nouns, like Latin.'

'Ah', I said, my indifference a little shaken, 'and are the characters in this book handsome?'

'Characters? Who is speaking of characters, unfortunate Axel! You did say "characters", didn't you? Oh, you are taking this for a printed book? You are so ignorant! This is a manuscript, and a runic manuscript.'

'Runic?'

'Yes. Are you now going to ask me to explain this word to you?'

'There is certainly no need,' I replied in the tone of a man wounded in his pride.

But my uncle continued all the more, and told me things, despite my opposition, that I did not want to know.

'Runes', he said, 'were handwritten characters formerly used in Iceland and, according to the tradition, were invented by Odin himself! But look, irreverent boy, admire these forms which sprang from a god's imagination.'

I swear that, having no other reply to give, I was going to curtsey, the sort of response that necessarily pleases gods and kings, because it has the advantage of never embarrassing them, when an incident happened to set the course of the conversation off on a different path. This was the appearance of a dirty parchment, which slid out of the book and fell to earth.

My uncle rushed to pick up this trinket with an eagerness easy to understand. An old document locked up in an old book since time immemorial could not fail to have a great value in his eyes.

'What is it?', he exclaimed.

At the same time, he carefully spread the parchment out on his desk. It was five inches long and three inches wide, with horizontal lines of strange characters written on it.

What follows is the exact facsimile. I want to show these strange characters because they lead Professor Lidenbrock and his nephew to undertake the strangest expedition the nineteenth century has ever known:

Illsllwlele llcleoieklalle mmeemm
ofkfsdofjh ejifoepjifoej gjieoeiojeo
kdjfseuioi rjereorjiejri ojrieojreei

The professor examined the series of characters for a few moments. Then he said, lifting up his glasses: 'they are runes; the forms are absolutely identical to those in Snorri Sturluson's manuscript. But what does it mean?'

As runes seemed to me to be an invention by scholars to mystify ordinary people, I wasn't displeased to see that my uncle didn't understand anything. I thought it was the case because his fingers were beginning to shake.

'And yet it is Old Icelandic!', he muttered through clenched teeth.

Professor Lidenbrock surely knew what he was talking about, for he was reputed to be a genuine polyglot: although he did not speak fluently the two thousand languages and four thousand dialects spoken on the surface of this planet, he knew quite a few.

In front of this problem, he was going to give in to all the impulsiveness of his character, and I could foresee a violent scene, when two o'clock sounded on the wall-clock over the mantelpiece.

Marthe immediately opened the study door and said: 'the soup is ready.'

'I don't care about the soup', shouted my uncle, 'and the person who made it, and those who will eat it.'

Marthe fled. I followed closely behind and, without knowing quite how, found myself sitting at my usual place in the dining-room.

I waited for a few moments. The professor didn't come. It was the first time, to my knowledge, that he was missing the ceremony of dinner. And what a dinner! Parsley soup, ham omelet with sorrel and nutmeg, loin of veal with stewed plums; and, for dessert, prawns in sugar; we even drank a good Moselle wine.

That was what an old bit of paper was going to cost my uncle. Well, as a devoted nephew, I considered it my duty to eat for both him and me; which I did, very conscientiously.

'It is the first time I see this,' said Marthe, 'Mr. Lidenbrock not at table.'

'It's unbelievable.'

'This does not augur well', said the maid, shaking her head.

In my opinion, it portended nothing at all, except for a terrible scene when my uncle found his dinner already eaten.

I was just eating the last prawn when a resounding voice called me from the delights of dessert. I was in the study in a single bound.

Chapter 3.

'It's quite obviously runic,' said the professor, knitting his brows, 'but there is a secret, and I am going to discover it. If not...'

A violent gesture completed his thought.

'Sit down here', he added, indicating the table with his fist, 'and write.'

In a moment I was ready.

'Now I'm going to dictate the letter in our alphabet corresponding to each of the Icelandic characters. We will see the result. But, by God, be careful not to make a mistake.'

The dictation began. I concentrated as hard as I could. Each letter was spelled out one after the other, to form the incomprehensible succession of words that follows:

Illsllwlele llcleñlklalle mmeemm
ofkfllofjh ejifoepjifoej gjieoe!!!eo
kdjfsouioi rjerççrjiejri ojrieojreei

When this work was finished, my uncle eagerly snatched up the sheet on which I had been writing, and examined it for a long time with great care.

'What does it mean?', he said quick as a flash.

I swear I couldn't have told him anything. Actually, he did not ask me and continued speaking to himself: 'this is what we call a cipher, in which the meaning is hidden in letters which have deliberately been mixed up, and which, if properly laid out, would form an intelligible sentence. When I think that there is perhaps here the explanation or indication of a great discovery!'

For my part, I thought there was absolutely nothing, but kept my opinions carefully to myself.

The professor then took the book and the parchment and compared them with each other.

'The two documents are not in the same hand', he said, 'the cipher is posterior to the book, for I can see an immediate and irrefutable proof: the first letter is a double *m* that would be sought in vain in Sturluson's book, since it was added to the Icelandic alphabet only in the fourteenth century. Consequently, at least two hundred years elapsed between the manuscript and the document.'

I must admit it was quite logical.

'I am therefore led to think', said my uncle, 'that one of the owners of the book must have written out these mysterious characters. But who the devil was this owner? Might he not have inserted his name at some point in the manuscript?'

My uncle lifted his glasses up, took a strong magnifying glass, and carefully worked his way over the first few pages of the book. On the back of the second one, the half-title page, he discovered a sort of stain, which to the naked eye looked like an ink blot. However, looking closer, it was possible to distinguish a few half-erased characters. My uncle realized that this was the interesting part, so he concentrated on the blemish and, with the help of his big magnifying glass, he ended up distinguishing the following symbols, which were runic characters he spelled out without hesitation:

Illsllwlele llcleoieklalle

'Arne Saknussemm!', he cried in a triumphant voice, 'but this is a name, and an Icelandic one: the name of a scholar of the sixteenth century, a famous alchemist!'

I looked at my uncle with a certain admiration.

'Those alchemists like Avicenna, Bacon, Lull, Paracelsus, were the real scholars of their time. They made discoveries at which we can reasonably be astonished. Why might this Saknussemm not have hidden some surprising invention in the incomprehensible cryptogram? This must be the case, indeed.'

The professor's imagination caught fire at this assumption.

'Maybe', I dared to reply, 'but what would be the point of a scholar hiding a great discovery in such a way?'

'Why? Why? How should I know? Didn't Galileo do the same with Saturn? Besides, we will soon see: I will find the secret of this document, and will neither eat nor sleep until I have discovered it.'

'Oh', I thought.

'Nor will you, Axel!', he added.

'My God', I said to myself, 'what luck I ate for two!'

'First', said my uncle, 'we must find out the language of this cipher: it cannot be difficult.'

At his words, I looked up quickly. My uncle continued his soliloquy:

'Nothing could be easier. There are 132 letters in the document, of which seventy-nine are consonants and fifty-three vowels. The southern languages conform approximately to this ratio, while the northern tongues are infinitely richer in consonants: it is therefore a language of the south.'

These conclusions were accurate.

'But what language is it?'

It was there that I expected to find a scholar, but discovered instead a brilliant analyst.

'This Saknussemm', he said, 'was an educated man. When he was not writing in his mother tongue, he must naturally have chosen the language customarily used amongst the educated people of the sixteenth century: I mean Latin. If I am wrong, I will try Spanish, French, Italian, Greek, or Hebrew. But the scholars of the sixteenth century used to write in Latin. I have therefore the right to say, a priori, that this is Latin.'

I almost jumped off my chair. My memories as a Latinist protested at the claim that this baroque series of words could belong to the sweet language of Virgil.

'Yes, Latin,' repeated my uncle, 'but Latin scrambled up.'

'Fine', I thought, 'if you can decrypt it, I will call you a smart guy.'

'Let's have a proper look at it,' he said, again picking up the sheet on which I had written. 'This is a series of 132 letters, presented in apparent disorder. There are words where the consonants are encountered on their own, like the first one, "llcl"; others in contrast where the vowels are abundant, for example the fifth word, "lele", or the second to last word "eoiek". This arrangement is clearly not deliberate: it is given mathematically by the unknown formula governing the succession of the letters. I think the original sentence must have been written normally, then jumbled up following a rule we have yet to discover. The person who got access to the key of the cipher would be able to read it easily: but what is this key? Axel, do you have the key?'

I replied nothing to his question, and for a good reason: I was gazing at a charming portrait on the wall, the picture of Gräuben. My uncle's ward was then in Altona, staying with one of her relatives. Her absence made me very sad, because, I can admit it now, the pretty Vironian girl and the professor's nephew loved one another the German way: with patience and calm. We had got engaged without my uncle knowing; he was too much of a geologist to understand such feelings. Gräuben was a charming blond girl with blue eyes, of a slightly serious character; but she did not love me any the less for that. For my part, I adored her (I am not certain this verb exists in the Germanic languages). Hence, the picture of my little Vironian girl immediately switched me from the world of reality to the land of fairy tales and memories.

In my mind I was looking at the faithful companion of my work and pleasure. Each day she helped me to put away my uncle's precious minerals, and labelled them with me. Fräulein Gräuben was a very good mineralogist. She would have borne comparison with more than one scholar. She liked to get to the bottom of the most difficult scientific questions. We spent many charming hours studying together, and many times I envied the fate of the feelingless stones she manipulated with her graceful hands!

Then, when the time for recreation had come, the two of us would go out. We used to walk through the bushy paths of the Alster and head together for the old tar-covered mill which looked so fine at the far end of the lake. On the way, we would chat while holding hands. I would tell her things and she would laugh as best she could. We would arrive on the banks of the Elbe; then, having said goodnight to the swans gliding around amongst the great white water lilies, we would come back by steam ferry to the quayside.

I was just at this point in my daydream when my uncle, hitting the table with his fist, brought me violently back to reality.

'Let's see', he said, 'in order to mix up the letters of a sentence, it seems to me that the first idea to come into one's mind ought to be to write the words vertically instead of horizontally.'

'Ah!', I thought.

'We must see what it produces. Axel, write any sentence at all on this scrap of paper; but, instead of writing the letters one after the other, put them in vertical columns made up of groups of fives or sixes.'

I understood what was required and I immediately wrote from top to bottom:

I y l e b

l o i G e

o u t r n

v m t a ,

e y l u ,

'Well,' said the professor without reading it, 'now write these words in a horizontal line.'

I did so and obtained the following sentence: **Iyleb loiGe outrn vmta, eylu,.**

'Perfect', said my uncle, tearing the paper out of my hands. 'This is beginning to look like the old document: the vowels and the consonants are both grouped together in the same confusion. There are even capitals in the middle of the words, and commas as well, just as in Saknussemm's parchment.'

I couldn't help thinking that these remarks were highly intelligent.

'Now', said my uncle again, addressing me directly, 'in order to read the sentence that you have just written and which I do not know, all I have to do is take the first letter of each successive word, then the second letter, then the third, and so on.'

And my uncle, to his great amazement and even more to mine, read out: I love you, my little Gräuben.

'What?', said the professor.

Without being aware of it, like a clumsy lover, I had written out this compromising sentence.

'Oh, so you're in love with Gräuben, aren't you?', said my uncle in an authentic guardian's tone.

'Yes... No... ', I spluttered.

'So, you're in love with Gräuben', he repeated mechanically. 'Well, let's apply my procedure to the document in question.'

My uncle had returned to his mesmerizing rumination and had already forgotten my risky words: I say 'risky' because the scholar's mind could never understand the matters of the heart. Fortunately, the vital question of the document took precedence.

He was about to perform his critical experiment, when his eyes threw sparks out through his glasses. His hands trembled as he picked the old parchment up again. He was really excited. Finally he coughed loudly, and in a solemn voice, calling out successively the first letter of each word, then the second, he dictated the following series to me:

Ertl`KO`p,kldlpel.se,lpe`pp
Çserelppa`Og,lsññseoéeee.

He finished and, I must admit, I was excited. These letters, called out one after another, had not produced any meaning in my mind. I was therefore waiting for the professor to pronounce a sentence of Latin gracefulness. But who could have foreseen it? A violent blow from his fist shook the table. The ink spurted; the pen jumped from my hands.

'It is wrong!', shouted my uncle, 'it does not make sense.'

Then, crossing the study like a cannon-ball, and going downstairs like an avalanche, he threw himself into the street and run away.

Chapter 4.

'Has he gone out?', cried Marthe, running up at the slam of the front door, which had just shaken the house to its very foundations.

'Yes, completely gone!'

'What about his dinner?'

'He won't have dinner!'

'And his supper?'

'He won't have supper!'

'What?', said Marthe clasping her hands.

'Yes, Marthe, he has given up food, and so has the entire household. Uncle John has put us all on a strict diet until he has deciphered an old grimoire that is totally undecipherable!'

'Goodness, we will all die of starvation!'

I didn't dare admit that with such an uncompromising individual as my uncle, this fate seemed inevitable.

Very worried, the maid went back into the kitchen sighing.

Once alone, I thought of going to tell Gräuben everything. But how could I get out of the house? The professor might come back at any moment. What if he called me? Or if he wanted to start to work again on that word-puzzle which even old Oedipus couldn't have solved? And if I wasn't there when he called for me, what might happen then?

The most intelligent reaction was to stay here. Moreover, a mineralogist from Besançon had just sent us a collection of siliceous geodes that needed sorting out. I set to work. I classified these hollow stones with their little crystals moving inside; then, I labelled them and put them in the presentation cases.

But this activity didn't require all my concentration. The problem of the old document did upset me. My head was swirling and I felt vaguely anxious. I had the feeling that something terrible was about to happen.

An hour later, my geodes were stacked in neat little rows. I fell into the massive Utrecht armchair, my arms lolling over the sides and my head leaning back. I lit my pipe, the one with the long curved stem and the bowl carved into a casually reclining water-nymph; and then had great fun watching it burn, slowly turning my naiad into a black woman. From time to time I listened out for steps hammering up the stairs, but there was nothing. Where could my uncle be at this moment? I imagined him running around under the beautiful trees on the Altona road, gesticulating, firing at the walls with his walking stick, flattening the grass at a stroke, beheading the thistles, an disturbing the lonely storks from their sleep.

Would he come back triumphant or discouraged? Who would win: him or the secret? I was wondering about such matters and, without thinking, I picked up the sheet of paper on which I had written the incomprehensible sequence of letters. I repeated to myself: 'what can it possibly mean?'

I tried to group the letters into words. I couldn't! Whether you put them into twos, threes, fives, or sixes, nothing came out that made sense. The fourteenth, fifteenth, and sixteenth letters did produce the English word *ice*. The eighty-fourth, eighty-fifth, and eighty-sixth ones gave *sir*. In the middle of the document, in the third line, I spotted the Latin words *rota*, *mutabile*, *ira*, *nec*, and *atra*.

'It's amazing!', I thought, 'these last few words seem to confirm my uncle's view about the language of the document! In the fourth line I can even see *luco*, which means "sacred wood". It's true that the third line also includes *tabiled*, which sounds completely Hebrew, and the last one, *mer*, *arc*, and *mère*, which are undoubtedly French.'

It was enough to drive you out of your mind. Four different languages in the same silly sentence! What possible connection could there be between ice, sir, anger, cruel, sacred wood, changeable, mother, bow, and sea? Only the first and last were easily linked: in a document written in Iceland, it was hardly surprising that there should be a 'sea of ice'. But putting the rest of the puzzle back together was another matter entirely.

I was struggling with an insoluble problem; my brain started to overheat and my eyes were blinking at the sheet. The 132 letters seemed to fly around me, like those silver drops which float above your head when there is a sudden rush of blood to it.

I was having a sort of hallucination; I was suffocating; I needed some fresh air. Without thinking, I fanned myself using the piece of paper, with the back and the front passing alternately before my eyes.

What a surprise when I thought I caught sight of perfectly intelligible words during a quick turn of the sheet, just as the other side came into view: Latin words like *craterem* and *terrestre*!

Suddenly my mind sparked; through the fleeting glimpses I had caught sight of the truth; I had discovered how the code worked. To understand the document, you didn't even need to read it through the paper. Far from it. In its original form, exactly as it had been spelled out to me, it could easily be decoded. The professor's ingenious attempts were all finally paying off. He had been right about the way the letters were arranged and right about the language the document was written in. A mere 'nothing' had stopped him reading the Latin sentence from beginning to end, and this self-same 'nothing' had just fallen into my lap by pure chance.

You can imagine how excited I felt. My eyes went out of focus. I couldn't use them anymore. I had spread the piece of paper out on the table. All I had to do now to possess the secret was to glance at it.

At last I managed to calm down. I forced myself to walk around the room twice to calm my nerves; then I came back and immersed myself again in the huge armchair.

I drew a large supply of air into my lungs, and said to myself: 'read!'

I bent over the table. I placed my finger on each successive letter and, without stopping, without slowing down at all, I read the whole sentence aloud.

What a terrifying surprise! At first, it was like being hit by a blow you didn't expect. What I had just discovered had really happened! A man had been daring enough to penetrate...

'No!', I cried jumping, 'no, I am not going to tell my uncle. It would be a very bad idea to tell him about such a journey. He would just want to have a go himself. Nothing would stop him, a geologist of such determination. He would leave anyway, against all obstacles. And he would take me with him, and we wouldn't come back. Never. Never!'

I was terribly anxious.

'No, no, no! It will not happen!', I said firmly, 'and since I can prevent any such idea from crossing the mind of my dictator, I will do so. By turning this document in every direction, he might accidentally discover the code. Let's destroy it.'

The fire hadn't quite gone out. I picked up the sheet of paper, together with Saknussemm's parchment. My trembling hand was just about to throw the whole lot on the embers, and thus destroy the dangerous secret, when the study door opened. My uncle came in.

Chapter 5.

I barely had time to put the wretched document back on the desk.

Professor Lidenbrock seemed engrossed. His obsessive idea wasn't giving him a moment's rest. He had obviously pondered and dissected the problem during his walk, called on every resource of his imagination. He had come back to try out some new combination.

Actually, he sat down in his armchair and, pen in hand, began to write down formulas that looked like algebraic calculations.

I watched his shivering hand: I was hypnotized. What kind of surprising new result was going to spring forth? I was afraid but it did not make any sense since the correct combination, the only one, had already been discovered; therefore, any other research was doomed to failure.

For three long hours, my uncle worked without a word, without looking up, rubbing out, starting again, crossing out, starting again a thousand times.

I knew that if he managed to put the letters into every single order possible, then the right sentence would come out. But I also knew that a mere twenty letters can form two quintillion, four hundred and thirty-two quadrillion, nine hundred and two trillion, eight billion, one hundred and seventy-six million, six hundred and forty thousand combinations. There were 132 letters in the sentence, and these 132 letters produced a total number of sentences that had at least 133 digits, a number that is virtually impossible to enumerate and goes completely beyond the bounds of imagination.

I felt reassured about this heroic means to solve the problem.

Nevertheless, time passed, night came, the street noises died down but my uncle, still bent over his work, didn't see anything. He didn't notice that good old Marthe half-opened the door. He heard nothing, not even the voice of the faithful maid saying: 'will Sir be having supper tonight?'

Marthe had to go away again without a response. As for me, after fighting it for some time, an irresistible drowsiness came over me, and I fell asleep on the end of the sofa, while my uncle kept on calculating and crossing out.

When I woke again the following morning, the tireless coal miner was still working. His red eyes, pale face, disheveled hair and purple cheekbones were the result of hours of a terrible mental struggle against the impossible.

I was genuinely sorry for him. In spite of the reproaches I probably had the right to make, I felt considerable pity. The poor man was so possessed by his idea that he had quite forgotten to be angry. His whole energy was concentrated on a single point, and since it could not escape through its normal outlet, it was to be feared that it might simply explode at any moment.

I could easily undo the iron hoop wrapped tight around his brain; one word could free him but I said nothing!

However, I had a kind heart. Why didn't I speak in such circumstances? For my uncle's own sake.

'No, no', I repeated, 'no, I won't speak. I know him, he would only want to go there; nothing would stop him. He has a volcanic imagination and he would risk his life to do what no geologist has ever done before. I won't say anything; I will keep this secret given to me by chance. To let it out would be tantamount to killing Professor Lidenbrock. Let him guess if he can. I don't want to feel responsible one day for having sent him to his death!'

Once my mind was made up, I crossed my arms and waited. But I hadn't reckoned with something that happened a few hours later.

When good old Marthe tried to go out to the market, she found the door locked. The big key was not in the keyhole. Who had taken it out? Obviously my uncle, when he had come back from his hasty excursion the day before.

Was it on purpose? Was it by accident? Did he want us to starve? That seemed to be going a bit far. Why should Marthe and I suffer because of a situation that had nothing to do with us? But apparently this was the case, and I recalled a frightening precedent. A few years before, when my uncle had been working on his grand mineral classification, he had remained forty-eight hours without eating, and his whole household had had to follow this scientific diet. As a result, I acquired stomach cramps that were not much fun for a boy of a fairly ravenous nature.

It now seemed that lunch was going to go the same way as supper the day before. Nevertheless I resolved to be heroic and not to give in to the demands of hunger. God old Marthe took it very seriously and was very upset. As for me, being unable to leave the house worried me more, with good reason, as I am sure you will understand.

My uncle was still working; his mind was lost in a world of combinations; he lived far from the Earth and truly beyond worldly needs.

At about twelve o'clock, though, hunger began to cause me serious problems. Marthe, very innocently, had devoured the supplies in the larder the day before, and so there was nothing left in the whole house. I held on, however. I considered it a matter of honour.

Two o'clock chimed. The situation was becoming ridiculous, and even intolerable. My eyes were wide open. I started to tell me that I was exaggerating the importance of the document; that in any case my uncle wouldn't believe what it said; that he would regard it as a mere practical joke; that if the worst came to the worst he could be restrained against his will if he wanted to attempt the expedition; and that he might easily find the code himself, in which case all my efforts at abstinence would have been in vain.

These reasons, which I would have indignantly rejected the day before, seemed excellent to me now. I even considered it a stupid idea to have waited so long: I decided to reveal everything.

I was therefore looking for a way into the subject, one that wasn't too sudden, when, without warning, the professor stood up, put his hat on, and got ready to go out.

What! Leave the house, and shut us in again! Never!

'Uncle John!', I said.

He didn't appear to have heard.

'Uncle John!', I repeated, raising my voice.

'What?' he said, like someone abruptly woken up.

'What about the key?'

'What key? The door?'

'No,' I cried. 'The key to the document!'

The professor looked at me over his glasses. He must have noticed something unusual in my face. He firmly grabbed me by the arm and, unable to say a word, he looked questioningly at me. Nevertheless, never was a question asked more clearly.

I moved my head up and down.

He shook his, with a sort of pity, as if dealing with a lunatic.

I made a more positive sign.

His eyes shone brighter; his hand became threatening.

Given the situation, this silent conversation would have fascinated the most indifferent spectator. I had in fact really reached the point of not daring to say anything, such was my fear of my uncle suffocating me when he first began to joyfully embrace me. But he became so insistent that I just had to speak.

'Yes, the code... Purely by chance...'

'What are you saying?', he cried with a visible emotion.

'Look', I said, giving him the paper with my writing on, 'read.'

'But it doesn't mean anything!', he replied, screwing it up.

'... It doesn't mean anything when you begin at the beginning, but when you start at the end...'

I hadn't finished before the professor produced a shout, more than a shout, an actual roar! A revelation had just occurred in his brain. He was transfigured.

'Oh, clever old Saknussemm!', he cried, 'so you wrote your message backwards?'

And throwing himself on the sheet of paper, with his blurred vision and trembling voice, he spelled the whole document out, working his way from the last letter back to the first.

This was what he read: 'In Snefells Yoculis craterem kem delibat umbra Scartaris Julii intra calendas descende, audas viator, et terrestre centrum attinges. Kod feci. Arne Saknussemm.'

Which, when translated from this poor Latin, reads as follows: 'Audacious traveller, go down into the crater of Snaefell Yocul, which the shadow of Scartaris caresses before the calends of July, and you will reach the centre of the Earth. I did so. Arne Saknussemm.'

As he read, my uncle jumped as if he had been electrocuted by a Leyden jar. His courage, joy and certainty were impressive. He walked up and down; he held his head in both hands; he moved the chairs around; he piled the books up; it is unbelievable but he juggled with his precious geodes! He threw a punch here, a blow there. At last, his nerves calmed down and, like a man exhausted after discharging too much fluid, he flopped back in his armchair.

'So what time is it?', he asked after a few moments' silence.

'Three o'clock', I replied.

'H'm, dinner has gone down quickly. I'm dying of hunger. Let us eat something. And then, after that...'

'After?'

'You will pack my trunk.'

'What?'

'And yours too!', concluded the merciless professor, walking into the dining-room.

Chapter 6.

These last words sent a shiver through my whole body but I kept my self-control. I even resolved to put on a brave face. Only scientific arguments could stop Professor Lidenbrock. And there were good arguments against such a journey. Go to the centre of the Earth! What madness! But I kept my reasoning for a more suitable moment and, instead, I gave my full attention to the meal.

There would be little point in reproducing here my uncle's curses when he saw the cleared-away table. Things were duly explained to him, and Marthe freed again. Running to the market, she managed so well that an hour later my hunger was satisfied, and I could begin to be aware of the situation once more.

During the meal, my uncle had been almost cheerful: there escaped from him some of those scholars' jokes that never become really dangerous. After the last course, he beckoned me into his office.

I obeyed. He sat at one side of his desk, with me at another.

'Axel', he said in a voice that was almost kindly, 'you are a highly gifted boy; you were of great assistance to me when I was worn out by my efforts and about to give up looking for the combination. Where would I have ended up? No one can guess. I will never forget that, my boy, and you will have your fair share of the fame we are going to achieve.'

'Now is my chance!', I thought, 'he is in a good mood: it is the moment to examine this fame.'

'... Above all', my uncle continued, 'total secrecy must be maintained, do you hear? In the scientific world, there is no shortage of people jealous of me, and many of them would dearly love to tackle this journey. But they will have no inkling of it until we get back.'

'Do you really believe there'd be so many takers?'

'Most definitely! Who would think twice about gaining such celebrity? If people knew of the document, a whole army of geologists would rush to follow in Arne Saknussemm's footsteps!'

'That's where I'm not totally convinced, Uncle John, for nothing proves that this document is genuine.'

'What! And the book that held it?'

'All right, this Saknussemm wrote the message, but does it mean he actually carried out the journey? Couldn't the old parchment just be a practical joke?'

I half-regretted this last word, which was a bit daring. The professor's thick eyebrows frowned, and I was afraid that the rest of the conversation might not go as I wished. But fortunately it didn't turn out like that. My stern questioner started to smile and replied: 'this is what we are going to find out.'

'H'm!', I said, a little offended, 'allow me first to exhaust all possible objections concerning the document.'

'Don't be afraid to speak up my boy: I allow you to express your opinion. You are no longer my nephew, but my colleague.'

'Well, I will first ask you what Yocul, Snaefell, and Scartaris mean, since I have never even heard of them.'

'That's easy. I have just received a map from my friend August Peterman of Leipzig. It couldn't have arrived at a better time. Take down the third atlas on the second section in the big bookcase, series Z, shelf 4.'

I got up and, thanks to the precise instructions, I quickly found the required atlas. My uncle opened it and said: 'this is Anderson's, one of the best maps of Iceland, and I think it will answer all your questions.'

I leant over the map.

'Look at this island consisting of volcanoes', said the professor, 'and notice that they all bear the name "Yokul". This word means "glacier" in Icelandic and, at that northerly latitude, most of the eruptions reach the light of day through the layers of ice. Hence this name "Yokul" applied to all the fire-producing peaks of the island.'

'Fine. But what about Snaefell?'

I hoped there would be no answer to this question. I was wrong. He added: 'follow me along the western coast of Iceland. Do you see Reykjavik, the capital? Yes. Good. Work your way up along the countless fjords of these shorelines eaten by the sea, and stop a little before the line of 65° N. What do you see?'

'A peninsula rather like a bare bone, with an enormous kneecap at the end.'

'Not an inappropriate comparison, my dear boy. Now, do you see anything on the kneecap?'

'Yes, a mountain that looks as if it has sprouted in the middle of the sea.'

'Good. This is Mount Snaefell.'

'Mount Snaefell?'

'The one and only. A five-thousand-foot-high mountain, one of the most remarkable on the island, and definitely the most famous in the whole world if its crater leads to the centre of the globe.'

'But it's impossible!', I said, shrugging my shoulders in protest at such a conjecture.

'Impossible?', answered Professor Lidenbrock severely, 'and why should that be?'

'Because this crater is obviously blocked up with lava and molten rock; consequently...'

'And supposing it is an extinct crater?'

'Extinct?'

'Yes. There are now only about three hundred volcanoes in activity on the surface of the Earth, but the number of extinct ones is much greater. Mount Snaefell falls into this latter category and, in historical times, it has only had a single eruption, the 1219 one. Since then, its glowing vociferations have gradually died down, and it is no longer considered an active volcano.'

I had no reply at all for these categorical statements; so, I focused on the other mysteries hidden in the document.

'But what does the word "Scartaris" mean, and what have the calends of July got to do with anything?'

My uncle concentrated for a few seconds. My hope came back for a moment, but only for a moment, for soon he replied to me as follows: 'what you call a mystery is crystal clear for me. It proves with what care and ingenuity Saknussemm wanted to indicate his discovery. Mount Snaefell is composed of several craters; it was therefore necessary to pinpoint which is the one that leads to the centre of the globe. What did the Icelandic scientist do? He observed that, as the calends of July approached (towards the end of June), one of the mountain peaks (called Scartaris) cast its shadow as far as the opening of the relevant crater, and he noted this fact in his document. Could he have found a more precise indication and, once we are on the summit of Mount Snaefell, can there be a moment's hesitation as to the path to follow?'

Decidedly, my uncle had an answer for everything. I saw full well that he was unassailable on the words of the ancient parchment. So, I stopped plying him with questions about it and, since the most important thing was to convince him, I turned to the scientific objections, which were much more worrisome in my opinion.

'All right, I am forced to accept that Saknussemm's message is clear and can leave no doubt in one's mind. I even grant that the document looks perfectly authentic. So, this scientist went to the bottom of Mount Snaefell; he saw the shadow of Scartaris touch the edge of the crater just before the calends of July; he heard the people of his time recounting legends that this crater led to the centre of the Earth. But as to whether he went down there himself, whether he carried out the journey and came back, whether undertook it: no, a hundred times no!'

'And the reason?', asked my uncle in a singularly mocking tone.

'Because all the scientific theories demonstrate that this is impossible!'

'All the theories say that?', replied the professor, putting on a good-natured appearance. 'Oh the nasty theories. They are going to upset us these blasted theories!'

I could see that he was making fun of me, but I continued: 'yes, it is well known that the temperature increases by approximately one degree centigrade for every seventy feet you go below the surface of the globe. Now, assuming that this ratio remains constant, and given that the radius of the Earth is about fifteen thousand leagues, the temperature at the centre will be well over 200,000°. The substances at the Earth's core exist therefore as hot gases, for even metals like gold or platinum, even the hardest rocks, cannot resist such a temperature. That is why I wonder whether it is possible to get into such an environment!'

'So, Axel, it is the heat that bothers you?'

'Yes, it is. If we were to attain a depth of only twenty-five miles, we would have reached the limit of the Earth's crust, for the temperature would already be more than 1,400°.'

'And you are afraid of melting?'

'Find the truth', I replied sharply.

'The truth is', retorted Professor Lidenbrock with contempt, 'that neither you, nor anyone else, knows for certain what happens in the Earth's interior, given that scarcely a twelve-thousandth part of its radius is known. Science can always be improved: each existing theory is constantly replaced by a new one. Was it not believed before Fourier that the temperature of interplanetary space went down indefinitely, and is it not known now that the greatest cold in outer space does not go beyond 40 or 50° below zero? Why should it not be the same for the internal heat? Why should it not encounter, at a certain depth, a limit that cannot be crossed, instead of reaching the point where the most fire-resistant minerals liquefy?'

Since my uncle was making assumptions, I could not answer anything.

'Well, Axel, I can tell you that real scientists, amongst them Poisson, have proved that if a temperature of 200,000° actually existed inside the globe, the hot gases produced by the fusion of the solids would acquire such force that the Earth's crust could not resist and would explode like the walls of a boiler under steam pressure.'

'It is Poisson's point of view, Uncle John, and nothing more.'

'Of course, but it is also the opinion of other distinguished geologists that the interior of the globe is not formed of gas, nor of water, nor of the heaviest stones that we know. The reason is that, if it were, the Earth would only weigh half as much as it does.'

'Oh, you can prove anything you want with figures!'

'And can you do the same, my boy, with facts? Is it not true that the number of volcanoes has considerably decreased since the first days of the world? And if there is indeed heat in the centre, can one not deduce that it is also tending to diminish?'

'Uncle John, you cannot oppose assumptions.'

'And I have to say that my opinion is shared by highly competent scientists. Do you remember a visit that the famous British chemist Sir Humphry Davy paid me in 1825?'

'Not at all: I was born nineteen years later!'

'Well, Sir Humphry came to see me as he was passing through Hamburg. Amongst other things, we had a long discussion about the hypothesis that the innermost core of the Earth was liquid. We both agreed that a molten state could not exist, for a reason to which science has never found a response.'

'What reason is that?', I said, slightly stunned.

'Because the liquid mass would be subject, like the ocean, to the moon's attraction, which would produce internal tides twice a day, push up the Earth's crust and cause regular earthquakes!'

'But it is obvious that the surface of the globe was once exposed to combustion, and one can suppose that the outer crust cooled down first while the heat retreated to the centre.'

'This is a mistake. The Earth heated up through combustion on its surface, not from any other cause. The surface was composed of a great quantity of metals such as potassium and sodium, which have the property of catching fire as soon as they are in contact with air and water. These metals started to burn when the water vapour in the atmosphere fell to the ground as rain. Little by little, as the water worked its way into the cracks in the Earth's crust, it produced further fires, explosion, and eruptions, what explains the large number of volcanoes during the first days of the world.'

'What an ingenious hypothesis!', I cried, rather in spite of myself.

'Which Sir Humphry brought to my notice by means of a highly simple experiment on this very spot. He constructed a ball made mainly of the metals I have just mentioned, and which perfectly represented our globe. When water was sprayed on its surface, it blistered, oxidized, and produced a small mountain. A crater opened at the summit; an eruption took place; and it transmitted so much warmth to the whole ball that it became too hot to hold.'

To tell the truth, I was beginning to have doubts about my own opinion because of the professor's arguments. What didn't help either was that he was presenting them with his usual vigour and enthusiasm.

'You see, Axel, the state of the central core has produced various hypotheses amongst geologists; nothing is less proven than the idea of an internal heat. In my view, it does not... it cannot possibly exist. Moreover, we will discover it for ourselves and, like Arne Saknussemm, we will understand this important matter at last.'

'Yes, we will that!', I shouted, won over by his enthusiasm, "if there is enough light to see!'

'And why not? Can't we count on electrical phenomena to light the way, and even on the atmosphere, which the pressure may make more and more luminous as the centre approaches?'

'Yes, yes! It is possible after all.'

'It is certain', retorted my uncle in triumph, 'but it must be kept secret, do you hear? All this must be kept secret so that no one else may have the idea of discovering the centre of the Earth before us.'

Chapter 7.

Our memorable session ended here. The discussion had given me a fever. I left my uncle's study and I felt dizzy; there was not enough air to calm me down in all the streets of Hamburg put together. So I reached the banks of the Elbe, near the steamboat service connecting the town with the Harburg railway line.

Was I really convinced by what I had just been told? Hadn't I been won over by Professor Lidenbrock's forceful manner? Could I take seriously his decision to go to the centre of the Earth? Had I just heard the senseless speculations of a lunatic or the scientific analyses of a genius? On this matter, where did the truth end and error begin?

I drifted amongst a thousand contradictory hypotheses, without being able to catch hold of any of them.

However, I did remember being convinced, although my enthusiasm was now beginning to wane: I would in fact have preferred to set off immediately so as not to have time to think. Yes, I would easily have been able to pack my suitcase at that very moment.

Yet I have to confess that an hour later my excitement had vanished. I felt relaxed: I had now forgotten the chthonic depths and was coming back to the surface.

'It's preposterous!', I exclaimed, 'it does not make any sense. It's not the kind of serious proposal you make to a sensible boy. None of all that exists. I didn't sleep properly. I must have had a bad dream.'

I had meanwhile walked along the banks of the Elbe and reached the other side of the town. I had worked my way along the port and arrived at the Altona road. A strange feeling had guided me, a justified feeling, for soon I caught sight of my little Gräuben walking nimbly back to Hamburg.

'Gräuben!', I shouted from afar.

The girl stopped; I think she was a little flustered to hear her name called on the public highway. Ten strides later I was in front of her.

'Axel!' she said, surprised, 'you came to meet me, didn't you?'

But when she looked at me, Gräuben could not avoid noticing my worried, upset appearance.

'What's wrong?', she said, taking my hand.

'What's wrong?', I cried.

In two seconds and three sentences my pretty Vironian girl was informed. She remained silent for a few seconds. Was her heart pounding as hard as mine? I don't know, but the hand holding mine wasn't trembling. We continued for a hundred yards without a word.

'Axel', she said at last.

'Dear Gräuben!'

'It will be a wonderful journey.'

I was surprised by her answer.

'Yes, Axel: a journey worthy of a scholar's nephew. A man should try to prove himself by some great adventure!'

'What, Gräuben, you're not trying to stop me from going on such an expedition?'

'No, dear Axel, and I would like to go with you and your uncle, but a poor girl like me would only be a burden.'

'Are you telling the truth?'

'Yes, of course.'

'Ah! Women, girls, feminine hearts: we never understand you! When you are not the shyest of creatures, you are the most courageous. Reason is not your cup of tea. It is incredible: this child was encouraging me to take part in such an expedition! She wouldn't have been afraid to do the journey herself! She wanted me to do it, although she loved me!

I was disconcerted, and also ashamed.

'Gräuben', I tried again, 'we will see if you talk this way tomorrow.'

'Tomorrow, dear Axel, I will say the same thing.'

We continued on our way, holding hands but not saying anything. I was exhausted by the day's events.

'After all', I thought, 'the calends of July are still ages off, and before then any number of things can occur to cure my uncle of his craze for underground travel.'

Night had fallen by the time we arrived at the house on the Königstrasse. I expected to find the house quiet, with my uncle in bed as usual and Marthe giving the dining-room one last feather-dusting.

But I had forgotten about the professor's impatience. I found him shouting and gesticulating in the middle of a troop of porters who were unloading goods on the garden path: the maid did not know which way to turn.

'Come here, Axel, and hurry up', shouted my uncle from afar as soon as he saw me. 'Your trunk is not packed, my papers are not in order, I have lost the key for the travelling-bag, and my gaiters have not yet arrived.'

I was stupefied and speechless. I was hardly able to pronounce: 'So we are leaving?'

'Yes, lucky boy: you are going to have a walk instead of staying here.'

'We are leaving!', I repeated faintly.

'Yes, the day after tomorrow, very early in the morning.'

I couldn't bear to hear any more, and I ran up to my little room. There could no longer be any doubt. During the afternoon, my uncle had been buying the articles and utensils needed for his journey. The path was blocked with rope-ladders, knotted cords, torches, water bottles, iron crampons, pickaxes, alpenstocks, the total needing at least ten men to carry it.

I spent an awful night. In the morning I was called early. I decided not to open the door. But how could I resist a gentle voice saying: 'dear Axel?'

I came out. I thought that my haggard face, the whiteness of my skin, my eyes reddened by lack of sleep, would affect Gräuben and make her change her mind.

'So, my dear Axel, I see you feel better today, and have calmed down during the night.'

'Calmed down!'

I rushed to the mirror. To my surprise, I looked less bad than I had thought. It was unbelievable.

'Axel,' said Gräuben, 'I have had a long talk with my guardian. He is a valiant scholar, a man of great courage, and you should always remember that his blood runs into your veins. We spoke about his aims, his hopes, why and how he will achieve his goal. He will get there; I'm sure. Dear Axel, it's such a great thing to devote oneself to science! How famous Mr. Lidenbrock and his companion will become. When you come back, Axel, you will be a man, his equal, free to speak, free to act, free at last to...'

The girl, turning red, did not finish her sentence. Her words restored my strength. But I still couldn't believe that we were about to leave. I dragged Gräuben into the professor's office.

'So, Uncle John', I said, 'are you really willing to go?'

'What! Aren't you convinced?'

'Of course I am', I said in order not to contradict him, 'but I'm just wondering what all the hurry is.'

'Time is the hurry, time fleeing inexorably!'

'But it is only the 26th of May, and until the end of June... '

'So, silly boy, you think that it is easy to get to Iceland! If you had not left like a madman, I would have taken you with me to the branch office of Liffender & Co. of Copenhagen. There, you would have seen that there is only one service from Copenhagen to Reykjavik, on the 22nd of each month.'

'Well then?'

'Well then, if we waited until the 22nd of June, we would arrive too late to see the shadow of Scartaris touching Mount Snaefell's crater! We have to get to Copenhagen as quickly as possible and try to find some means of transport there. Go and pack your trunk.'

There was nothing more I could say. I went back up to my room. Gräuben came with me. She immediately took charge, carefully packing into a small suitcase the things needed for my journey. She was no more excited than if it had been a day-trip to Lübeck or Heligoland. Her little hands went back and forth unhurriedly. She talked calmly, she gave me the most sensible reasons for doing our expedition. She beguiled me and I felt very angry with her. At times, I wanted to get angry, but she took no notice and continued her calm and methodical work.

Finally, the suitcase was packed. I went downstairs again. Throughout the day, more and more suppliers of scientific instruments, firearms, and electrical apparatus arrived. Marthe was in a tizzy.

'Is Sir mad?', she cried.

I nodded.

'And he is taking you with him?'

I nodded again.

'Where?'

I pointed to the centre of the Earth.

'To the cellar?'

'No, further!'

The evening came. I was no longer aware of the passing of time.

'See you tomorrow', said my uncle, 'departure: six sharp.'

At ten o'clock, I fell on my bed like a lifeless mass.

During the night, terror took hold of me again.

I spent it dreaming of chasms. I was raving. I felt myself seized by the vigorous hand of the professor, dragged along, engulfed, bogged down. I was falling to the bottom of bottomless pits with the increasing speed of bodies abandoned in space. My life was just one endless fall.

I woke at five, exhausted and restless. I went down to the dining-room. My uncle was at table. He was wolfing food down. I looked at him with horror. Gräuben was there. I didn't say anything. I was unable to eat.

At half past five, wheels were heard rumbling in the street. A large carriage arrived to take us to Altona station. It was soon piled up with my uncle's packages.

'And your trunk?'

'It is ready', I replied, almost fainting.

'Hurry up and bring it down or we will miss the train.'

Fighting against destiny seemed impossible for the moment. Going up to my room I let my case slide downstairs, rushing headlong down after it.

Meanwhile my uncle was solemnly putting the reins of his house in Gräuben's hands. My pretty Vironian girl was as calm as usual. She kissed her guardian, but she could not hold back a tear when she touched my cheek with her sweet lips.

'Gräuben', I said.

'Go, dear Axel, go. You are leaving a fiancée but you will come back to a wife.'

I held Gräuben briefly in my arms, then got into the carriage. She and Marthe waved us a last goodbye from the front door. Then the two horses, urged on by the whistling of the driver, galloped off towards Altona.

Chapter 8.

In less than twenty minutes, we had crossed the border into Holstein Province. Altona, really a suburb of Hamburg, is the terminus of the line from Kiel, along which we were due to travel to the coast of the Belts.

At half past six the carriage pulled up in front of the station. My uncle's numerous packages and bulky cases were unloaded, carried in, weighed, labelled, and loaded into the luggage van. At seven o'clock we were sitting opposite each other in our compartment. The steam-whistle blew and the locomotive moved off. We had left.

Was I resigned to my fate? No, not yet. But the fresh morning air and the view constantly changing with the motion of the train soon took my mind off its main worry.

The professor's thoughts were obviously flying ahead of the train, moving too slowly for his impatience. We were alone in the coach, but we did not speak. My uncle checked his pockets and travelling-bag with the most painstaking care. I could see that not one of the items needed for carrying out his projects was missing.

Amongst them was a carefully folded sheet of headed notepaper from the Danish consulate, signed by Mr. Christiensen, consul-general in

Hamburg and a friend of his. It was intended to afford us every facility in Copenhagen with a view to being granted recommendations to the governor-general of Iceland.

I also saw the famous document, carefully hidden away in the most secret compartment of my uncle's wallet. Still cursing it from the bottom of my heart, I began to examine the countryside. It was an endless succession of plains, which were boring, monotonous and silty, but relatively fertile and highly suitable for laying down a railway, given its potential for those straight lines so popular with the rail companies.

But this monotonous countryside did not have time to annoy me for, only three hours after leaving, the train stopped at Kiel, a stone's throw from the sea.

Since our luggage was registered for Copenhagen, we had no need to bother with it. Nevertheless, the professor watched with an anxious expression as it was loaded onto the steamship. Then, it disappeared in the bilge.

In his hurry, my uncle had so carefully calculated the connections between the train and the steamer that we had nearly a whole day to kill, for the *Ellenora* was not due to leave until after nightfall. Hence, the cantankerous traveller criticized, for nine hours, the shipping and railway companies, and the governments which allowed such abuses to happen. I was forced to back him up while he berated the captain of the *Ellenora* on this very subject. He wanted him to start up the boilers without wasting a moment. The captain sent him away with a flea in his ear.

In Kiel, as elsewhere, it is impossible to alter the timeline. By dint of walking along the luxuriant banks of the bay leading to the town, by trampling through the bushy woods which make the town look like a nest amidst a network of branches, by admiring the bungalows each with its own little cold-bath-house, and by rushing and grumbling, we somehow managed to reach ten in the evening.

The whorls of smoke rose from the *Ellenora* into the sky; the deck trembled because of the vibrations coming from the boiler; we had already embarked and were the proud owners of a bunk bed in the only passenger cabin on board.

At quarter past ten the moorings were cast off, and the steamer moved rapidly over the dark waters of the Great Belt.

It was a pitch-black night; there came the wind and a strong sea; a few lights from shore appeared in the darkness. Later, a flashing lighthouse shone briefly over the waves from some mysterious point. That is all I can remember of our first crossing.

At 7 a.m. we disembarked at Korsor, a little town on the west coast of Zealand. There, we quickly climbed into another train, which carried us over a countryside just as flat as the Holstein one.

It still took three more hours to reach the capital of Denmark. My uncle hadn't shut his eyes all night. In his impatience, I think he was even pushing the carriage along with his feet.

Finally he caught sight of the sea.

'*The Sound*!', he shouted.

On our left was a big construction looking like a hospital.

'A lunatic asylum', said one of our travel companions.

'Well', I thought, 'this is a place where we ought to end our lives! And however big it is, that hospital would still be too small for all the professor's madness!'

At 10 a.m., we finally alighted in Copenhagen. The luggage was loaded onto a cab and driven with us to the *Phoenix hotel* on *Bredgale*, taking half an hour, for the station is out of town. Then, after a quick wash, my uncle dragged me out of my room. The hotel porter spoke German and English; but the professor, in his capacity as polyglot, spoke to him in good Danish, and it was in good Danish that we were told where the Museum of Northern Antiquities was.

This curious establishment contained stacks of marvels allowing one to reconstitute the country's history, with its old stone weapons, its goblets, and its jewels. Professor Thomson, the director, was a scholar and a friend of the consul in Hamburg.

My uncle had a warm letter of recommendation to give him. In general, one scholar does not receive another very well. But, here, things were different. Professor Thomson, a man who liked to help, gave Professor Lidenbrock and even his nephew a kind welcome. To say that our secret was kept from the excellent director goes without saying. We wished simply to visit Iceland as disinterested amateurs.

Mr. Thomson put himself entirely at our disposal, and together we combed the quays looking for a ship about to sail.

I had hoped that no means of transport would be available; but I was wrong. A little Danish schooner, the *Valkyrie*, was due to sail for Reykjavik on the 2nd of June. Mr. Bjarne, the captain, was on board. His passenger-to-be, overjoyed, shook his hand hard enough to break it. This simple man was surprised by such a handshake. He found it quite easy to go to Iceland since it was his job. My uncle found it extraordinary. The worthy captain took advantage of his enthusiasm to make us pay twice the price for the trip. But we weren't bothered by such trifles.

'Be on board by 7 a.m. on Tuesday', said Mr. Bjarne, thrusting a wad of dollars into his pocket.

We thanked Mr. Thomson for all his help and returned to the *Phoenix Hotel*.

'Everything's going well, very well indeed!', my uncle kept on saying. 'What a stroke of luck to have found that boat ready to leave! Now let's eat and visit the town.'

We headed for Kongens Nytorv, an irregularly shaped square with a plinth containing two innocent cannons which are ready to open fire but frighten nobody. Just beside it, at No. 5, there was a restaurant run by a French chef called Vincent. We ate our fill there for the modest price of four marks each.

Then I took a childish pleasure in exploring the town, with my uncle allowing himself to be dragged along. He saw nothing: neither the insignificant Royal Palace, nor the pretty seventeenth-century bridge across the canal in front of the museum, nor the huge memorial to Thorvaldsen, covered in hideous murals and with the works of this sculptor inside, nor, in a rather beautiful park, the candy-box Rosenborg Castle, nor the admirable Renaissance building of the Stock Exchange, nor the church tower made of the intertwined tails of four bronze dragons, nor even the great windmills on the ramparts, whose immense wings swelled up like a ship's sails in a strong sea-wind.

What delightful walks we could have gone on, my lovely Vironian girl and I, around the port where the double-deckers and frigates slept peacefully under their red roofs, along the lush shores of the strait, or through the bushy shade concealing the fortress, whose cannon push their black mouths between the branches of the elders and willows...

But unfortunately my poor Gräuben was far away. Did I have any hope of ever seeing her again?

And yet, if my uncle noticed nothing of these enchanted sites, he was bowled over when he saw a certain church tower on the Island of Amager, in the south-eastern part of Copenhagen.

I was instructed to head in that direction. We climbed onto a small steam-powered boat serving the canals and, soon, it pulled in at the quay known as 'The Dockyard'.

Having made our way through narrow streets where convicts dressed in grey-and-yellow-striped trousers were working under stick-wielding warders, we arrived at the Vor Frelsers Kirke. The church itself was not special in any way. But its high tower had caught the professor's eye: starting from the platform, an outside staircase worked its way round the spire, with its spirals in the open air.

'Up we go', said my uncle.

'But what if we get giddy?'

'All the more reason: we have to get used to it.'

'But...'

'Come on, I tell you, we're wasting time.'

There was no choice but to obey. A caretaker who lived on the other side of the street gave us the key, and our ascent began.

My uncle went first, treading firmly. I followed but I was terrified, for my head turned deplorably easily. I had neither the eagle's sense of balance nor its steady nerves.

As long as we were imprisoned in the staircase inside the tower everything went well. But after 150 steps the air suddenly hit me in the face: we had arrived on the platform. This was where the open-air staircase began, protected by a thin rail, with the steps getting ever narrower, apparently climbing up to infinity.

'I can't!'

'You are not a coward, are you? Start climbing!', replied the pitiless professor.

The only option was to follow, hanging firmly on. The open air made my head turn. I could feel the tower swaying in the gusts of wind. My legs began to weaken. Soon I was climbing on my knees, then on my stomach. I closed my eyes; I was suffering from vertigo.

At last, with my uncle pulling me up by the collar, I arrived near the ball.

'Look', he said, 'and look properly. You need to take lessons in precipices!'

I opened my eyes. Through the smoky mist I caught sight of houses without any depth, as if crushed by a great fall. Above my head passed disheveled clouds which, by some optical illusion, seemed to have become stationary while the tower, the ball, and I were being carried away at an incredible speed. In the distance, the green countryside stretched out on one side, while on the other the sea sparkled under a sheaf of sunrays. The Sound unwound to the Point of Elsinore, speckled with a few white sails exactly like seagulls' wings; in the eastern mist waved the coast of Sweden, only slightly smudged. This huge expanse swirled every time I looked at it.

Nevertheless, I had to get up, stand straight up, and look. My first lesson in dizziness lasted an hour. When at last I was allowed down and could set foot again on the firm paving of the streets, I was aching all over.

'We'll do the same tomorrow', declared my teacher.

In fact, I practiced this dizzy-making exercise each day for five days. Whether I liked it or not, I made noticeable progress in the art of 'contemplation from high places'.

Chapter 9.

The time came when we were due to leave. The day before, the obliging Mr. Thomson had brought the warmest letters of recommendation for Count Trampe, the governor of Iceland, Mr. Petursson, the bishop's coadjutor, and Mr. Finsen, the mayor of Reykjavik. In return, my uncle granted him his heartiest handshake.

At 6 a.m. on the 2nd of June, our precious luggage was already on board the *Valkyrie*. The captain led us down to cabins that were rather narrow and situated under the quarterdeck.

'Is the wind with us?', enquired my uncle.

'Yes, it is,' replied Captain Bjarne. 'It is a wind blowing from the south-east. We will leave the Sound on a broad reach and all sails set.'

A few moments later, the schooner, with its foresail, mainsail, gaff topsail, and topgallant, cast off and sailed full speed into the strait. An hour later, the capital of Denmark seemed to sink below the distant waves as the *Valkyrie* grazed the coast of Elsinore. In the state of nervousness I was in, I expected to see Hamlet's shadow walking along the legendary terrace.

'Sublime fool', I said, 'you would probably agree with us! You might even have wanted to come with us to the centre of the globe to seek a solution to your eternal doubt!'

But nothing appeared on the aged ramparts. Moreover, the castle is much younger than the heroic prince of Denmark. It serves now as a luxurious lodge for the watchman of this strait of the Sound, through which fifteen thousand ships of all nations pass each year.

Kronborg Castle soon disappeared into the mist, as did Helsingborg Tower on the Swedish coast. The schooner leaned over slightly in the breeze from the Kattegat.

The *Valkyrie* was a good sailing ship, but with sails you never know exactly what to expect. It was carrying coal, household utensils, pottery, woolen clothing, and a cargo of wheat to Reykjavik. Five crew members, all Danish, were enough to maneuver it.

'How long will the crossing take?', asked my uncle.

'About ten days', responded the captain, 'if we don't have too many north-western squalls near the Faroe Islands.'

'But you don't normally encounter significant delays?'

'No, Mr. Lidenbrock. Don't worry, we'll get there.'

In the evening, the schooner rounded Cape Skagen, the northernmost point of Denmark then, during the night, it crossed the Skagerrak, passed by the tip of Norway opposite Cape Lindesnes and ventured into the North Sea.

Two days later, we sighted the coast of Scotland in the region of Peterhead, and the *Valkyrie* headed towards the Faroe Islands, passing between the Orkneys and the Shetlands.

Soon, our schooner was lashed by the waves of the Atlantic; it had to tack against the north wind, and reached the Faroes only with some difficulty. On the 8th, the captain caught sight of Mykines, the easternmost of the Faroes, and from that moment on headed straight for Portland Point, on the southern coast of Iceland.

The crossing did not involve any special incident. I resisted seasickness quite well; whereas my uncle, to his great annoyance and even greater shame, was ill all the time.

As a result, he was unable to raise the subject of Mount Snaefell with Captain Bjarne, or the availability of means of communication and transport. He had to put off these questions until he arrived, and spent all his time lying in his cabin, whose walls creaked whenever the ship rocked. It must be admitted that he had, to a certain degree, deserved his fate.

On the 11th, we sighted Cape Portland. The weather, clear at this point, allowed us to see Mýrdalsjökull standing up behind the cape, which consists of a steep-sided hill. There was nothing else on this beach.

The *Valkyrie* kept a reasonable distance from the coast, going towards the west while encircled by many whales and sharks. Soon appeared a huge rocky outcrop with daylight showing through a hole where the foaming sea furiously surged. The Westman Islands looked as if they had emerged directly from the ocean, like rocks planted in the liquid plain. From this point forward, the schooner kept well out so as to leave a lot of space while rounding Cape Reykjanes, which forms the western corner of Iceland.

The sea was very rough, stopping my uncle from coming on deck to admire these jagged coasts lashed by the south-westerly wind.

Forty-eight hours later, after leaving behind a storm which had forced the schooner to run with all sails furled, we sighted to the east the beacon of Point Skagen, whose dangerous rocks extend a long way out under the waves. An Icelandic pilot came on board, and three hours later the *Valkyrie* dropped anchor in Faxa Bay, beside Reykjavik itself.

The professor finally came out of his cabin, a little pale, a little shaky, but still enthusiastic, and with a gleam of satisfaction in his eye.

The population of the town, enthralled by the arrival of a ship in which each expected something, congregated on the quayside.

My uncle was in a hurry to flee his floating prison-cum-hospital. But before leaving the deck of the schooner, he dragged me forward; there, near the northern part of the bay, stood a high mountain with two points on top: a double cone covered with perpetual snows.

'Mount Snaefell', he roared, 'Mount Snaefell!'

He made a sign indicating total secrecy, and then he climbed down into the waiting boat. I followed him. Soon we were standing on the soil of Iceland itself.

The first man to appear had a pleasant countenance and a general's uniform. He was, however, a mere civilian, the governor of the island, Baron Trampe himself. The professor realized whom he was dealing with. He presented the governor with the letters from Copenhagen and launched into a short conversation in Danish, which I took no part in at all, for a very good reason. But the result of this first interview was that Baron Trampe put himself entirely at Professor Lidenbrock's disposal.

My uncle received a warm welcome from the mayor, Mr. Finsen, whose uniform was no less military than the governor's, but whose temperament and function were just as peaceful.

As for the coadjutor, Mr. Petursson, he was, at present, carrying out an episcopal visit to the northern diocese; so, we had to postpone being introduced to him. But a charming citizen, whose help became extremely precious, was Mr. Fridriksson, who taught natural sciences at Reykjavik School.

This humble scholar spoke only Icelandic and Latin: he came and offered me his services in the language of Horace, and I felt that we were bound to understand each other. He was, in fact, the only person I could converse with during my entire stay in Iceland.

Of the three rooms making up his household, this excellent man put two at our disposal, and soon we were ensconced there with our luggage, whose quantity slightly surprised the inhabitants of Reykjavik.

'Well, Axel', said my uncle, 'things are working out. We are over the worst.'

'The worst?', I exclaimed.

'I mean it's downhill all the way!'

'In that sense, you're right; but, having gone down, won't we eventually have to come back up?'

'Oh, it does not worry me! Look, there is no time to be lost. I am going to visit the library. It might contain some manuscript of Saknussemm's, and if so I would very much like to have a look at it.'

'Well then, during that time I'll visit the town. Aren't you going to have a look yourself?'

'To tell the truth, I am not very much drawn by all that. What is interesting in this country of Iceland is below the ground, not above.'

I went out, and walked around at random.

To get lost in the two streets of Reykjavik would have been difficult. I did not therefore have to ask my way, which can cause problems when you speak with your hands.

The town stretches out over rather low and marshy ground between two hills. A huge lava bed protects it on one side as it descends in gentle stages towards the sea. On the other side stretches the vast Faxa Bay, encircled to the north by the huge glacier of Snaefell, and where the *Valkyrie* lay at anchor, alone for the moment. Normally, the British and French fish-patrols remain at anchor further out; but at this period they were working on the eastern coastline of the island.

The longer of Reykjavik's streets runs parallel to the shore. This is where the shopkeepers and tradesmen work, in log cabins made of horizontal red beams. The shorter street, lying further to the west, heads towards a little lake, passing between the houses of the bishop and other people who are not merchants.

I had soon finished my tour of these bleak, gloomy avenues. From time to time, I caught sight of a scrap of faded lawn, looking like an old woolen carpet threadbare through use, and some places resembling a kitchen garden, with rare vegetables (like potatoes, cabbages and lettuces) which would not have seemed out of place on a Lilliputian table. A few sickly wallflowers endeavored to imitate the sun.

Not far from the middle of the residential street, I found the public cemetery, enclosed by an earthen wall and with plenty of room left inside. Then, only a few yards away, I reached the governor's house, a farmhouse in comparison with Hamburg Town Hall, but a palace beside the huts of the Icelandic population.

Between the little lake and the town lay the church, in the Protestant style, built out of calcined rocks provided by the volcanoes themselves. During the strong westerly winds, the red tiles of its roof clearly had a habit of flying into the air, to the considerable danger of the congregation.

On a nearby hillock, I saw the National School where, as our host later told me, Hebrew, English, French, and Danish were taught, four languages of which, to my shame, I knew not a single word. I would have been the last amongst the forty pupils at this tiny school, and unworthy to sleep with them in those two-compartment cabinets where more sensitive people might easily have suffocated on the very first night.

In three hours, I had visited not only the town but even its surroundings. Their appearance was especially dismal. No trees, no vegetation to speak of. Everywhere the bare bones of the volcanic rocks. The Icelandic habitations are made of earth and peat, and their walls slope inwards. They look like roofs placed on the ground, except that the roofs themselves constitute relatively fertile fields. Thanks to the heat from the houses, grass grows here in abundance. It is carefully cut at haymaking time, for otherwise the animals from the houses would come and gently graze on these lush cottages.

During my excursion, I encountered few locals. When I got back to the street containing the shops, I found most of the population busy drying, salting, and loading cod, the main export. The men seemed robust but heavy, like blond Germans with pensive eyes. They must feel slightly outcast from humanity: exiles on this frozen land. Nature should really have turned them into Eskimos when she condemned them to live on the Arctic Circle. I tried in vain to surprise a smile on their faces; they sometimes laughed in a sort of involuntary contraction of the muscles, but never actually smiled.

Their clothing consisted of a black wool pea jacket, known in Scandinavian countries as wadmal, a hat with a very broad rim, a pair of trousers with red piping, and a piece of folded leather in the way of shoes.

Women wore sad, resigned faces, of a fairly pleasant type but rather expressionless, and were dressed in a blouse and black wool skirt. As for girls, they wore a small brown knitted bonnet on their hair, which was plaited into garlands. Married women wore a coloured kerchief around their head, with a crest of white linen on top.

After a good walk I returned to Mr. Fridriksson's house: my uncle was already there, together with his host.

Chapter 10.

Dinner was ready. Professor Lidenbrock devoured it: its stomach had become a deep chasm during the forced abstinence on board. The meal, more Danish than Icelandic, involved nothing remarkable in itself; but our host, more Icelandic than Danish, reminded me of the heroes of classical hospitality. It was clear that we were more part of his household than the man himself.

Conversation used the native tongue, interspersed for my sake with German by my uncle and Latin by Mr. Fridriksson. It concerned scientific subjects, as is appropriate for scholars; but Professor Lidenbrock maintained a very strict reserve, and at each sentence his eyes told me to keep a total silence about our future plans.

First Mr. Fridriksson questioned my uncle about the results of his research in the library.

'Your library! It consists of lonely books on almost deserted shelves.'

'What! We have eight thousand volumes, many of which are valuable and rare, including works in old Scandinavian, plus all the new books that Copenhagen sends us each year.'

'Where do you keep those eight thousand volumes? For my part...'

'Professor Lidenbrock, they are all over the country. We enjoy studying in our frozen old island. Every farmer, every fisherman knows how to read, and does read. We believe that books, instead of rotting behind bars, far from the captivated minds, are meant to be worn out by the readers' eyes. So, these books are passed from person to person, looked at, read and re-read; and often do not come back to the shelves for a year or two.'

'And in the meantime', replied my uncle with some annoyance, 'the poor foreigners...'

'It cannot be helped. Foreigners have their own libraries at home and, above all, our farmers need to educate themselves. As I have mentioned, the love of study is in the Icelandic blood. Thus, in 1816, we founded a Literary Society which is still thriving; foreign scholars are honoured to become members; it publishes books for the enlightenment of our fellow citizens, and performs a real service for the country. If you wished to be one of its corresponding members, Professor Lidenbrock, we would be delighted.'

My uncle, who already belonged to a hundred or so scientific societies, accepted with good grace, which greatly pleased Mr. Fridriksson.

'Now', he said, 'kindly indicate the books you hoped to find in our library, and I can perhaps provide some information on them.'

I looked at my uncle. He could not decide whether or not to reply. This matter concerned his projects directly. However, after thinking for a while, he decided to speak.

'Mr. Fridriksson, I would like to know whether you have, amongst the oldest books, those of a certain Arne Saknussemm.'

'Arne Saknussemm! You are referring to that scholar of the sixteenth century who was a great naturalist, a great alchemist, and a great traveller?'

'Precisely.'

'One of the stars of Icelandic literature and science?'

'As you so well put it.'

'One of the most illustrious of men?'

'Most certainly.'

'And whose courage was as great as his genius?'

'I see you know him perfectly.'

My uncle was in ecstasy to hear his hero spoken of in this way. He was eyeing Mr. Fridriksson greedily.

'Well?', he asked, 'what about his works?'

'H'm... his works, we do not have.'

'What, even in Iceland?'

'They do not exist, in Iceland or anywhere else.'

'And why ever not?'

'Because Arne Saknussemm was persecuted for heresy, and his books were burned in Copenhagen, in 1573, by the hand of the executioner.'

'Good! Splendid!', shouted my uncle, greatly shocking the biology teacher.

'What?'

'Yes, everything is explained, everything fits together, all is clear, and now I understand why Saknussemm, having been put on the Index and forced to hide the discoveries of his genius, had to conceal the secret in an incomprehensible word-puzzle...'

'What secret?', enquired Mr. Fridriksson keenly.

'A secret that... by means of which...', spluttered my uncle.

'Do you, by any chance, have some special document?'

'No... I was making a pure supposition.'

'Fine', replied Mr. Fridriksson, who had observed my uncle's confusion and was kind enough not to insist. 'I hope', he added, 'that you will not leave our island without delving into its mineral riches?'

'Certainly, but perhaps I arrive a little late in the day; have any scholars been through here already?'

'Yes, Mr. Lidenbrock; the work of Ólafsson and Povelsen, carried out by order of the king, Troil's studies, Gaimard and Robert's scientific mission on board the French corvette *La Recherche*, and, recently, the observations of scholars on the frigate *La Reine Hortense*, have all contributed very considerably to our knowledge of Iceland. But believe me, there are still things to be done.'

'Do you really think so?', said my uncle a shade naively, trying to make his eyes shine less.

'Yes. How many mountains, glaciers, volcanoes there are to be studied, still hardly explored! Look, without going any further, consider that mountain on the horizon. It is called Mount Snaefell.'

'Mount Snaefell...'

'Yes, a most unusual volcano, whose crater is rarely visited.'

'Extinct?'

'Oh yes, extinct for the last five hundred years.'

'Well', replied my uncle, frantically crossing and uncrossing his legs so as not to jump into the air, 'I feel like beginning my geological studies with this Seafall... Feeless... what did you call it?'

'Snaefell', repeated the excellent Mr. Fridriksson.

This part of the conversation took place in Latin. I had followed everything, hardly able to keep a straight face when I saw my uncle trying to keep his satisfaction in, flowing as it was from every pore. He was trying to put on an innocent air, which made him look like a grimacing old devil.

'Yes', he said, 'your words have made up my mind! We will try to climb this Snaefell, perhaps even study its crater!'

'I very much regret that my duties do not allow me to leave Reykjavik; I would have accompanied you with pleasure and profit.'

'Oh, no, no, no!', responded my uncle tit for tat, 'we don't want to bother anybody, Mr. Fridriksson. I thank you with all my heart. To have a scholar like you with us would have been very useful, but your professional duties...'

I like to think that our host, in the innocence of his Icelandic soul, did not suspect my uncle's blatant tricks.

'It seems a very good idea, Professor Lidenbrock, to begin with this volcano. You will make many interesting observations there. But tell me, how are you planning to reach the Snaefell peninsula?'

'By sea, crossing the bay. It is the quickest route.'

'No doubt; but it cannot be taken.'

'Why not?'

'Because we do not have a single small boat in Reykjavik.'

'My God!'

'You will have to go by land, following the coast. It will take longer, but it will be more interesting.'

'Good. I will try to find a guide.'

'As a matter of fact, I have one to offer you.'

'A reliable and intelligent man?'

'Yes, he lives on the peninsula. He is an eider hunter, highly skilled, and with whom you will be pleased. He speaks Danish fluently.'

'And when can I see him?'

'Tomorrow if you wish.'

'Why not today?'

'Because he will only be here tomorrow.'

'Tomorrow then', my uncle replied with a sigh.

This decisive conversation finished a few moments later with warm thanks from the German professor to the Icelandic teacher. During the dinner, my uncle had gathered some vital information, including the story of Saknussemm, the reason for his mysterious document, the fact that his host would not be accompanying him on the expedition, and the news that a guide would be at his orders the very next day.

Chapter 11.

In the evening, I went for a brief walk along the seafront of Reykjavik, came back early, then lay down on my bed of rough planks. I slept well.

On waking up, I heard my uncle talking volubly in the next room. I quickly got up and joined him.

He was speaking Danish with a tall man, robustly built. This great strapping figure was clearly of unusual strength. His eyes, in a head of very considerable size and a certain naivety, appeared intelligent to me. They were of a dreamy blue colour. His long hair, which would have been considered red even in Britain, fell on athletic shoulders. This native was supple in his movements, but moved his arms little, like a man who didn't know the language of gestures or didn't bother to use it. Everything about him revealed a perfectly calm nature, not lazy, but composed. You felt that he didn't require anything from anyone, that he worked as it suited him, that his philosophy of life couldn't be astonished or disturbed by anything in this world.

I was able to detect the nuances of the Icelander's character by the way he listened to the passionate flow of words addressed to him. He remained with his arms crossed, not moving despite my uncle's repeated gesticulations; to say no, his head turned from left to right; to say yes, downwards, but so little that his long hair hardly moved. He was not so much economical with his movements as tight-fisted.

Certainly, looking at this man, I would never have guessed that he was a hunter. He wouldn't frighten the game, for sure, but how could he possibly get near it?

Everything became clear when Mr. Fridriksson reminded me that this calm person was only a hunter of eider, a bird whose plumage constitutes the main resource of the island. Actually, this plumage is called eiderdown, and you do not need to move a great deal to collect it.

During the first days of summer, the female eider, a kind of beautiful duck, goes and builds its nest amongst the rocks of the fjords which fringe the coast. The nest built, it covers it with fine feathers that it tears from its stomach. Straightaway the hunter, or rather merchant, arrives, takes the nest, and the female starts its work again. This continues as long as it has any down left. When it is completely bare, the male follows the same procedure. But as the hard, rough feathers of the male have no commercial value, the hunter does not bother to steal the future brood's bed. So, the nest is completed; the female lays its eggs; the babies hatch; and, the following year, the hunting of the eiderdown starts again.

However, since the eider does not choose steep rocks to build its nest on, but easy, horizontal ones sloping down into the sea, this Icelandic hunter could carry on his profession without too much commotion. He was a farmer who didn't have to sow the seed or cut his harvest, but merely gather it in.

This serious, phlegmatic, silent type was called Hans Bjelke; and he came with Mr. Fridriksson's recommendations. He was our future guide. His manner contrasted singularly with my uncle's.

Nevertheless, they got on well from the start. Neither of them discussed prices; the one was ready to accept whatever was offered, the other to pay whatever was asked. Never was a deal easier to reach.

According to their agreement, Hans undertook to guide us to the village of Stapi, on the southern coast of the Snaefell peninsula and at the very foot of the volcano. The distance by land was about twenty-two miles, or two days' journey according to my uncle's opinion.

But when he learned that these were Danish miles, of twenty-four thousand feet apiece, he had to adjust his calculations, and plan on seven or eight days' travel, given the poor quality of the tracks.

Four horses were to be put at our disposal, two for riding and two for luggage. Hans would travel on foot, which he was used to. He knew this part of the coast like the back of his hand, and promised to take us by the shortest route.

His contract with my uncle did not expire when we arrived at Stapi. He remained in his service for the total time necessary for his scientific excursions, at the price of three dollars per week. It was expressly agreed that this sum would be paid to the guide each Saturday evening, failing which his contract would be null and void.

It was decided we would leave on the 16th of June. My uncle wanted to give the hunter an advance on the agreement, but was rebuffed with a single word.

'Efter.'

'After', said the professor for my edification.

Once the agreement had been reached, the hunter promptly left.

'He's great', exclaimed my uncle, 'but he can hardly realise the brilliant part he is going to play.'

'So, he is coming with us...'

'Yes, Axel, to the centre of the Earth.'

There were still forty-eight hours left, but, to my great regret, I had to devote them to the preparations. All our intelligence was employed organizing things in the most useful way, the instruments here, the firearms there, the tools in this package, the food in that one. Four groups in all.

The instruments included:

1. A Eigel thermometer, graduated to 150°, which didn't seem quite right to me. Too much if the temperature went up as far as that, since we would be cooked. But not enough to measure the temperature of hot springs or other molten substances.

2. A manometer operated by compressed air, designed to show pressures greater than that at sea level. An ordinary barometer would not have been sufficient, given that the atmospheric pressure was due to increase proportionally with our descent underground.

3. A chronometer by Boissonnas the Younger of Geneva, perfectly set to the Hamburg meridian.

4. Two compasses to measure positive and negative inclination.

5. A spyglass.

6. Two Ruhmkorff lamps which used an electric current to give a highly portable source of light, reliable and not too bulky.

The weapons consisted of two rifles from Purdley More & Co. and two Colt revolvers. Why did we have weapons? I didn't imagine we were going to encounter many savages or wild beasts. But my uncle seemed very attached to his arsenal and his instruments, and especially to a considerable quantity of guncotton, which is unaffected by damp and whose explosive power is far greater than that of ordinary powder.

The tools were two ice axes, two pickaxes, a rope ladder, three alpenstocks, one axe, one hammer, a dozen iron wedges and pitons, and several long knotted ropes. It was a large packet, for the ladder alone was three hundred feet in length.

Finally there were the provisions. The packet was not big but reassuring, for I knew that it contained six months' supply of dried meat and biscuits. Gin was the only liquid, with water totally absent: we had flasks, and my uncle counted on springs to fill them. The objections I raised as to their quality, temperature, and even existence were ignored.

To complete our list of travel items, I will mention a portable medical kit containing blunt-bladed scissors, splints for fractures, a beige strap, bandages and compresses, sticking-plaster, a basin for bloodletting: terrifying objects. There was also a whole series of bottles containing dextrin, ethanol, liquid acetate of lead, ether, vinegar, and ammonia, all drugs of a frightening nature. As for the Ruhmkorff lamps, they had put the chemicals they required in the package.

My uncle was careful not to forget a supply of tobacco, powder for hunting, and tinder, nor a leather belt which he wore around his waist and which contained an adequate supply of money in gold, silver, and paper form. Six stout pairs of shoes, waterproofed by means of a coating of tar and latex, fell into the category of 'tools'.

'With such clothing, shoes, and equipment, there is no reason we shouldn't go far', said my uncle.

The 14th was entirely taken up with organizing the various items. In the evening we dined at Baron Trampe's, in the company of the mayor of Reykjavik and Dr. Hyaltalin, the most distinguished physician in the country. Mr. Fridriksson was not amongst the guests; I learned later that the governor and he were in disagreement on an administrative matter and did not speak to each other. As a result I didn't have the opportunity of understanding a single word of what was said during this semi-official dinner. I noticed only that my uncle spoke all the time.

The following day, our preparations were finished. Our host delighted the professor by presenting him with a map of Iceland which was incomparably better than Anderson's: it was the map drawn up by Mr. Olaf Nikolas Olsen, on a scale of 1/480,000, published by the Icelandic Literary Society and based on Messrs. Scheel and Frizac's geodesic work and Mr. Björn Gunnlaugsson's topographical survey. It constituted a precious document for a mineralogist.

The last evening was spent in close conversation with Mr. Fridriksson, for whom I felt the warmest sympathy; after the talk came a rather agitated sleep, for me at least.

At five o'clock, I was woken up by four horses whinnying and stamping below my window. I dressed quickly and went outside. Hans was finishing loading the luggage, almost without moving. He worked, however, with an unusual degree of skill. My uncle was blowing hot air and the guide seemed to be taking very little notice of his recommendations.

Everything was ready by six. Mr. Fridriksson shook our hands. With a great deal of warmth and in Icelandic, my uncle thanked him for his kind hospitality. As for myself, I strung together a cordial farewell in my best Latin. Then we climbed into the saddles, and Mr. Fridriksson accompanied his final goodbye to me with that line from Virgil that seemed ready-made for us, uncertain travellers on the road: *Et quacumque viam dederit fortuna sequamur* (and whatever route fortune gives, we will follow).

Chapter 12.

We left in overcast but settled weather. No exhausting heat to fear, no disastrous rain. Weather for tourists.

The joy of riding through an unknown land made me easy to please at the beginning of our venture. I was caught up in the happiness of those who go on journeys, a feeling of hope mixed with a sense of freedom. I began to feel involved in the trip.

'Besides, what do I risk? Travelling through a fascinating country, going up a remarkable mountain, at worst climbing down an extinct crater! It's clear that Saknussemm did not do anything else. As for the existence of a tunnel leading straight to the centre of the globe, it is pure fantasy! It is impossible! So, let's get whatever good we can out of this expedition without quibbling.'

By the time my thoughts had got this far, we had left Reykjavik.

Hans walked in front, at a quick but regular and unchanging pace. The two horses with our luggage followed him without having to be led. My uncle and I came last: we did not look ridiculous on our small but hardy mounts.

Iceland is one of the biggest islands in Europe. Its surface stretches across fourteen hundred miles, but it has only sixty thousand inhabitants. Geographers have divided it into four parts, and it was the Region of the South-West Quarter, 'Sudvestr Fjordungr', that we had to cross, almost diagonally.

On leaving Reykjavik, Hans had immediately followed the seashore. We crossed thin pastures that made great efforts to be green; yellow had more success. The rugged summits made of a trachytic substratum faded away amongst the mists on the eastern horizon. From time to time, patches of snow, concentrating the diffuse light, shone on the slopes of distant mountains. A few peaks, standing up more firmly, pointed through the grey clouds, to reappear above the shifting mists like bare reefs in an open sky.

Often these chains of dry rocks pushed out towards the sea, eating into the pasture, but there was always room to get past. Besides, our horses instinctively chose the best route without ever slowing their pace. My uncle did not even have the consolation of using his voice or whip to urge his mount forward: he had no excuse to be impatient. I couldn't help smiling when I saw him so big on his little horse for, with his long legs skimming the ground, he looked like a six-legged centaur.

'Nice animal, nice animal!', he said. 'You will see, Axel, that a creature more intelligent than the Icelandic horse does not exist. Snow, storms, blocked paths, rocks, glaciers: nothing stops it. It is brave, it is intelligent, it is reliable. It never trips, it never gets nervous. Should a stream appear, a fjord to be crossed, and they will appear, you will see it throw himself unhesitatingly into the water, like an amphibian, and swim across to the other side. If we do not upset it, if we let it do as it wishes, we will cover our twenty-five leagues a day, the one carrying the other.'

'We will, I'm sure; but what about the guide?'

'Oh, I am not worried about him. That sort of person walks without noticing. Our guide moves so little that he cannot possibly get tired. Moreover, I would give him my horse if he were tired. I would soon get cramps if I did not take some exercise. My arms feel all right, but one must not neglect one's legs.'

We carried on meanwhile at a considerable pace. The countryside was already virtually deserted. Here and there an isolated farm appeared, a lonely house built of wood, earth, and blocks of lava, like a beggar beside a sunken lane. These dilapidated huts seemed to be imploring the charity of passers-by, and one would almost have offered them alms. In this region, roads and even paths were completely lacking, and the vegetation however slow-growing, soon hid the traces of the rare travellers.

And yet this part of the province, a stone's throw from the capital, was considered one of the inhabited and cultivated parts of Iceland. What do the more deserted areas looked like? After half a mile, we had still not seen a single farmer at the door of his cottage, nor a single wild shepherd grazing a flock less wild than himself; only some cows and a few sheep left to their own devices. What would the regions in turmoil be like, broken by eruptions, born of volcanic explosions and underground upheavals?

We were due to make their acquaintance later; but when I consulted Olsen's map, I saw that we were avoiding them by following the winding edge of the shore. The main eruptive movements are in fact concentrated in the interior of the island. There, the horizontal strata of superimposed rocks called *trapps* in the Scandinavian languages, the trachytic strips, the eruptions of basalt, of tuff, of all the volcanic aggregates, the streams of lava and of molten porphyry, have produced a country of supernatural horror. I hardly realized at this stage what a sight awaited us on the Snaefell peninsula, where the damage of an impulsive nature forms a fearsome chaos.

Two hours after leaving Reykjavik, we arrived at the Aoalkirkja (main church or settlement) of Gufunes. It contained nothing special. Just a handful of houses. Hardly enough for a hamlet in Germany.

Hans decided to stop there for half an hour; he shared our frugal breakfast, replied 'yes' or 'no' to my uncle's questions about the nature of the road, and when asked where he intended to spend the night, he answered : 'Gardär'.

I looked at the map to find out what Gardär was. I located a small community of this name on the shore of the Hvalfjörd, four miles away from Reykjavik. I showed it to my uncle.

'Only four miles!', he said, 'four out of twenty-two! Just a pleasant stroll.'

He tried to say something to the guide, who did not reply but took up his position at the head of the horses and set off again.

Three hours later, still travelling over the faded grass of the pastures, we had to work our way around the Kollafjörd, as detouring round this estuary was easier and quicker than crossing it. Soon we had reached a *pingstaoer* (village administrative unit) called Ejulberg, whose church tower would have struck twelve, if the Icelandic churches had been rich enough to possess a clock; but they closely resemble their parishioners, who have no watches, but manage quite well without.

The horses were given food and water there. Afterwards, they took us along a shore squeezed in between the sea and a chain of hills. Then, they carried us without stopping to the *aoalkirkja* of Brantär, and then, a mile further, to Saurboer *annexia* (church annex), situated on the southern shores of the Hvalfjörd.

It was now four o'clock, and we had covered four 'miles'. The fjord was at least half a 'mile' wide at this point; the waves crashed noisily onto the sharp rocks; this bay opened out between high rocky walls, a sort of peak three thousand feet high, with remarkable brown strata separated by tuff beds of a reddish tinge. However intelligent our horses were, I was not looking forward to crossing a real strip of water on the back of a four-legged animal.

'If they really are smart', I said, 'they won't try to cross. Anyway, I'm planning to be smart on their behalf.'

But my uncle didn't want to wait. He spurred his horse on towards the shore. His mount sniffed slightly at the swell lapping at the edge and stopped. My uncle, who had his own instinct, urged it on all the more. Another refusal from the beast which shook his head. Next, oaths and an application of the whip, but kicks from the animal which began to unsaddle the rider. Finally, the small horse, bending his knees, withdrew from the professor's legs and left him standing there on two seashore rocks, like the Colossus of Rhodes.

'Cursed animal!', shouted the rider, suddenly converted into a pedestrian, as humiliated as a cavalry officer turned infantryman.

'*Färja*', said the guide, touching him on the shoulder.

'What, a ferry?'

'*Der*', replied Hans, pointing to a boat.

'Yes', I called out, 'there's a ferry.'

'You should have said so earlier! Well, come on!'

'*Tidvatten*', said the guide

'What is he saying?'

'He is saying "tide"', translated my uncle from the Danish.

'We presumably have to wait for the tide?'

'*Förbida*?'

'*Ja*.'

My uncle stamped his foot, while the horses headed for the ferry.

I perfectly understood the need to wait for a particular moment of the tide before starting to cross the fjord: the moment when the sea has reached its highest level and so is not moving. The ebb and flow are not felt then and the ferry is not in danger of being carried to the bottom of the bay or out to the open sea.

The right time only arrived at six o'clock. My uncle, myself, the guide, two ferrymen, and the four horses had got onto a sort of flatboat which looked rather fragile. Accustomed as I was to the steam ferries on the Elbe, I found the boatmen's oars a sad mechanical device. It took more than an hour to cross the fjord; but finally we arrived without incident.

Half an hour later, we had reached the aoalkirkja of Gardär.

Chapter 13.

It should have been dark, but on the sixty-fifth parallel I was not surprised to see light during the night: in June and July, in Iceland, the sun never sets.

Nevertheless, the temperature had gone down. I was cold and, above all, hungry. Most welcome was the *boer* which received us.

It was a peasant's house but worth a king's in terms of hospitality. When we arrived, the master came to shake our hands and, without further ado, indicated we should follow him into the house.

'Follow him', for it would have been impossible to go in at the same time. A long, narrow, dark passage led into this dwelling constructed of beams that had hardly been squared off. It gave access to each of the rooms. There were four: the kitchen, the weaving workshop, the *badstofa* (family bedroom) and, the best of all, the visitors' bedroom. My uncle, whose height had not been remotely considered when the house was built, duly hit his head three or four times against the projections of the ceiling.

We were shown into our room, which was quite large and had an earthen floor and a window with panes made of rather opaque sheep membranes. The bed was dry straw heaped into two wooden frames painted red and ornamented with maxims in Icelandic. I did not expect such comfort. Unfortunately, the house was pervaded with a strong smell of dried fish, marinated meat, and sour milk which rather upset my nose.

After setting down our travelers' saddlery, we heard our host's voice inviting us into the kitchen, the only room with a fire even during the coldest weather.

My uncle hastened to follow this hospitable suggestion. I followed him.

The kitchen chimney was of the classical sort: just a primitive stone as a hearth in the middle of the room, with a hole in the roof to let the smoke out. The kitchen also served as the dining-room.

When we came in, our host, as if seeing us for the first time, greeted us with the word 'saellvertu', which means 'be happy', and came and kissed us on the cheek.

His wife pronounced the same word in turn, accompanied by the same greeting; then the two of them, putting their right hands on their hearts, bowed deeply.

I hasten to add that the Icelandic woman was the mother of nineteen children, some small and some big and all chaotically teeming in the spirals of smoke filling the room from the hearth. At each moment I caught sight of another little blond head of some melancholy emerging from the cloud. It was exactly like a line of angels who had forgotten to wash their faces.

My uncle and I gave a very warm welcome to the brood; soon we had three or four of the urchins on our shoulders, the same number on our laps, and the others between our knees. Those who could speak repeated 'saellvertu' in all imaginable pitches. Those who could not merely shouted louder.

The concert was interrupted by the meal being announced. At this moment the hunter came back, having seen to the horses' food by thriftily letting them out on the countryside. The poor beasts had to be satisfied with chewing the rare mosses on the rocks and some seaweed which did not provide a lot of energy. However, the following day they would willingly come and continue the work of the day before.

'Saellvertu', said Hans.

Then, calmly, automatically, without one kiss being different from another, he greeted the host, the hostess, and their nineteen children.

Once the ceremony was over, we moved to table, all twenty-four of us, and consequently some literally on top of the others. The luckiest ones had only two urchins on their knees.

However, silence fell across the whole community when the soup arrived, and the natural Icelandic taciturnity, even amongst the youngsters, came back. Our host served us a lichen soup which was not unpleasant, then an enormous portion of dried fish swimming in butter that had been soured for twenty years, and was consequently much to be preferred to fresh butter according to the gastronomic ideas of Iceland. With it was some *skyr*, a sort of curdled milk, served with biscuits and sweetened with the juice of juniper berries; and finally, as a drink, whey mixed with water, called *blanda* in this country. If this remarkable food was good or not, I was unable to judge. I was hungry and, when the dessert came, I swallowed a thick buckwheat porridge down to the last bite.

After the meal was finished, the children disappeared; the adults grouped around the fireplace which was burning with peat, heather, cowpats, and the bones from the dried fish. Then, after this 'taking of the heat', the various groups went to their respective rooms. The hostess, as was the custom, offered to take off our stockings and trousers but, following our gracious declining of this offer, she did not insist, and I was finally able to curl up in my straw bedding.

The following day, at five o'clock, we bade the Icelandic farmer farewell, although my uncle had great difficulty in making him accept sufficient payment; and finally Hans gave the signal for departure.

Less than a hundred yards from Gardär, the appearance of the landscape began to change: the ground became marshy and the going less easy. On the right, the chain of mountains extended indefinitely, in a huge system of natural fortifications, of which we were following the counterscarp; often there were streams which had to be forded, without getting the bags too wet.

The wasteland was getting more and more deserted. Sometimes, nevertheless, a human shadow in the distance seemed to flee. If the bends of the path unexpectedly brought us near one of these ghosts, I felt a sudden disgust at the sight of a swollen head with shiny skin, devoid of hair, and repulsive wounds barely hidden by miserable rags.

The unhappy creature did not come to hold out his deformed hand; he ran away instead, but not before Hans had had time to greet him with the customary 'saellvertu'.

'*Spetelsk*', he said.

'A leper!'

This single word produced a frightful effect. The horrible affliction of leprosy is relatively common in Iceland; it is not contagious, but is hereditary: accordingly the wretched creatures are forbidden to marry.

These wraith-like figures were hardly calculated to add joy to the countryside, which was becoming deeply depressing, as the last patches of grass died under our feet. Not a single tree, if one excludes a few thickets of dwarf birches similar to brushwood. Not a single animal, except a few horses their owner could not feed and which wandered over the sad plains. Sometimes a falcon glided amongst the grey clouds and fled in full flight towards some southern lands; I let myself become absorbed in the melancholy of this untamed Nature, and my memories took me back to my native country.

Soon we had to cross several insignificant little fjords, and finally a real bay; the sea, motionless at this time, allowed us to traverse without waiting and thus reach the hamlet of Alftanes, a mile further on the other side.

In the evening, after fording across two rivers teeming with trout and pike, the Alfta and Heta, we were obliged to spend the night in an abandoned cottage, worthy of being haunted by all the goblins of Scandinavian mythology; the god of cold had clearly taken up residence there, and he was up to his tricks the whole night.

The following day presented no particular incident. Still the same marshy ground, the same uniform view, the same sad features. In the evening we had covered half the total distance, and we slept in the *annexia* at Krösolbt.

On the 19th of June, a bed of lava extended beneath our feet for about a mile; this kind of ground is called *hraun* locally; the lava, wrinkled on the surface, produced shapes like thick ropes, either simply stretched out or coiled up on themselves. A huge lava flow came down from the neighbouring mountains, now extinct volcanoes, but whose remnants testified to the violence of the past. A few wreaths of steam from hot springs still crept here and there.

We had little time to marvel at these phenomena; we had to push on. Soon the marshy ground came back under our horses' feet, crisscrossed by little lakes. We were now proceeding in a westerly direction; we had worked our way round the great Faxa Bay, and the two white peaks of Mount Snaefell stood erect amongst the clouds less than five miles away.

The horses were moving well; the problems of the terrain did not stop them. For my part I was beginning to feel very tired; my uncle remained as stiff and as upright as on the first day; I could not help admiring him as much as the hunter, who considered this expedition a simple stroll.

On Saturday, the 20th of June, at 6 p.m., we got to Büdir, a village on the seacoast, and the guide asked for his agreed pay. My uncle settled the sum. It was Hans's own family, his uncles and first cousins, who offered their hospitality. We were kindly welcomed, and without wishing to abuse the generosity of these good people, I would have been very glad to recover from the fatigues of the journey in their house. But my uncle, who had nothing to recover from, didn't see it that way and, the following day, we had to straddle our good old mounts once more.

The ground was affected by being near the mountain: its granite roots emerged from the earth like those of an old oak tree. We were working our way round the huge base of the volcano. The professor couldn't take his eyes off it; he waved his arms, he seemed to be sending challenges to it, as if saying: 'that's the giant I am going to tame!' Finally, after four hours' ride, the horses stopped of their own accord at the front door of Stapi parsonage.

Chapter 14.

Stapi is a settlement of about thirty shacks, built on the lava itself and in the rays of the sun reflected from the volcano. It lies at the end of a little fjord which forms part of a basalt wall of a most curious appearance.

We know that basalt is a dark brown rock of igneous origin. It takes on regular forms which produce surprising patterns. Nature proceeds geometrically here, working in the human fashion, as if she had used a set square, a pair of compasses, and a plumb line. If in every other case her art consists of great heaps strewn in disorder, barely formed cones, imperfect pyramids, strange successions of lines, here, wanting to provide an example of regularity, and working before the architects of the first ages, she has constructed a severe order which has never been surpassed, even in the marvels of Babylon or the wonders of Greece.

I had of course heard of the Giants' Causeway in Ireland and Fingal's Cave on one of the Hebrides, but I had never actually seen the display of a basalt construction.

Here at Stapi, I was able to appreciate the full beauty of the phenomenon.

The walls of the fjord, like the whole coast of the peninsula, were made up of a series of vertical columns, thirty feet tall. These straight shafts of perfect proportions supported an archivolt made of horizontal columns, whose overhang produced a half-vault over the sea. At intervals in this natural *impluvium*, one's eye detected arched openings of a superb design, through which rushed and foamed the waves from the open sea. A few basalt sections, torn off by the ocean's furies, were stretched out on the ground like the remains of a classical temple, ruins eternally young, over which the centuries would pass without leaving any mark.

This was the last overnight stop of our overland journey. Hans had brought us here with intelligence, and I drew some reassurance from the thought that he was to accompany us further.

When we arrived at the door of the rector's house, a simple low-built croft that was no finer and no more comfortable than its neighbours, I found a man shoeing a horse, hammer in hand and dressed in a leather apron.

'*Saellvertu*', said the hunter.

'*God dag*', replied the blacksmith in perfect Danish.

'*Kyrkoherde,*' said Hans, turning to my uncle.

'The rector! It seems, Axel, that this good man is the rector.'

In the meantime the guide had been explaining the situation to the *kyrkoherde*. He stopped his work and shouted out in a way presumably designed for horses and horse dealers, and immediately a big, ugly woman came out of the croft. If she was not six feet tall, the difference wasn't worth mentioning.

I was afraid that she might offer the travellers an Icelandic kiss; but this didn't happen and nor did she demonstrate very good grace in showing us in her house.

The guest-room seemed to me the worst in the parsonage, narrow, dirty, and foul-smelling. But we had no choice. The rector apparently didn't practice the traditional hospitality. Far from it. Before the day was out, I could see that we were dealing with a blacksmith, a fisherman, a hunter, a carpenter, and not at all with a minister of the Lord. We were in mid-week, it has to be admitted. Perhaps he made up for it on Sundays.

I don't want to criticize these poor priests who are, after all, perfectly wretched: they get a ludicrous income from the Danish government and receive a quarter of a tithe from their parish, which does not even add up to sixty marks at present-day values. Hence, they need to work for a living. But by fishing, hunting, and shoeing horses, one ends up adopting the manners, tone, and habits of hunters, fishermen, and other slightly rustic people. That same evening I noticed that amongst our host's virtues, sobriety did not figure.

My uncle quickly understood what sort of man he was dealing with: instead of a fine, dignified scholar, he found a heavy, rude countryman. He accordingly resolved to begin his great expedition as soon as possible and to leave this inhospitable rectory. Ignoring his tiredness, he decided we would spend a few days in the mountains.

Consequently, the preparations for leaving were made the day after arriving at Stapi. Hans hired the services of three Icelanders to replace the horses carrying the luggage; once we got to the bottom of the crater, these locals would have to turn back, leaving us on our own. That point was made clear.

At this juncture, my uncle had to tell the hunter of his intention to continue his exploration of the volcano to its furthermost limits.

Hans merely inclined his head. Whether he went there or somewhere else, whether he plunged into the innards of his island or travelled over its surface, made no difference to him. As for me, I had rather forgotten about the future, distracted until this point by the events of the journey, but now felt my emotions taking hold of me more than ever. What could I do? If I had wanted to try and stand up to Professor Lidenbrock, it should have been in Hamburg and not at the foot of Mount Snaefell.

One idea above all others worried me tremendously, a terrifying idea that might unsettle nerves stronger than mine.

'So', I said to myself, 'we're going to climb Mount Snaefell. Fine. We're going to have a look at its crater. Good. Some people have done so and they are still alive. But that is not all. If a path appears going down into the bowels of the Earth, if that wretched Saknussemm told the truth, we're going to get lost in the underground galleries of the volcano. But there is no indication that Mount Snaefell is really extinct! What proves that an eruption is not in preparation? The monster has been asleep since 1229 but does it necessarily mean it won't wake up again? And if it does wake up, what will happen to us?'

It was certainly worth thinking about, which I was doing most seriously. I couldn't sleep without dreaming of eruptions. And playing the part of scoria seemed to me rather difficult.

In the end I couldn't stand it anymore. I decided to put the case to my uncle as skillfully as possible, presenting it as a hypothesis which couldn't possibly be put into practice.

I went and found him. I shared my fears with him, and then retreated so that he could explode unhindered.

'I've been thinking about it', was his only reply.

What did these words mean? Was he going to listen to the voice of reason? Was he thinking of giving up his projects? It seemed too good to be true.

After a few moments of silence, during which I did not dare to question him, he continued: 'I had thought of it. Since we arrived in Stapi,

I have anxiously considered the critical question you have just put to me, for we must not be hasty.'

'No, we mustn't', I said emphatically.

'Although Mount Snaefell has been silent for six hundred years, it might speak again. But eruptions are always preceded by perfectly well-known phenomena. I have therefore questioned the local inhabitants, I have surveyed the ground, and I can assure you, Axel, that there will not be an eruption.'

I stood flabbergasted at this statement, and was not able to reply.

'Don't you believe me?', said my uncle, 'well then: follow me!'

I obeyed without thinking. Leaving the rectory, the professor took a direct route which led through a gap in the basalt rock face, heading inland. Soon we were out in open country, if that term can be used for a huge accumulation of volcanic material. The country appeared flattened under a hail of huge boulders, trap rocks, basalt, granite, and all the inosilicate minerals.

Here and there I could see gas and smoke rising in the air: these white mists, called *reykir* in Icelandic, came from hot springs, and their intensity showed the volcanic activity of the ground. This seemed to me to justify my fears. So I was surprised to hear my uncle say: 'do you see all that steam, Axel? Well, it proves that we have nothing to fear from the fury of the volcano!'

'It is amazing!', I cried.

'Listen carefully. When an eruption is on the way, the steam increases considerably; but then disappears completely when the phenomenon is actually happening, for the expanding gas no longer has the required pressure, and heads for the craters instead of escaping through the cracks of the globe. If therefore this steam stays in its normal state, if its force does not increase, if you add to such an observation that the wind and rain are not replaced by a heavy, calm atmosphere, you can safely say that there will not be an immediate eruption.'

'But...'

'Enough. When science has spoken, one can only remain silent afterwards!'

I returned to the parsonage a little hangdog. My uncle had defeated me by means of scientific arguments. However, I had one remaining hope: that once we got to the bottom of the crater, it would be impossible, for lack of a gallery, to go any deeper, in spite of all the Saknussemms in the world.

I spent the night in the clutches of a nightmare; I was in the middle of a volcano in the depths of the Earth, I felt as if I was being thrown into interplanetary space in the form of eruptive rock.

The following day, the 23rd of June, Hans was waiting for us with his companions, who were loaded down with food, tools, and instruments. Two alpenstocks, two rifles, and two cartridge belts were set aside for my uncle and me. Hans, a man of foresight, had added to our bags a full goatskin water bottle which, together with our flasks, meant that we had water for eight days.

It was 9 a.m. The rector and his tall bad-tempered wife were waiting in front of the door. They presumably wished to give us the last farewell that a host addresses to the traveller. But this farewell took the unexpected shape of a formidable bill, which charged even for the air of the pastoral house, far from fresh air I may say. The worthy couple held us to ransom like a Swiss innkeeper and put a high price on their overrated hospitality.

My uncle paid without quibbling. A man who leaves for the centre of the Earth spares no expense.

Once the matter was settled, Hans gave the signal for departure, and a few moments later we had left Stapi.

Chapter 15.

Mount Snaefell is five thousand feet high. Its double cone marks the end of a trachytic strip which is separate from the main relief system of the island. From our point of departure we couldn't see its two peaks in profile against the greyish background of the sky. I could only see an enormous snowy cap lowered on the giant's forehead.

We were walking in single file, following the hunter; he was climbing up narrow paths where two men couldn't have proceeded abreast. All conversation therefore became more or less impossible.

Beyond the basalt wall of Stapi fjord we encountered first a peaty soil, fibrous and herbaceous, the remains of the age-old vegetation of the marshes on the peninsula; these quantities of fuel, which have never been put to use, would be sufficient to heat the whole population of Iceland for a century. The huge peat bog, to judge from the bottom of the ravines in it, was often seventy feet deep and consisted of successive layers of carbonized rubbish, separated by thin sheets of pumiceous tuff.

As a true nephew of Professor Lidenbrock, and despite my worries, I examined with interest the mineralogical curiosities displayed in this vast natural history collection. At the same time my mind ran through the whole geological history of Iceland.

This extraordinary island clearly emerged from the watery depths at a relatively recent period. It is perhaps still rising imperceptibly. If indeed so, its origin can only be attributed to the work of underground fires. Accordingly, in such a case, Sir Humphry Davy's theory, Saknussemm's document, my uncle's claims, all went up in smoke. This hypothesis led me to examine the nature of the ground closely, and I was soon able to observe the successive phenomena governing its formation.

Iceland, which has no sedimentary terrain at all, is composed uniquely of volcanic tuff, that is to say of an agglomeration of stones and rocks of a porous texture. Before the volcanoes appeared, it consisted of a trappean massif, slowly lifted above the waves by the pressure of the forces in the centre. The central fires had not yet burst out.

But later a wide slit cut its way diagonally from the south-west to the north-east of the island, and the whole trachytic magma gradually poured out. At that time the phenomenon happened without violence, for the exit was very large, and the molten matter, thrown up by the bowels of the Earth, spread quietly out in vast sheets or hilly formations. The feldspars, syenites, and porphyries appeared during this period.

Thanks to this effusion, the thickness of the island increased considerably, and consequently its resistance. One can imagine what quantities of elastic fluid were built up inside when there was no longer any way out after the cooling of the trachytic crust. There came therefore a moment when the mechanical force of these gases was such as to lift up the heavy crust and to create high chimneys. Hence, this phenomenon shaped this volcano.

After the eruptive phenomena came the volcanic ones. Through the recently made openings escaped first the basaltic streams, of which the plain we were crossing at this moment offered us the most splendid specimens. We were walking over these heavy dark-grey rocks that the cooling down had molded into prisms with hexagonal bases. In the distance could be seen a large number of flattened cones, each of which was formerly a fire-vomiting mouth.

Then, when the basaltic eruption was exhausted, the volcano, which drew its strength from that of the extinct craters, gave passage to the lavas and to those tuffs made up of cinders and scoria whose long spread-out flows I could see on its sides, like a cascading mane.

Such were the successive phenomena that had constructed Iceland. All of them came from the effect of the internal fires, and to suppose that the interior did not remain in a permanent state of white-hot flux was pure madness. It was madness, especially, to claim to be able to reach the centre of the globe!

So I was reassuring myself about the results of our undertaking as we moved in to attack Mount Snaefell.

The route was becoming more and more difficult; the ground was climbing; the loose rocks were easily displaced and it needed the most careful concentration to avoid dangerous falls.

Hans carried calmly on, as if moving over unbroken ground. Sometimes he passed behind huge boulders and we lost sight of him for a moment, but then a piercing whistle would spring from his lips to tell us which way to go. Often he would stop, pick up loose pieces of rock and arrange them into signs in a recognizable fashion, so as to mark the way back. An admirable precaution in itself, but one that would be made useless by future events.

Three hours' tiring march had only brought us as far as the base of the mountain. At this point Hans called a halt, and we shared a quick lunch. My uncle took double mouthfuls to save time. Since this halt was also a rest period, he was forced to wait the guide's decision: he gave the signal for departure an hour later. The three Icelanders, as taciturn as their hunter companion, didn't utter a single word and ate soberly.

We now began to move up the slopes of Mount Snaefell. By an optical illusion common with mountains, its snow-covered summit seemed to me very close but it took many long hours to reach it! I was exhausted! The stones, not held together by earth or grass, rolled from under our feet and disappeared towards the plain at the speed of an avalanche.

In some places, the sides of the mountain made an angle of at least 36° with the horizon. It was impossible to climb them, and we had to work our way round these steep rock-strewn slopes with considerable difficulty. In such cases we helped each other by means of sticks.

I have to say that my uncle kept close to me as often as possible. He never lost sight of me and on quite a few occasions his arm provided solid support. He himself undoubtedly had an innate sense of balance for he never hesitated. The Icelanders climbed with the sure-footedness of highlanders, despite their heavy loads.

To judge from the height of Mount Snaefell, I assumed it was impossible for us to reach it from this side, unless the angle of the slope decreased. Fortunately, after an hour of tiring efforts and considerable feats, a sort of staircase suddenly appeared in the middle of a vast carpet of snow built up on top of the volcano, and this helped our climb. It was formed by one of those rivers of stones (called *stinâ* in Icelandic) thrown out by the eruptions. If this river hadn't been stopped dead by the shape of the mountain's flanks, it would have thrown itself into the sea, and thus formed new islands.

As it was, it helped a great deal. The steepness of the slope increased, but the stone steps meant that it could be climbed without problem. So quick was our progress that, remaining behind for a moment while my companions carried on up, I saw that they were already reduced to a microscopic size by the distance.

By seven in the evening, we had climbed the two thousand steps of the staircase. We stood at the top of a big swelling of the mountain, a sort of base on which rested the cone forming the crater.

The sea stretched out at a depth of 3,200 feet. We were above the snow line, at a relatively low level in Iceland because of the constant humidity of the climate. It was bitterly cold. The wind blew hard. I felt utterly exhausted. The professor saw clearly that my legs were refusing to carry me and decided to stop, despite his impatience. He therefore made a sign to the hunter, who shook his head saying:

'*Ofvanför.*'

'Apparently we need to go higher.'

He asked Hans the reason for his reply.

'*Mistour.*'

'*Ya, mistour,*' repeated one of the Icelanders in a frightened tone.

'What does the word mean?', I asked anxiously.

'Look there', replied my uncle.

I turned to look at the plain. An immense column of ground-up pumice stone, sand, and dust was climbing, swirling like a cloudburst. The wind was driving it against the flank of Mount Snaefell, which we were now clinging to. This opaque curtain, spread out before the sun, threw a large shadow over the whole mountain. If this cloudburst leaned over, it would inevitably embrace us in its swirls. Such a phenomenon, called *mistour* in Icelandic, is quite common when the wind blows in from the glaciers.

'*Hastigt, hastigt*', shouted the guide.

Without knowing Danish, I understood that we had to follow Hans as quickly as possible. He began to work his way round the cone of the crater, at an angle to make the going easier. Soon the cloudburst crashed down on the mountain, which quivered at the shock; the stones caught up in the eddies rained down as if in an eruption. Fortunately, we were on the other side and sheltered from all danger. If it hadn't been for the guide's precaution, our torn bodies would have been pulverized and dropped far away like the product of some unknown meteor.

However, Hans didn't consider it prudent to spend the night on the side of the cone. We continued our zigzagging ascent. The fifteen hundred feet still to be covered took nearly five hours, for the detours, shortcuts, and retreats measured at least eight miles. I couldn't go on: I was overcome by cold and hunger. The air was slightly rarefied and insufficient to fill my lungs.

Finally, at eleven at night, very much in darkness, we reached the summit of Mount Snaefell. Before going to shelter inside the crater, I caught sight of the midnight sun at the lowest point in its life's course, sending its pale rays over the island sleeping at my feet.

Chapter 16.

Supper was quickly swallowed and the posse settled down as well as it could. The ground was very hard, the shelter fragile, the situation very uncomfortable at five thousand feet above sea level. But my sleep was especially calm that night, one of the best I had spent for a long time. I didn't even dream.

In the morning, we woke up half-frozen by a glacial temperature, but in the rays of a fine sun. I got up from my granite bed to go and enjoy the magnificent spectacle laid out before my eyes.

I was standing on the southern summit of Snaefell's twin peaks. The panorama extended over most of the island. As at all great heights, the perspective lifted up the shores while the central parts seemed to have sunk. You would have thought that one of Helbesmer's relief-maps was spread beneath my feet. I saw deep valleys crisscrossing in every direction, chasms opening up like shafts, lakes turned into ponds, rivers become rivulets. On my right were endless glaciers and repeated peaks, some of them plumed with light smoke. The undulations of these infinite mountains, whose layers of snow made them appear foaming, reminded me of the surface of a rough sea. If I turned towards the west, the ocean spread out its magnificent expanse like a continuation of these foam-flecked summits. I could hardly see where the land stopped and the swell began.

I plunged into that high-blown ecstasy produced by lofty peaks, without feeling dizzy this time, as I was finally getting used to these sublime contemplations. My dazzled eyes bathed in the clear irradiation of the sun's rays. I forgot who I was, where I was, and lived the life of elves and sylphs, those imaginary inhabitants of Scandinavian mythology. I was intoxicated by the voluptuous pleasure of the heights, oblivious of the depths my fate was shortly going to plunge me into. But I was brought back to reality by the arrival of the professor and Hans, joining me at the very summit.

Turning to the west, my uncle pointed towards a slight mist, a haze, a hint of land above the line of the waves.

'Greenland.'

'Greenland?'

'Yes, we're less than thirty-five leagues away, and during the thaws the polar bears come as far as Iceland, carried down from the north on ice floes. But that is of little importance. We have reached the top of Mount Snaefell, with its twin peaks: one to the north and the other to the south. Hans will tell us what the Icelanders call the one bearing us at this instant.'

The hunter duly replied to his question: 'Scartaris.'

My uncle glanced at me triumphantly.

'To the crater!', he said.

The crater of Mount Snaefell formed an inverted cone whose mouth was probably slightly more than half a league across. It seemed to me to be about two thousand feet deep. One should imagine the state of such a receptacle when it was filling up with thunder and flames. The bottom of the funnel was only about five hundred feet in circumference, so its relatively gentle slopes allowed one to reach the lower part with ease. I couldn't help comparing this crater to an enormous widened-out blunderbuss; and the comparison terrified me.

'To climb down into a blunderbuss', I thought, 'it may be loaded and could go off at the least shock: you've got to be crazy.'

But there was no going back. With an indifferent expression, Hans took the lead. I followed him without a word.

In order to make the going easier, Hans described greatly lengthened ellipses on the inside of the cone. We had to pass amongst stones from eruptions, some of which, when loosened from their crevices, would rebound and rush down to the bottom of the chasm. Their fall produced waves of strange-sounding echoes.

Parts of the cone were covered with internal glaciers. Hans moved forward here with tremendous caution, prodding the ground with his alpenstock, looking for crevasses. At some of the difficult parts, we had to tie ourselves together with a long rope, so that if by chance one of us happened to slip, he would be held up by his companions. This solidarity constituted a useful precaution, but did not remove all danger.

Despite the difficulties of climbing down slopes unknown to the guide, we covered the distance without incident, except for the fall of a packet of ropes which slipped from the hands of one of the Icelanders, and took the shortest route towards the bottom of the chasm.

We arrived at midday. I looked up and saw the high mouth of the cone framing part of the sky: an almost perfect circle, but with a dramatically reduced circumference. Only at one point did the peak of Scartaris stand out and plunge into the huge space.

At the bottom of the crater opened three vents through which, at the time when Mount Snaefell used to erupt, the central fire forced its lava and its steam. Each of these chimneys was about a hundred feet across. There they were, wide open, beneath our feet. I didn't dare to look down into them. As for Professor Lidenbrock, he had quickly examined their shape and size. He was breathing heavily, running from one to the other, waving his arms and shouting unintelligible words. Hans and his companions sat on hummocks of lava and watched: they clearly took him for a lunatic.

Suddenly my uncle cried out. At first I thought he had just fallen into one of the three holes. But then I saw him, standing with arms outstretched and legs apart in front of a granite boulder placed at the centre of the crater, like an enormous pedestal designed for a statue of Pluto. He stood like a man dumbstruck, but it soon turned instead into an exaggerated happiness.

'Axel, Axel! Come here, down here!'

I ran down. Hans and the Icelanders stayed exactly where they were.

'Look!', said the professor.

Dumbstruck like him, but markedly less happy, I read on the western side of the boulder, in runic characters gnawed by time, the thousand-times-accursed name: Arne Saknussemm!

'Arne Saknussemm!', shouted my uncle, 'can you have any doubt now?'

I didn't reply, but came back to my lava seat in a state of total confusion. I was crushed by the evidence.

How long I spent sunk in my thoughts? I don't know! All I know is that, when I looked up again, I found my uncle and Hans alone at the bottom of the crater. The Icelanders had been dismissed, and were now climbing down the outer slopes of Mount Snaefell on their way back to Stapi.

Hans was quietly sleeping at the foot of a rock, in a lava channel where he had improvised a bed. My uncle was walking up and down the floor of the crater, like some wild animal in a trap dug by a hunter. I had neither the strength nor the desire to get up, and, imitating the guide, I slipped into a harrowing doze, thinking I could hear noises or feel shivers coming from the sides of the mountain.

That was how our first night at the bottom of the crater was spent.

The following day, a grey sky, cloudy and heavy, lowered over the summit of the cone. I noticed this less from the darkness of the chasm than from the anger that took hold of my uncle.

I understood why, and a last feeling of hope came back to me. The reason was as follows: of the three routes that were under out feet, only one had been followed by Saknussemm. According to the Icelandic scholar, it was to be identified by the particularity described in the cryptogram, namely that the shadow of Scartaris came and touched its edge during the last few days of the month of June.

This sharp peak could thus be considered the style of a huge sundial, whose silhouette on a given day marked the way to the centre of our globe.

If by chance the sun was not there: no shadow! Consequently, no sign! It was the 25th of June. Should the sky stay overcast for six more days, the observation would have to be put off for another year.

I will not attempt to describe Professor Lidenbrock's impotent rage. The day passed without a shadow coming down to the bottom of the crater.

Hans didn't move from where he was, although he must have wondered what we were waiting for, if he wondered anything! My uncle didn't address a single word to me. His eyes, invariably turned to the sky, blended into the grey and misty background.

On the 26th, still nothing. Rain mixed with snow fell during the day. Hans built a hut with pieces of lava. I took some pleasure from watching the thousands of improvised cascades running down the sides of the cone, with each of its stones adding to the deafening murmur.

My uncle could no longer hold himself back. The most patient man could legitimately be irritated, for this really was like sinking while coming into harbour.

But Heaven constantly mixes great joys with great sorrows, and it was preparing a satisfaction for Professor Lidenbrock equal to his terrible disappointments.

The sky was still covered the following day. But on Sunday, the 28th of June, the third last day of the month, the change of moon coincided with a change in the weather. The sun poured its abundant rays down into the crater. Each hummock, each rock, each boulder, each bump, had its share of the luminous flow and instantly cast its shadow on the ground. That of Scartaris, especially, stood out like a sharp stone and began to turn imperceptibly with the radiant orb.

My uncle turned with it.

At 12 o'clock, it came and briefly touched the edge of the middle chimney.

'It is there! There it is!', shouted the professor. 'To the centre of the globe!', he added in Danish.

I looked at Hans.

'*Forüt!*', he said calmly.

'Forward!', replied my uncle.

It was thirteen minutes past one.

Chapter 17.

The real journey began. Until now things had been more tiring than difficult; but henceforth problems were literally going to spring forth under our feet.

I had still not looked down at the bottomless pit into which I was going to engulf myself. The moment had arrived. I could still either take part in the venture or else refuse to try it. But I felt ashamed to turn back in the hunter's presence. Hans accepted the adventure so calmly, with such indifference, such unconcern at all danger, that I blushed at the idea of being less brave than him. On my own, I would have launched into a whole series of important arguments, but since the guide was there I remained silent. My memory flew back towards my pretty Vironian girl, and I approached the middle chimney.

I have already mentioned it was a hundred feet across, or about three hundred feet right round. I leant over an overhanging rock, and looked. My hair stood on end. An impression of void took hold of my being. I felt my centre of gravity moving through me and dizziness going to my head like an intoxicating beverage. Nothing more dizzying than this attraction of the abyss. I was about to fall. A hand held me back. Hans's. Decidedly, I hadn't had enough 'lessons in chasms' at the Frelsers Kirke in Copenhagen.

However, little I had dared to look down into the well, I had realized what shape it was. Its walls, almost perpendicular, had many projections which were certainly going to make them easier to climb down. But if there was an adequate staircase, there was no banister. A rope attached at the mouth would have provided sufficient support, but how to untie it when we got to its end?

My uncle employed a very simple method to get round this difficulty. He unrolled a rope as thick as a thumb and four hundred feet long. First he dropped half of it down, then wound it round a block of lava which projected outwards, and finally threw the other half into the chimney. Each of us could then climb down while holding together the two halves of the rope, which couldn't slip. Two hundred feet further on, nothing would be easier than bringing it down by letting one end go and pulling on the other. We would then be able to repeat this exercise ad infinitum.

'Now', said my uncle, 'having finished these preparations, let's think about the luggage. It will be split into three, and each of us will strap a package to his back, I refer only to the fragile objects.'

The bold professor clearly didn't include us in the last category.

'Hans will carry the tools and a third of the food; you, Axel, another third of the food and the firearms; I will take the rest of it and the delicate instruments.'

'But what about the clothing and this great pile of ropes and ladders, who will take charge of them?'

'They will go down by themselves.'

'How?'

'You will see.'

My uncle liked to employ strong-arm methods, without hesitating. On his command, Hans tied the non-fragile objects into a single packet, which was roped solidly together, and then quite simply dropped down into the abyss.

I heard the lowing sound produced by the movements of the layers of air. My uncle, leaning over the gulf, watched the descent of our luggage with a satisfied air, and stood up again only after losing sight of it.

'Right. We are next.'

I ask any man of good faith if it is possible to listen to such words without getting cold shivers.

The professor attached the package of instruments to his back; Hans took the implements; I took the firearms. The descent began in the following order: Hans, my uncle, myself. It proceeded in deep silence, broken only by rock debris falling into the abyss.

I allowed myself to flow, so to speak, with one hand desperately holding on to the double rope, and the other using my alpenstock to slow me down. A single idea obsessed me: I was afraid of losing all means of support. This rope seemed to me very fragile for bearing the weight of three people. I used it as little as possible, performing miracles of balance on the lava projections that my foot tried to hold on to like a hand.

When one of these precarious steps happened to dislodge under Hans's feet, he would say in his calm voice: '*gif akt!*'

'Careful!', repeated my uncle.

After half an hour we had reached the top of a boulder solidly attached to the wall of the chimney.

Hans pulled one of the ends of the rope, and the other rose in the air. Having gone round the rock at the top, it fell back, dragging down pieces of rock and lava, a sort of rain or rather hail, full of danger.

Leaning over our narrow platform, I noticed that the bottom of the hole could still not be seen.

The rope manoeuvre began again, and half an hour later we had got two hundred feet deeper.

I don't know if, during such a descent, the most fanatical geologist would have tried to study the nature of the formations surrounding him. As for me, I hardly thought about them; I was not really bothered whether they were Pliocene, Miocene, Eocene, Cretaceous, Jurassic, Triassic, Permian, Carboniferous, Devonian, Silurian, or Primitive. But the professor undoubtedly made observations or else took notes, for during one of our halts he said: 'the further I go, the more confident I become. The arrangement of these volcanic formations absolutely confirms Davy's theory. We are in the middle of the primordial ground, the ground in which the chemical reaction between the metals burning on contact with the air and water occurred. I absolutely refuse to accept the theory of a heat in the centre. But we will see for ourselves.'

Still the same conclusion. It goes without saying that I didn't bother to discuss it. My silence was taken for agreement, and the descent began again.

After three hours, I had still not caught a glimpse of the bottom of the chimney. When I looked up, I could see the mouth, which was getting quite a lot smaller. Because of the small angle between the walls, they looked as though they were coming together. It was slowly getting darker and darker.

We were still going down. It seemed to me that the rocks disturbed from the walls were swallowed up with a duller reverberation and that they ought to be reaching the bottom of the abyss quickly.

As I had carefully noted the operations of the rope, I was able to calculate the precise depth and time elapsed.

We had used the rope fourteen times, taking half an hour each time. So, we had spent seven hours, plus fourteen rest periods of fifteen minutes, or three and a half hours. Ten and a half in total. Since we had left at one, it had to be about eleven now.

As for the depth reached, the fourteen operations of the rope gave 2,800 feet.

At that moment Hans's voice was heard: 'halt!'

I stopped dead at the precise moment when my feet were about to collide with my uncle's head.

'We have arrived', he said.

'Where?', I asked, slipping down beside him.

'At the bottom of the vertical chimney.'

'And there is no way out?'

'Yes there is, I can just see a sort of corridor at an angle towards the right. We will have a look tomorrow. Let's eat, and then we can sleep.'

It was still not completely dark. We opened the food bag, ate, and lay down, each doing his best to make a bed amongst the stone and lava debris.

Lying on my back, I opened my eyes and caught sight of a brilliant object at the other end of the three-thousand-foot-long tube, converted into a gigantic telescope.

It was a star, but not twinkling at all. According to my calculations it was Beta of the Little Bear.

Then I fell into a deep sleep.

Chapter 18.

At eight in the morning, a ray of daylight came and woke us up. The thousand facets of the lava on the walls picked it up on the way down and scattered it everywhere like a shower of sparks.

These gleams were enough for us to be able to distinguish the surrounding objects.

'Well, Axel, what do you say?', exclaimed my uncle, rubbing his hands together.

'Have you ever spent a more peaceful night in our house on the Königstrasse? No noise of cartwheels, no cries from the market, no yelling boatmen!'

'It is admittedly very calm at the bottom of this well, but such quiet is, in itself, quite frightening.'

'Well, if you are frightened already, what will you be like later? We have not gone a single inch into the bowels of the Earth!'

'What do you mean?'

'I mean that we have only reached ground level on the island! This long vertical tube leading down from the crater of Mount Snaefell stops at approximately sea level.'

'Are you certain?'

'Yes I am. Have a look at the barometer.'

The mercury, after rising in the instrument as we descended, had indeed stopped at twenty-nine inches.

'You see. The pressure is still only one atmosphere, and I am looking forward to the manometer replacing the barometer.'

The barometer was indeed going to become useless when the weight of the air was greater than its pressure as calculated at sea level.

'But shouldn't we be afraid that the ever-increasing pressure will become highly uncomfortable?'

'No, we will descend slowly, and our lungs will get used to breathing a denser atmosphere. Aeronauts eventually lack air when they climb up into the highest layers whereas we may perhaps have too much. But I prefer that. Let's not waste a moment. Where is the package that came down the inside of the mountain before us?'

I remembered then that we had looked for it the evening before but not found it. My uncle questioned Hans, who looked carefully with his hunter's eyes, then replied: '*der huppe*!'

'Up there!'

The package was indeed hanging from a projecting rock a hundred feet above our heads. The agile Icelander immediately climbed up like a cat and, a few moments later, it had caught up with us.

'Now,' said my uncle, 'let's have breakfast, but a breakfast like people who perhaps have a long journey ahead of them.'

The dried meat and biscuit were washed down with a few mouthfuls of water mixed with gin.

Once we had finished, my uncle pulled from his pocket a notebook designed for observations. He took each of the various instruments in turn and wrote down:

Monday, 1 July.
Chronometer: 8.17 a.m.
Barometer: 29 p. 7 l.
Thermometer: 6°.
Direction: ESE.

The last observation referred to the dark corridor, as indicated by the compass.

'Now, Axel', cried the professor enthusiastically, 'we are really going to penetrate the globe's bowels. This is the precise moment when our journey begins.'

Saying that, with one hand he took the Ruhmkorff lamp, which was hanging round his neck. With the other he applied the electric current to the filament of the lamp, and a fairly bright light chased the darkness from the tunnel.

Hans carried the second lamp, which was also switched on. This ingenious application of electricity allowed us to go for a long time thanks to the production of artificial daylight, in spite of the presence of inflammable gases.

'Let's go!', said my uncle.

Each of us picked up his bundle. Hans took charge of pushing the packet of ropes and clothing in front of him, and, with me in third position, we entered the gallery.

Just as I plunged into the black passage, I raised my head and looked through the long tube at the sky of Iceland 'that I would never see again'.

During its last eruption in 1229, the lava had forced its way through this tunnel. It had carpeted the inside with a thick, shiny coating: the electric light was now reflected in it, becoming a hundred times brighter.

The only difficulty consisted of not sliding down the slope too quickly, for it was at an angle of about 45°. Fortunately, worn-away parts and blisters acted as steps, and all we had to do was let our packages slide, held back by a long rope.

But what acted as steps under our feet became stalactites on certain walls. The lava, porous in places, was covered with little round bulbs; crystals of opaque quartz, decorated with clear drops of glass, hung from the vaulted ceiling like chandeliers: they seemed to light up as we passed. It was as if the spirits of the underground were lighting up their palace to welcome their guests from the Earth's surface.

'It's magnificent!', I shouted in spite of myself. 'What a sight, Uncle John! Look at the shades of the lava which slowly go from reddish-brown to bright yellow. And these crystals that look like luminous spheres!'

'At last, Axel! At last, you find this beautiful my boy! You will see many others, I hope. Off we go!'

He should have said 'off we slide', for we were able to simply let ourselves go on these inclined slopes, without straining ourselves. It was Virgil's *facilis descensus Averni*. The compass, which I often consulted, showed the direction as south-east with an unflinching precision. The lava flow deviated to neither side. It had the inflexibility of a straight line.

Meanwhile it wasn't getting appreciably warmer. This confirmed Davy's theories, and several times I looked at the thermometer with surprise. Two hours after we had left, it still only indicated 10°, in other words an increase of 4°. That made me think that our journey was more horizontal than vertical. As for knowing the exact depth reached, nothing was easier. The professor measured the precise vertical and horizontal angles of our route but kept the results to himself.

At about eight in the evening, he gave the signal to stop. Hans immediately sat down. The lamps were hung from a lava projection.

We were in a sort of cavern where there was no lack of air. On the contrary: we felt a wind blowing. What was causing it? What movement in the atmosphere did it arise from? I wasn't really interested in answering the question at that moment. Hunger and tiredness made me unable to think. A descent of seven hours without stopping produces a great depletion of energy. I was exhausted, and had been very glad to hear the word 'halt'. Hans spread out a few provisions on a block of lava and each of us ate hungrily. One thing worried me, though: half our supply of water had been used up. My uncle planned to replenish it at underwater springs, but there hadn't been a single one so far. I couldn't help mentioning it to him.

'Are you surprised by the absence of streams?', he replied.

'Yes, and even worried. We have water left for only five days.'

'Don't worry, Axel, my reply is that we will find water, and more than we want.'

'When?'

'When we have left this lava envelope. How do you think that springs can get through these walls?'

'But the lava flow may continue to a great depth. And we don't seem to have gone very far yet in the vertical direction.'

'What makes you say that?'

'Because if we had gone a long way into the interior of the Earth's crust, the heat would be greater than it is.'

'According to your system. What does the thermometer say?'

'Hardly 15°, which is only 9° more than when we left.'

'And your conclusion?'

'I conclude as follows. From the most precise observations, we know that the temperature increases by one degree for every hundred feet you go into the interior of the globe. But local conditions can sometimes alter that figure. Thus, in Yakutsk, in Siberia, it has been observed that the increase is one degree for every thirty-six feet. The difference clearly depends on the conductivity of the rocks. One can also add that in the neighbourhood of an extinct volcano, through the gneiss, the increase is only one degree for every 125 feet. Let us therefore take this last hypothesis, which is the most favorable, and let us calculate.'

'Calculate, my boy.'

'It's easy,' I said, jotting the figures down in my notebook. 'Nine times 125 feet gives 1,125 feet deep.'

'So it does.'

'Well?'

'Well, according to my observations, we are now ten thousand feet below sea level.'

'Is it possible?'

'Yes, or else figures are no longer figures!'

The professor's calculations were correct. We had gone six thousand feet further than the greatest depths achieved by man, such as the mines of Kitzbühel in the Tyrol or those of Wuttemberg in Bohemia. The temperature, which should have been 81° at this spot, was barely 15°. It gives you food for thought.

Chapter 19.

At 6 a.m. the following day, Tuesday, 30 June, the journey began again.

We were still following the lava gallery, truly a natural ramp, as gentle as those inclined planes that still replace staircases in old houses. This continued until 12.17, the precise moment when we caught up with Hans, who had just stopped.

'Ah', exclaimed my uncle, 'we have reached the end of the chimney.'

I looked around. We were in the middle of an intersection, with two paths heading forward, both of them dark and narrow. Which one were we to take? We had a problem.

But my uncle didn't want to appear to hesitate before either me or the guide: he pointed to the eastern tunnel, and soon all three of us had plunged into it.

In any case, any deliberation about the choice of path could have gone on indefinitely, for no clue could possibly determine the choice of one or the other: we had to trust entirely to chance.

The slope of the new gallery was very gentle, and the cross-section varied a great deal. Sometimes a succession of arches unfolded before us like the aisles of a Gothic cathedral. The artists of the Middle Ages could easily have studied here all the forms of religious architecture generated by the ogive. A mile further on, we had to bow our heads under low semicircular arches in the Roman style, with thick pillars forming part of the rock itself, bending under the spring of the vaults. At certain places, these forms gave way to low substructures that looked like beavers' work, and we crawled and slid through narrow passageways.

The heat stayed at a tolerable level. I couldn't help thinking about its intensity when the lavas vomited by Mount Snaefell had rushed through this path, so peaceful today. I imagined the rivers of fire broken at the angles in the tunnel and the build-up of superheated steam in this enclosed space!

'I hope', I thought, 'the old volcano will not decide to go back into its old ways!'

I didn't mention these ideas to Uncle John: he wouldn't have understood. His sole thought was to go forward. He walked, he slid, he tumbled down even, with a degree of conviction that it was better, after all, to admire.

At 6 p.m., following a relatively easy march, we had covered two leagues in a southerly direction, but scarcely a quarter of a mile in depth.

My uncle gave the signal to stop. We ate without talking very much, and then went to sleep without thinking very much.

Our arrangements for the night were very simple: travel blankets, which we rolled ourselves up in, were our sole bedding. We had no fear of cold, nor of surprise visits. Those travellers who penetrate the middle of the deserts of Africa or the heart of the forests of the New World are forced to watch over each other during the hours of sleep. But here, absolute solitude and complete safety. Savages or wild beasts: none of these harmful races were to be feared.

In the morning we woke fresh and restful. We started off again. We were following a lava route like the day before. Impossible to recognise what sort of formations we were passing through. Instead of going down into the bowels of the globe, the tunnel was becoming more and more horizontal. I even thought it was heading back up towards the surface of the Earth. At about 10 a.m., the tendency became so clear, and consequently so tiring, that I had to slow our progress.

'Well, Axel?', the professor said impatiently.

'Well, I'm totally exhausted.'

'What, after three hours of strolling along such an easy route!'

'Easy, perhaps, but most certainly tiring.'

'But all we have to do is descend!'

'Climb, with respect!'

'Climb?', said my uncle, shrugging his shoulders.

'Definitely. For the last half-hour, the gradient has been different, and were we to follow it to the end, we would certainly get back to Iceland.'

The professor shook his head like someone unwilling to be convinced.

I tried to pursue the conversation. He didn't reply, but just gave the signal for departure. I saw clearly that his silence was nothing but concentrated ill humour.

However, I valiantly picked up my burden and hurried after Hans, who was following my uncle. I didn't want to be left behind for I was tremendously worried about losing sight of my companions. I trembled at the thought of getting lost in the depths of this labyrinth.

Besides, if the ascending route was becoming more difficult, I consoled myself by thinking that it was bringing me closer to the surface of the Earth. It was a hope. Every step confirmed it, and I rejoiced at the idea of seeing my little Gräuben again.

At midday the appearance of the walls of the tunnel changed. I noticed this from the dimming of the electric light reflecting from them. The covering of lava was being replaced by bare rock. The massif was made up of layers at an angle, often in fact completely perpendicular. We were in the middle of the Transition Era, in full Silurian Period.

'It's obvious', I said to myself, 'during the Second Era of the Earth, the sediments from the water formed these schists, these limestones, these sandstones! We are turning our backs on the granite massif. We are like people from Hamburg who take the Hanover road to go to Lübeck.'

I should have kept my remarks to myself. But my geologist's temperament overcame my caution, and Uncle John overheard my exclamations.

'What is the matter then?'

'Look!', I replied, showing him the successive varieties of sandstones and limestones and the first signs of shale formations.

'Well?'

'Here we are at the period when the first plants and animals appeared!'

'Do you really think so?'

'But look, examine, observe!'

I made the professor shine his lamp on the walls of the tunnel. I expected some exclamation from him. But he didn't say a word: he continued on his way.

Had he understood me or not? Didn't he want to admit, because of his self-respect as an uncle and a scientist, that he had made a mistake in choosing the eastern tunnel; or did he want to explore the passage to the end? It was clear in any case that we had left behind the route taken by the lava, and that this path couldn't lead to the source of Mount Snaefell's heat.

However, I wondered whether I wasn't placing too much importance on the change in the formation. Was I not deluding myself? Were we really crossing the layers of rock superimposed on the granite foundation?

'If I'm right', I thought, 'I'll surely find traces of primitive plants, and it will be self-evident to anyone. Let's look.'

I hadn't gone a hundred yards further before irrefutable proof appeared before my eyes. It was to be expected, for during the Silurian Period there were more than fifteen hundred species of vegetables and animals in the seas. My feet, used to the hard ground of the lava, were suddenly treading on a dust composed of fragments of plants and shells. On the walls could be clearly seen the outlines of seaweeds and clubmosses. Professor Lidenbrock could no longer entertain any doubt, but he closed his eyes, I think, and continued on his way at a steady pace.

This was obstinacy taken beyond all limit. I couldn't stand it anymore. I picked up a perfectly preserved shell, one that had belonged to an animal more or less like the present-day woodlouse. Then I caught up with my uncle and said to him: 'see!'

'Well', he replied calmly, 'it is the shell of a crustacean of the extinct order of trilobites. Nothing else.'

'But don't you conclude that...?'

'What you conclude yourself? Yes. Fine. We have left the granite stratum behind, together with the route followed by the lava. It is possible that I made a mistake; but I will only be certain of my error when I have reached the end of the gallery.'

'You're right to follow such a course of action, Uncle John, and I would support it, if we weren't in greater and greater danger.'

'Of what?'

'Of the shortage of water.'

'Well, we will ration it, Axel.'

Chapter 20.

Rationing was indeed necessary. We didn't have enough water left for more than three days, as I found out that evening at supper-time. Nor could we have much hope of coming across an open spring in the ground of the Transition Era: what a dismal perspective!

The whole of the following day, the tunnel lined up its endless arches before us. We walked almost without a word. Hans's silence was catching.

The route was not climbing, at least not noticeably. Sometimes it even seemed to be going down. But such a tendency, in any case very slight, can't have reassured the professor, for the nature of the strata didn't change, and the signs of the Transition Era became more and more obvious.

The electric lamp produced a wonderful sparkling on the schists, the limestone, and the old red sandstones of the walls. You might have thought you were in a trench excavation in Devon, the county which gave its name to this sort of formation. Magnificent marble specimens covered the walls, some, an agate grey with white veins, standing out in various places, others crimson, or yellow with red spots. Further on were samples of griotte marble in dark colours, but with limestone providing bright highlights.

Most of the marble displayed the outlines of primitive animals. Since the day before, creation had made clear signs of progress. Instead of rudimentary trilobites, I spotted evidence of a more perfect order: amongst others, ganoid fish and those saurians where the paleontologist's eye has discerned the first reptile forms. The Devonian seas were inhabited by a large number of animals of this latter species, and deposited thousands and thousands of them onto the newly formed rocks.

It became obvious that we were moving back up the scale of animal life, of which man forms the peak. But Professor Lidenbrock didn't seem to be paying attention to this.

He was hoping for one of two things: either that a vertical shaft would somehow open up beneath his feet and thus allow him to descend again; or that he would be blocked by some obstacle. But evening came without either hope being fulfilled.

On the Friday, after a night when I began to be tortured by thirst, our little team plunged again into the tunnel's meanders.

After ten hours' march, I noticed that the reflection of our lamps on the surfaces was decreasing to a remarkable degree. The marble, the schist, the limestone, and the sandstone of the walls were giving way to a dark and dim covering. At a moment when the tunnel was especially narrow, I leaned on the left-hand wall.

When I withdrew my hand, it was completely black. I looked closer. We were in the middle of a coal deposit.

'A coal mine!', I exclaimed.

'A mine without miners.'

'Who knows?'

'I know', replied the professor firmly, 'and I am certain that this tunnel cutting through the coal seams was not made by human hands. But I do not really care whether it is Nature's work or not. The time for dinner has arrived. Let us therefore have dinner.'

Hans prepared some food. I hardly ate anything, but drank the few drops of water that made up my ration. The guide's half-full flask was all that remained for three men.

After the meal, my two companions stretched out on their blankets and found a remedy to their tiredness in sleep. I couldn't sleep: I counted the hours till morning.

On Saturday, we left at six. Twenty minutes later, we arrived at a huge excavation. I realized then that human hands could not have hollowed out this coalpit, for in that case the arches would necessarily have been underpinned.

Here they literally held up only by some miracle of equilibrium. This cavernous space was 100 feet wide by 150 feet high. The earth had been violently pushed aside by some underground upheaval. The solid ground, subjected to some huge force, had split wide open, leaving this spacious void where, for the first time, some inhabitants of the Earth were wandering.

On these dark walls was written the whole history of the coal period, and a geologist could easily read its successive stages. The beds of coal were separated by strata of sandstone or compacted clay, as if crushed under the uppermost layers.

During this age of the world which preceded the Secondary Era, the Earth became covered in immense vegetation due to the tropical heat combined with a permanent humidity. An atmosphere of steam enveloped all parts of the globe, shielding it from the sun's rays.

Hence, the high temperatures could not have come from that new source of heat. Perhaps the sun was not ready to play its brilliant role. But in any case 'climates' did not yet exist, and a torrid heat spread across the entire surface of the globe, the same at the poles as at the equator. Where did it come from? From the centre of the globe.

Despite Professor Lidenbrock's theories, a violent fire smoldered in the bowels of the spheroid. Its effects were felt even in the outermost layers of the Earth's crust. The plants, shielded from the life-giving radiation of the sun, did not produce flowers or scent, but their roots drew strength from the burning soils of the first days.

There were few trees, only herbaceous plants, huge grassy areas, ferns, club-mosses, and sigillarias and asterophyllites, rare families whose species were then numbered in thousands.

It was this exuberant vegetation which produced the coal. The Earth's crust, still elastic, followed the movements of the liquid mass it encased and generated a large amount of cracking and subsiding. The plants, dragged under water, gradually built up considerable piles of matter.

Next came the action of Nature's chemistry: on the bottom of the seas, the vegetable masses became peat. Then, thanks to the effect of the gases and the heat from fermentation, they underwent a complete mineralization.

In this way were formed the huge layers of coal. These, however, will be used up by over-consumption in less than three centuries, if the industrialized nations do not take care.

These ideas passed through my mind while I looked at the coal riches accumulated in this section of the Earth's mass. Such riches will probably never be opened up. The exploitation of these far-away mines would require too much effort. What would be the point in any case, when coal is spread over the Earth's surface, so to speak, in a large number of countries? So, these untouched strata I saw will probably remain exactly the same when the Earth's last hour sounds.

We carried on walking meanwhile, and I was the only one of the three companions to forget how long the route was, deeply engrossed as I was in my geological considerations. The temperature remained virtually the same as during our passage through the lavas and the schists. On the other hand, my nose was distressed by a very pronounced smell of methane. I immediately realized that in this tunnel there was a significant amount of the dangerous gas which miners call firedamp, and whose explosions have so often caused terrible disasters.

Fortunately, our lighting came from the ingenious Ruhmkorff lamps. If, by misfortune, we had carelessly explored this tunnel holding torches, an awful explosion would have terminated the journey by destroying the travellers.

Our excursion through the coal lasted until evening. My uncle could hardly control the impatience that the horizontality of the route was generating in him. The darkness, impenetrable at more than twenty yards, prevented any estimation of how far the tunnel ran. I was beginning to believe that it must be endless, when suddenly and without warning, at 6 p.m., a wall appeared right in front of us. There was no way through, whether to the left or to the right, above or below. We had reached the end of a cul-de-sac.

'Well, so much the better!', bellowed my uncle, 'at least I know what I'm up against. We are not on Saknussemm's route, and our only choice is to turn round and go back. Let's rest for a night, and within three days we will be back at the point where the two tunnels fork.'

'Yes, if we are strong enough.'

'And why should we not be?'

'Because tomorrow there will be no water left at all!'

'And no courage left either?', asked the professor, looking at me sternly.

I did not dare reply.

Chapter 21.

The following day, we left very early. Speed was of the essence. We were five days' march from the parting of the ways.

I will not dwell on our suffering during the return. My uncle bore it with the anger of a man who knows that he is less strong; Hans with the resignation of his peaceful nature; myself, I must admit, with complaints and despair, for I was unable to just grin and bear it.

As I foresaw, the water ran out completely at the end of our first day's march. Our supplies of liquid were limited to gin, but this diabolical liquor burned your throat, and I couldn't even bear to look at it. I found the heat stifling. Tiredness prevented me from moving. More than once, I almost fell down in a faint. On such occasions a halt was called, and my uncle or the Icelander comforted me as best they could. But I could see that the professor was already reacting with difficulty against the extreme fatigue and the torment produced by the lack of water.

Finally, on Tuesday, 7 July, dragging ourselves along on our hands and knees, half-dead, we reached the point where the two tunnels split. I lay there, a lifeless mass, stretched out on the lava floor. It was ten in the morning.

Hans and my uncle, leaning back against the walls, tried to nibble a few crumbs of biscuit. Long groans escaped from my swollen lips. I fell into a heavy slumber.

After a time, my uncle drew near and lifted me up in his arms whispering in a sorrowful tone: 'poor child!'

I was touched by these words, not being used to such tenderness from the tough professor. I seized hold of his trembling hands in mine. He allowed me to do this, while looking at me. His eyes were damp.

I then saw him take the flask hanging at his side. To my amazement, he put it to my lips saying: 'drink.'

Had I heard properly? Had my uncle gone mad? I looked at him with a wild expression. I did not want to understand what he was saying.

'Drink', he repeated.

And tilting the flask, he emptied it between my lips. Oh! Infinite ecstasy! A mouthful of water came and wetted my burning lips and tongue, only one, but it was enough to bring back the life that was tiptoeing away from me.

I thanked my uncle by putting my hands together.

'Yes, one mouthful of water. The last, do you hear? The very last! I carefully kept it at the bottom of my flask. Twenty times, a hundred times, I had to resist a terrible desire to drink it. But no, Axel, I was keeping it for you.'

'Uncle John!', I whispered as large tears formed in my eyes.

'Yes, poor child, I knew that when you arrived at this junction, you would drop down half-dead, and I kept my last drops of water to bring you back to life.'

'Thank you, thank you!', I cried.

However little my thirst was quenched, I had nevertheless got back some strength. The muscles in my throat, contracted until this point, now relaxed, and the burning in my lips diminished. I could speak again.

'Look, we now have only one option: since we have no water, we must retrace our path.'

While I spoke, my uncle avoided looking at me. He hung his head, and his eyes avoided mine.

'We have to turn round, and follow the path back to Mount Snaefell. May God give us the strength to climb back up to the top of the crater!'

'Go back!', said my uncle, as if replying to himself rather than to me.

'Yes, go back, without wasting a moment.'

There came a long silence.

'So as a consequence, Axel,' said the professor in a strange tone, 'those few drops of water have not given you back your courage and energy?'

'Courage!'

'I see you are as overcome as before, giving voice to words of despair!'

What sort of man was I dealing with, and what plans was his fearless spirit still hatching?

'What, you don't want to… ?'

'Give up the expedition, at a moment when all the signs show it can succeed? Never!'

'So we must prepare to die?'

'No, Axel, no! Go if you want. I do not wish your death! Hans will go with you. Leave me alone!'

'Abandon you?'

'Leave me, I tell you! I began this journey; I will carry it out to the bitter end, or else not come back at all. Off you go, Axel. Go!'

My uncle spoke very agitatedly. His voice, tender for a moment, had now become hard and threatening. He was struggling with a sombre energy against the impossible! I did not want to abandon him at the bottom of this chasm; but, from another point of view, my instinct for self-preservation urged me to flee from him.

The guide followed this scene with his usual indifference. Yet he understood what was happening between his two companions. Our gestures were enough to show the different ways that each of us wanted to drag the other. But Hans did not appear to be especially interested in this question where his life was at stake: he seemed ready to leave if the signal was given, ready to remain at the least wish of his master.

What I would have given at that moment to be able to speak to him! My words, my complaints, my tone would have won his cold nature over.

The dangers the guide did not seem to suspect, I would have made him understand them in the most literal way. The two of us together might perhaps have convinced the stubborn professor. If necessary, we could have forced him to return to the heights of Mount Snaefell!

I went over to Hans. I put my hand on his. He did not move. I pointed at the route up to the crater. He still remained motionless. My gasping face showed all my suffering. The Icelander gently shook his head, and, calmly indicating my uncle, he said: 'master.'

'No, you fool! He is not the master of your life! We must flee, we must drag him with us! Do you hear? Do you understand?'

I seized Hans by the arm, trying to make him get up. I tried again. My uncle intervened.

'Calm down, Axel. You will not get anything out of this impassive servant. So hear what I have to offer.'

I crossed my arms, looking squarely at my uncle.

'Only the lack of water puts an obstacle to the achievement of my aims. In that eastern tunnel, made of lavas, schists, and coals, we did not find a single liquid molecule. We may possibly be more fortunate in the western tunnel.'

I shook my head with a look of utter disbelief.

'Hear me out', continued the professor in a louder voice. 'While you were lying there without moving, I went to reconnoitre the shape of the tunnel. It forces its way directly into the bowels of the Earth and will lead us, in a few hours, to the granite rock-formations. There we should meet abundant springs. The nature of the rock implies this: intuition and logic combine to support my conviction! Now, here is what I have to offer you. When Columbus asked his crews for three more days to reach the new lands, his crews, ill and terror-stricken, nevertheless granted his request, and he discovered a new world. I, the Columbus of these underground regions, am asking you for only one more day. If at the end of that time I have not encountered the water we need, I swear to you that we will return to the surface of the Earth.'

In spite of my irritation, I was touched by these words and by the way my uncle had to force himself to speak in such a way.

'All right!', I cried, 'let it be as you wish, and may God reward your superhuman energy. You have only a few hours left in which to tempt fate. Let us go!'

Chapter 22.

We set off again, this time down the other tunnel. Hans led the way as usual. We hadn't gone further than a hundred yards, when the professor, shining his lamp along the walls, bellowed: 'here: the Primitive formations! We are on the right route, come on, come on!'

When the Earth slowly cooled during the first days of the world, the decrease in volume produced disruptions, breakages, shrinkages, and cracks in the crust. Our present corridor was a fissure of this sort, through which the eruption of the liquid granite had formerly poured out. Its thousand paths formed an impossible maze through the primeval ground.

As we went further down, the succession of strata making up the Primitive system appeared more and more clearly. Geological science considers the Primitive system as the base of the mineral crust, and has analyzed it into three different strata: schists, gneisses, and mica-schists resting on that unbreakable rock called granite.

Never had mineralogists been in such perfect circumstances for studying nature in situ. The drill, a brutal and unintelligent machine, could not bring the internal texture back to the surface of the globe, but we were going to examine it with our eyes, touch it with our hands.

Through the layer of schists, coloured in wonderful green shades, meandered seams of copper and manganese, with traces of platinum and gold. I dreamed when I saw these riches hidden away in the bowels of the Earth, which human greed would never enjoy! These treasures were so deeply buried by the upheavals of the first days, that neither pickaxe nor drill will ever be able to tear them from their tomb.

After the schists came the layers of gneisses, remarkable for their regularity and their parallel folia; then the mica-schists laid out in huge laminae, standing out because of the scintillations of the white mica.

The light from the lamps, reflected by the tiny facets of the mass of rock, shone its fiery flashes at all angles, and I imagined I was travelling through a hollowed-out diamond with the rays disintegrating into a thousand dazzling lights.

At about six, this festival of light reduced noticeably and then almost stopped. The rock-faces took on a crystallized tint, but of a dark shade. The mica mixed more intimately with feldspar and quartz, to form that most rock-like of all rocks, the stone that is the hardest of all, the one that holds up the four storeys of the globe's formation without being crushed. We were walled up in a huge granite prison.

It was eight in the evening. There was still no water. I was in terrible pain. My uncle walked ahead. He wouldn't stop. He kept turning his head to one side in order to detect murmurs from any spring. But none came!

Meanwhile my legs refused to carry me any further. I resisted the agony so that my uncle would not have to call a halt. It would have been a terrible blow for him, as the day was coming to an end (the last one he had).

Finally my strength left me. I uttered a cry and fell down.

'Help! I'm dying!'

My uncle came back. He examined me, crossing his arms. Then the leaden words came from his lips: 'it's over!'

A terrifying gesture of anger struck my eyes one last time, and I closed them.

When I opened my eyes again, I saw my two companions motionless, rolled up in their blankets. Were they asleep? For my part, I could not find a moment's repose. My distress was too great, and above all the thought that my sufferings were not going to find any relief. My uncle's last words rang out in my ears: 'it's over!'... I was so weak that we couldn't even think about reaching the surface of the Earth again...

There was a league and a half of Earth's crust! This mass seemed to be leaning with all its weight on my shoulders. I felt crushed, and I wore myself out with violent struggles to turn over on my granite bed.

A few hours went by. A deep silence hung around us, the silence of the grave. Nothing reached us through these walls, each at least five miles thick.

Nevertheless, in the middle of my sleep, I thought I heard a noise. It was dark in the tunnel. I looked more carefully and thought I could see the Icelander slipping away with the lamp in his hand.

Why was he going? Was Hans leaving us to our fate? My uncle was asleep. I tried to cry out. My voice could not find a way through my dried-up lips. It was now very dark, and the last sounds had just died away.

'Hans is leaving us!', I cried, 'Hans, Hans!'

These words, I shouted them inside myself. They went no further. But after the first moment of terror, I felt ashamed of my suspicion of a man whose conduct had been beyond reproach until now. His departure could not be running away. Instead of going up the tunnel, he was heading down. Evil intentions would have taken him towards the top, not the bottom. This argument calmed me down a little, and I came back to another order of ideas. Only a serious reason could have torn Hans, that peaceful man, from his rest. Was he in search of something? Had he heard some murmur during the silent night, one that had not reached me?

Chapter 23.

For an hour, my delirious brain ran through all the conceivable reasons that could have made the calm hunter act in this way. The most absurd ideas intersected in my head. I thought I was about to go mad!

But finally the sound of feet could be heard in the depths of the chasm. Hans was coming back up. An indefinite light began to slide along the walls, then flowed through the mouth of the corridor. Hans reappeared.

He went up to my uncle, put a hand on his shoulder, and gently woke him. My uncle sat up.

'What is it?'

'*Vatten*', replied the hunter.

It must be the case that, under the inspiration of extreme suffering, everyone becomes multilingual. I did not know a single word of Danish, and yet I instinctively understood our guide's utterance.

'Water, water!', I shouted, clapping my hands and gesticulating like a lunatic.

'Water!' repeated my uncle. '*Hvar*?'

'*Nedat*', replied Hans.

Where? Below! I could understand everything. I had seized hold of the hunter's hands, and was holding them tight, while he looked calmly at me.

The preparations for departure didn't take long, and soon we were moving down a corridor with a gradient of one in three.

An hour later, we had covered about a mile and a quarter and gone down about two thousand feet.

At that moment, I distinctly heard an unusual sound running along the granite side-walls, a sort of muffled rumbling like a distant thunder. During the next half-hour of walking, not meeting the promised spring, I felt anxiety taking hold of me again; but then my uncle told me where the noise was coming from.

'Hans was not wrong. What you hear is the roaring of fast-flowing water.'

'A stream?'

'There can be no doubt about it. An underground river is flowing around us!'

We walked faster, overstimulated by hope. I forgot about my tiredness. The sound of babbling water was already refreshing me. It was increasing noticeably. The water, having for a long time remained over our heads, was now running behind the left-hand rock face, roaring and splashing. I frequently touched the rock with my hand, hoping to find traces of condensation or water oozing through. But in vain.

Another half-hour went by. Another mile and a quarter was covered.

It became clear at this point that, while he had been away, the hunter hadn't been able to continue his search any further. Guided by an instinct peculiar to mountain men, to water-diviners, he had 'felt' the presence of a stream through the rock, but had certainly not seen the precious liquid; and he had not drunk any.

Soon it became obvious that, if we continued walking, we would be moving away from the current, whose murmuring was now tending to diminish. We turned back. Hans stopped at the precise point where the stream seemed to be the closest.

I sat near the rock wall, while the waters ran with great violence only two feet away from me. But a granite wall stood between us.

Without thinking, without wondering whether some way of getting to this water didn't exist, I gave into an immediate feeling of despair.

Hans looked at me, and I thought I could see a smile playing on his lips.

He rose and picked up the lamp. I followed. He went up to the rock face. I watched him. He put his ear to the dry stone, and slowly moved it around, listening with great concentration. I understood that he was looking for the precise point where the noise from the stream was loudest. He located this spot in the left-hand wall, three feet above the ground.

I was highly excited. I didn't dare guess what the hunter planned to do. But I had to understand, and applaud, and embrace him passionately, when I saw him lift up the pickaxe to attack the very rock.

'Saved!', I cried out.

'Yes', repeated my uncle in a frenzy, 'Hans is right. Oh, he is such an intelligent hunter! We would never have thought of that!'

I cannot disagree. Such a solution, however simple, would not have entered our minds. Nothing could be more dangerous than striking a blow with a pick into the structure of the globe. What if a landslide happened and crushed us to death? What if the water, bursting through the rock, drowned us? These fears were far from imaginary; but at such a moment the danger of landslide or flood couldn't stop us. Our thirst was so strong that to quench it we would have dug into the ocean bed itself.

Hans set to work, a task which neither my uncle nor I could have completed. Our hands would have been so impatient that the rock would have flown into pieces under our hurried blows. The guide, in contrast, was calm and moderate, slowly chipping away at the rock with a long series of little blows, creating an opening six inches wide. I heard the noise of the stream increase, and I could already feel the life-giving water spurting on my lips.

Soon the pick had gone two feet into the granite wall. The work had lasted over an hour. I was writhing with impatience. My uncle wanted to bring in the big guns. I had difficulty holding him back, and he was already seizing his pickaxe, when suddenly a whistling noise was heard. A jet of water shot out of the rock and hit the opposite face.

Hans, almost knocked down by the blow, could not hold back a cry of pain. I understood why when I thrust my hand into the liquid jet, and in turn uttered a wild exclamation. The spring was boiling.

'Water at 100°!', I shouted.

'It will soon cool down', replied my uncle.

The corridor filled with steam, while a brook formed, and headed off into the underground meanders. Soon we were drinking our first mouthfuls.

Oh, what ecstasy! What indescribable gratification! What was this water? Where did it come from? I didn't care. It was water and, although still hot, it gave back to our hearts the life that was escaping from them. I drank without stopping, without even tasting.

It was only after a minute of delight that I shouted: 'but it's full of iron!'

'Excellent for the stomach', replied my uncle, 'and full of minerals! Our journey is as good as a trip to Spa or Toeplitz!'

'Oh, this is so good!'

'I am not surprised, water from five miles below ground. It tastes of ink, which is not unpleasant. A vital commodity Hans has given us! I propose therefore to call this brook after the person who was our salvation.'

'Agreed!'

The name 'Hans-Bach' was decided on the spot.

Hans did not become any the prouder because of this. Having drunk in moderation, he sat back in a corner with his usual calm.

'Now', I said, 'we mustn't let the water be lost.'

'Why? I do not imagine this source will ever dry up.'

'It makes no difference. Let's fill the water bottle and flasks, and then try to block up the hole.'

My advice was followed. Using granite chips and oakum, Hans tried to block the gash made in the wall. It was not easy. Our hands got scalded to no avail; there was too much pressure, and our attempts produced no result.

'It's obvious', I said, 'that the water-bearing beds are at too great a height, to judge from the strength of the jet.'

'There can be no doubt about it. If this water column is thirty-two thousand feet high, it will be at a pressure of a thousand atmospheres. But I have an idea.'

'What is it?'

'Why are we trying so hard to block the hole?'

'But, because…'

I was unable to find the correct answer.

'When our flasks are empty, would we be certain to be able to fill them again?'

'Clearly not.'

'Well then, we will let the water flow. It will work its way down naturally, and guide those who drink from it on the way!'

'Good idea! With this stream as companion, there is no reason for our projects not to succeed.'

'My boy, you are about to find the solution', said the professor, laughing.

'I'm doing better than that, I have found it already.'

'Not so quick! Let's begin by taking a few hours' rest.'

I had in truth forgotten that it was night-time. The chronometer soon confirmed the fact. Shortly afterwards, each of us, having eaten and drunk, fell into a deep sleep.

Chapter 24.

The following day, we had already forgotten our difficulties. I was amazed at first not to feel thirsty, and wondered why. The stream flowing and gurgling at my feet gave me the answer.

We ate and drank from the excellent ferrous water. I felt like a new man who wanted to go a long way. Why should a man as convinced as my uncle not succeed, with a hard-working guide like Hans and a determined nephew like me? These were the wonderful ideas which slid into my brain. Had someone suggested going back up to the top of Mount Snaefell, I would have indignantly refused.

But fortunately the only item on the agenda was descending.

'Let's go!', I shouted, waking, with my enthusiastic cries, the old echoes of the globe.

We started off again at 8 a.m. on Thursday. The granite corridor, twisting and turning in sinuous paths, produced unexpected corners, taking on the complexity of a maze; but, overall, its general direction was still towards the south-east. My uncle continually consulted his compass with the greatest care, so as to be able to note the ground covered.

The gallery proceeded almost horizontally, with a gradient of one in thirty-five at the very most. The stream followed unhurriedly at our feet, murmuring. I compared it to some familiar spirit guiding us down into the Earth, and I caressed the warm water nymph whose song accompanied our steps. My good mood was tinged with mythology.

As for my uncle, he was cursing the horizontality of the route, as 'the man of the perpendiculars'. His route was being indefinitely extended and instead of 'sliding down the Earth's radius', as he put it, he was almost going off at a tangent. But we had no choice, and as long as we were getting nearer the centre, no matter how slowly, there was no reason to complain.

However, from time to time, the slopes got steeper: the water nymph would start tumbling down and moaning, and we would go down deeper with her.

In sum, during that day and the following one, we covered a great deal of ground horizontally, but relatively little vertically.

On Friday evening, 10 July, according to our estimates we were about thirty leagues south-east of Reykjavik and at a depth of two leagues and a half.

Under our feet opened a rather frightening pit. My uncle couldn't resist clapping his hands when he calculated the steepness of the slope.

'It will take us a very long way', he exclaimed, 'and easily, for the projections of the rock form a veritable staircase.'

The ropes were placed in position by Hans in such a way as to prevent all accidents. The descent began. I do not dare call it a perilous descent because I was already familiar with this sort of operation.

This pit was a narrow slit cut into the mass of the rock, of the sort called 'faults'. It has clearly been produced during the contraction of the Earth's very structure, at the period when it was cooling down. If it had formerly served as a way through for the eruptive matters vomited by Mount Snaefell, I couldn't explain to myself how it was that these materials had left no trace. We were going down a sort of spiral staircase that you would have said was made by human hands.

Every quarter of an hour we were forced to stop and take a rest to allow our knees to recover. We invariably sat down on some projection with our legs dangling over it; we ate while chatting; and we drank at the brook.

It goes without saying that the Hans-Bach had become a waterfall in this fault and had lost much of its volume, but it was still more than sufficient to quench our thirst. In any case, when the slope became less steep, it would soon have to adopt its more peaceful course again. At the present point it reminded me of my worthy uncle, with his fits of impatience and anger, whilst, when following the gentler slopes, it was like the Icelandic hunter's calm.

On 11 and 12 July we worked our way round the spirals of the fault, penetrating two leagues further into the Earth's crust, which made five leagues below sea level. But on the 13th, at about midday, the fault took on a much gentler slope of about 45°, heading towards the southeast.

The path then became quite easy, and very boring. It would have been hard for it to have been anything else. There was no way that the journey could be varied by changes in the countryside.

Finally, on Wednesday the 15th we were seven leagues below ground and fifty leagues from Mount Snaefell. Although we were a little tired, our health was still in a reassuring state and the portable medical kit had not yet been used.

Every hour my uncle noted the measurements of the compass, the chronometer, the manometer, and the thermometer: the same notes that he published later in his scientific account of the journey. In this way he could easily deduce what our position was. When he told me that we had done this horizontal distance of fifty leagues, I couldn't hold back an exclamation.

'What's the matter?', he asked.

'Nothing, I was just thinking.'

'And what are you thinking of, my boy?'

'If our calculations are correct, we are no longer under Iceland.'

'Do you think so?'

'It is easy to check.'

I used my compasses to measure on the map.

'I was right', I said, 'we have gone right past Portland Point and these fifty leagues towards the south-east mean that we are now in the open sea.'

'Under the open sea', said my uncle, rubbing his hands.

'So,' I exclaimed, 'the ocean stretches above our heads!'

'Well, Axel, it is perfectly normal. At Newcastle, are there not coal mines which extend a great distance under the ocean?'

The professor might find the situation perfectly normal, but the thought of walking under the great weight of the waters wouldn't stop worrying me. And yet, whether the plains and mountains of Iceland were suspended over our heads, or the waves of the Atlantic, made very little difference in the end, provided that the granite structure remained solid. Anyway, I quickly got used to the idea, for the corridor (which was sometimes straight, sometimes winding, as capricious in its slopes as in its detours, but running regularly towards the south-east and working its way constantly down) was quickly leading us to great depths.

Four days later, on the evening of Saturday, 18 July, we reached a sort of grotto, of considerable size. My uncle gave Hans his three weekly dollars; and it was decided that the following day would be a day of rest.

Chapter 25.

Accordingly I woke up on the Sunday morning without the normal worry about leaving immediately and, although we were amongst the deepest chasms, it was very pleasant. Besides, we had got used to our troglodytic existence. I hardly thought about the sun, the stars, the moon, the trees, the houses, the towns: all the superfluous aspects of earthly life which terrestrial beings consider a necessity. Since we were fossils, we didn't care about such useless marvels.

The grotto formed a huge hall. Over its granite floor gently flowed the faithful stream. At such a distance from its source, its water was only the same temperature as the air, and we could drink it without difficulty.

After breakfast the professor wanted to spend a few hours putting his daily notes in order.

'First of all', he said, 'I am going to make a few calculations in order to find out exactly what our position is. When we get back, I want to be able to draw a map of our journey: a sort of vertical section of the globe giving the profile of the expedition.'

'That will be interesting, Uncle John, but will your observations be accurate enough?'

'Yes, I have carefully noted down the angles and the gradients. I am sure I have not made any mistakes. Let us first see where we are: take the compass and note the direction it indicates.'

I considered the instrument and, after a careful examination, I replied: 'East-a-quarter-south-east.'

'Good', said the professor, noting down the observation and making a few quick calculations. 'I conclude that we have covered 85 leagues from the point where we started.'

'So we're travelling underneath the Atlantic?'

'Yes we are.'

'And at this moment a storm is perhaps raging up there, with ships being shaken about above our heads by waves and hurricanes?'

'It is possible.'

'And the whales are coming to knock their tails on the roof of our prison?'

'Don't worry, Axel, they will not do it any harm. But let's get back to our calculations. We are 85 leagues from the base of Mount Snaefell in a southeasterly direction, and, according to my previous notes, I estimate the depth reached to be sixteen leagues.'

'Sixteen leagues?', I cried.

'Yes, sixteen leagues .'

'But that's the extreme limit that science has ascribed to the thickness of the Earth's crust.'

'Maybe.'

'And here, according to the law of increasing temperature, there should be a temperature of over 1,500°.'

'"Should be", my boy.'

'And all this granite couldn't remain in a solid state and would be completely melted.'

'You can see that this is not the case and that, as usual, the facts are able to contradict the theories.'

'I am forced to agree, but it still surprises me.'

'What temperature does the thermometer indicate?'

'27.6°.'

'The scientists are only out, therefore, by 1,474.4°. So, the proportional increase in temperature is an error. So, Sir Humphry Davy was right. So, I was not wrong to listen to him. What have you to say to that?'

'Nothing.'

In fact, I would have had quite a few things to say. I didn't accept Davy's theories at all: I still believed in the heat in the centre, although I could not feel any of its effects. To tell the truth, I preferred to think that this vent was the chimney of an extinct volcano, one that the lava had covered over with a coating that was refractory and so did not allow the temperature to spread through its walls.

But without stopping to seek new arguments, I merely accepted the situation as it was.

'Uncle John', I tried again, 'I believe that all your calculations are accurate, but allow me to draw a logical conclusion from them.'

'Go on, my boy, feel free.'

'At the point where we are now, on the same latitude as Iceland, the radius of the Earth is about 1583 leagues.'

'1583 leagues and a third.'

'Let's say 1600 as a round figure. Out of a journey of 1600 leagues we have done twelve.'

'As you say.'

'And this has been achieved at the expense of 85 leagues in a diagonal direction?'

'Perfectly.'

'In about twenty days.'

'In twenty days.'

'Now, sixteen leagues is a hundredth of the radius of the Earth. If we continue in this way, we will therefore take two thousand days, or nearly five and a half years, to get down.'

The professor did not say anything.

'And that's not counting the fact that, if the vertical journey of sixteen leagues has been at the expense of a horizontal one of eighty, that will make 8,000 leagues towards the south-east, and we will have come out through a point on the circumference long before we reach the centre.'

'The devil take your calculations!' cried my uncle with an angry gesture. 'The devil take your hypotheses. What do they rest on? Who can tell you that this corridor does not go straight to our goal? Moreover, I have a precedent on my side. What I am doing here, someone else has already done, and where he succeeded I will also succeed.'

'I hope so. But finally, I have the right…'

'You have the right to keep quiet, Axel, when you attempt to reason in that way.'

I could see clearly that the terrible professor was threatening to reappear under the skin of the uncle, and so I considered myself duly warned.

'Now', he said, 'consult the manometer: what does it indicate?'

'A considerable pressure.'

'Good. You can see that by going down gradually, by slowly getting used to the density of the atmosphere, we have not had any problems at all.'

'None at all, apart from a few earaches.'

'That's nothing, and you can get rid of the pain by putting the external air in rapid communication with the air contained in your lungs.'

'Absolutely', I replied, having decided not to upset my uncle anymore. 'There is even a real pleasure in being plunged into this denser atmosphere. Have you noticed how intensely the sound is propagated?'

'Yes I have; a deaf man would end up hearing perfectly.'

'But this density will undoubtedly increase?'

'Yes, following a law which has not been completely determined. It is true that the force of gravity will decrease in proportion to our descent. You know that it is at the surface of the Earth that its action is most strongly felt, and that objects no longer have any weight at the centre of the globe.'

'I know, but tell me, will this air not finish up having the density of water?'

'Probably, at a pressure of 710 atmospheres.'

'And further down?'

'Further down this density will increase still further.'

'How will we carry on then?'

'Well, we will just have to put stones in our pockets.'

'Uncle John, you have an answer for everything.'

I didn't dare venture any further into the area of hypotheses, for I would again have come up against some impossibility that would have made the professor hopping mad.

It was clear, however, that the air, at a pressure which could reach thousands of atmospheres, would end up solidifying, and then, even supposing that our bodies could have resisted this, we would have to stop, in spite of all the reasoning in the world.

But I did not communicate this argument; my uncle would have counter-attacked again with his perpetual Saknussemm, a precedent without value, for, even accepting as true the journey of the Icelandic scientist, there was a very simple thing that could be said in reply: in the sixteenth century, neither the barometer nor the manometer had been invented; so, how did Saknussemm know when he had reached the centre of the globe?

But I kept this objection to myself and waited to see what the future would bring.

The rest of the day was spent calculating and chatting. I was always in agreement with Professor Lidenbrock; and I envied the perfect indifference of Hans who, without seeking causes and effects to such an extent, carried blindly on wherever fate took him.

Chapter 26.

It must be admitted that things had gone well until now and it would have been ill-advised to complain. But if the average difficulty didn't increase, we couldn't miss reaching our goal. And what glory then! I had reached the point where I reasoned like Professor Lidenbrock. Seriously, was this due to the strange environment in which I was living? Maybe.

For a few days, steeper gradients, some of them even of an alarming perpendicularity, brought us deeper into the internal rock massif. On some days we gained between one and one league and a half towards the centre. Perilous descents, during which Hans's skill and his marvelous sang-froid were very useful to us. The impassive Icelander gave of himself with an incomprehensible honesty and, thanks to him, we survived more than one tricky situation which we wouldn't have been able to handle by ourselves.

What was surprising was that his silence increased every day. I believe that we were even beginning to behave like him. External objects have a real effect on the brain. The person who shuts himself up between four walls finishes up losing the ability to associate ideas and words. How many people in prison cells have become idiots, if not madmen, through lack of use of their intellectual faculties?

For the two weeks that followed our last conversation, nothing worth reporting happened. I can only find in my memory a single event of an extreme seriousness, but with good reason. It would be difficult for me to forget the smallest detail of it.

On 7 August our successive descents had brought us to a depth of thirty leagues; in other words, above our heads lay thirty leagues of rocks, oceans, continents and towns. We must have been about two hundred leagues from Iceland.

That day the tunnel was following a relatively gentle slope.

I was walking ahead. My uncle carried one of the Ruhmkorff lamps and myself the other one. I was examining the granite strata.

Suddenly, turning round, I noticed that I was alone.

'So', I thought, 'I've walked too quickly, or else Hans and my uncle have stopped on the way. It's best to join up with them again. Fortunately, the path doesn't climb very much.'

I went back the way I had just come. I walked for a quarter of an hour. I looked. Nobody. I called out. No reply. My voice was lost in the middle of the cavernous echoes that it suddenly awakened.

I began to feel worried. A shiver ran through my whole body.

'Let's be calm', I said out loud, 'I am certain to be able to find my companions again. There is only a single path. I was ahead: let's go back.'

I went up for half an hour. I listened out to see if some call was not addressed to me. In such a dense atmosphere it might reach me from a long way away. An extraordinary silence reigned in the immense tunnel.

I stopped. I couldn't believe that I was on my own. I wanted to think I had just gone astray: I was not lost. When you've strayed from your path, you can find it again.

'Let's see', I repeated, 'since there is only one route, since they are following it, I must meet up with them again. All I have to do is go further up. Unless, not having seen me, forgetting that I was ahead of them, they thought they had to go back. Well, even in that case, I will find them again if I hurry. It's obvious.'

I repeated these last words like a man who is not convinced. What is more, to put together such simple ideas and form them into reasoning, I had to employ a great deal of time.

A doubt then took hold of me. Was I really ahead? Certainly Hans had been following me, and he was in front of my uncle. He had even stopped for a few seconds to adjust the bags on his shoulder. The detail came back to me. It was at that very moment that I must have continued on my way.

'In any case', I thought, 'I have a sure means of not getting lost, a thread to guide me through this labyrinth, one which can never break: my faithful stream. All I have to do is go back up its course and I will automatically find my companions' traces again.'

This reasoning brought me back to life: I resolved to start off again without losing a second.

How I blessed, then, the foresight of my uncle when he prevented the hunter from blocking up the incision made in the granite wall. In this way, the health-giving source, having quenched our thirst en route, was going to guide me through the meanders of the Earth's crust.

Before starting back up, I thought a wash would do me good.

I bent over to wet my forehead in the water of the Hans-Bach.

My stupefaction can be imagined: under my feet was dry and uneven granite. The stream was no longer flowing at my feet!

Chapter 27.

I cannot depict my despair. No word in any human language would be adequate to describe my feelings. I was buried alive with the prospect of dying from agonies of hunger and thirst.

Without thinking, I moved my burning hands over the ground. How dried up this rock seemed to me!

But how could I have left the stream's course? For it wasn't there anymore! I understood then the reason for the strange silence when I had listened the last time to see if some call from my companions might not reach my ear. At the point when I had first started off on the wrong route, I hadn't noticed at all that the stream wasn't there. Clearly, at that moment, a forking in the gallery must have appeared in front of me, whilst the Hans-Bach, obeying the whims of another slope, had gone off with my companions towards unknown depths.

How could I get back? There were no traces at all. My feet left no imprint on the granite. I racked my brain, looking for a solution to this intractable problem. My position could be summed up in a single word: lost!

Yes, lost at a depth which seemed immeasurable to me: those thirty leagues of Earth's crust weighed down on my shoulders with a terrible weight. I felt crushed.

I tried to take my mind back to ordinary things. I could hardly do so. Terrified, I thought about Hamburg, the house in the Königstrasse, my poor Gräuben, this whole world under which I was lost. I relived the incidents of the journey in a violent hallucination, the events of the crossing, Iceland, Mr. Fridriksson, Mount Snaefell. I said to myself that if, in the present situation, I still kept the shadow of a hope, it would be a sign of madness; therefore, it was better to sink into despair.

Actually, what human power could bring me back up to the surface of the globe or break down these enormous vaults leaning over my head? Who could put me on the route back and help me catch my companions up?

'Oh, Uncle John', I shouted, in a tone of despair.

It was the only word of reproach that came from my mouth, for I understood that the unfortunate man must himself be suffering while looking for me.

When I saw myself without any human help, unable to try to do anything to save me, I thought of the help of Heaven. Memories of my childhood, of my mother whom I had known only at the time of kisses, came back into my mind. I prayed a God who was entitled to ignore my belated request; I implored him with fervor.

This return to Divine Providence made me a little calmer and I was able to concentrate all my intelligence on the situation.

I had three days' food left, and my flask was full. However, I could not remain alone any longer. But should I go up or down?

Go up, of course! Continue to go up!

I would reach the point where I had left the stream, the fateful fork. There, once I had the stream beside my feet, I would still be able to get back up to the summit of Mount Snaefell.

Why hadn't I thought of this sooner? There was clearly a chance of being saved. The most important thing to do was to find the course of the Hans-Bach again.

I got up and, leaning on my alpenstock, went back up the tunnel. The slope was quite steep. I walked with hope and without worrying, like a man who cannot choose the path to follow. For half an hour no obstacle stopped me. I tried to recognise my route from the form of the tunnel, the shape of some of the rocks and the location of some crevices. But no particular feature struck my mind and soon I had to admit that this gallery could not lead me back to the fork. It was a dead end. I bumped into an impenetrable wall and fell on a rock.

With what horror, with what despair I was seized then, I cannot say. I lay there overwhelmed. My last hope had just broken against this granite wall.

Lost in this labyrinth, whose multiple meanderings crisscrossed in all directions, I was unable to flee. I had to die from the most terrifying of deaths! It is strange but it came into my mind that if one day my fossilized body was found again, thirty leagues into the bowels of the Earth, it would raise serious scientific questions.

I wanted to speak aloud, but only rough sounds emerged from my dried-up lips: I could hardly breathe.

In the midst of these fears, a new terror took hold of my mind. My lantern had broken when it fell; and I had no means of repairing it. Its light was getting dimmer and was about to go out.

I watched the light fading away in the filament of the apparatus. Moving shadows were dancing on the darkened walls. I no longer dared to blink or move my eyes, for fear of losing the least molecule of this fleeing light. At each moment it seemed to me that it was vanishing and that blackness was taking hold of me.

Finally, a last gleam trembled in the lamp. I followed it; I swallowed it with my eyes. I concentrated the whole power of my eyes on it, as if it were the last sensation of light they would ever be able to see. I remained into the depths of an immense darkness.

What a terrible shout came from me! On Earth, in the middle of the darkest nights, light never entirely gives up its rights. It is diffuse, it is subtle, but however little remains, the retina ends up perceiving it. Here, nothing. Absolute darkness made me a blind man in the full sense of the word.

Hence, my head got lost. I raised my arms in front of me, trying to touch the harmful rocks. I was fleeing, rushing at random through this inextricable maze, going down all the time, running through the Earth's crust like an inhabitant of the underground faults, calling, shouting, vociferating, soon bruised on the rock projections, falling and getting up covered with blood, trying to drink this blood running down my face, but constantly waiting for some unexpected wall to come so that my head might bang into it.

Where did this mad running take me? I will never know. After several hours, undoubtedly exhausted, I fell like an inert mass along the wall and thought I did not exist anymore.

Chapter 28.

When I came back to life, my face was wet, wet with tears. How long this state of unconsciousness had lasted? I don't know. I no longer had any way of keeping track of time. No man had ever felt so lonely and abandoned.

After my fall, I had lost a lot of blood. I could feel myself covered in it. Oh, how I regretted not being dead and that 'it still had to be done'. I no longer wanted to think. I pushed every idea out of my head and, overcome by pain, I rolled over towards the opposite wall.

I could already feel fainting taking hold of me again, and with it the supreme annihilation, when a loud noise struck my ear. It resembled a long thunderclap; I heard the sound waves slowly disappear into the far depths of the abyss.

Where was this noise coming from? From some phenomenon happening in the heart of the Earth's mass. The explosion of gas or the collapse of some major rock foundation.

I listened again. I wanted to know whether this noise would occur again. A quarter of an hour went by. Silence reigned in the tunnel. I couldn't even hear the sound of my own heart beating anymore.

Suddenly, my ear, by chance applied to the wall, seemed to detect vague, imperceptible, distant words. I jumped.

'It is an hallucination', I thought. But no, by concentrating harder on listening, I distinctly heard whispering voices. I was too weak to understand what was being said. Someone was speaking though. I was quite certain of that.

For a moment I was terrified that it might be my own words coming back to me through an echo. I had perhaps shouted without realizing it. I tightly closed my mouth and, once more, I put my ear on the granite wall.

'Yes, they are talking and talking for sure!'

By moving only a few feet along the side of the tunnel, I could hear distinctly. I managed to catch strange, uncertain, incomprehensible words. They reached my ear as if spoken in a low voice or murmured. The word *förlorad* was repeated several times in a sorrowful tone.

What could it mean, and who was speaking? My uncle or Hans, of course! But if I could hear them, they might easily be able to hear me.

'Help!', I cried with all my strength, 'help!'

I listened; I waited, in the dark, for a reply, a cry, a sigh. But nothing could be heard. A few minutes passed. A whole world of ideas crossed my mind. I thought that my weakened voice might not reach my companions.

'It must be them', I repeated. 'What other men can be buried thirty leagues underground?'

I began to listen again. By moving my ear along the rock face, I found the mathematical point where the voices appeared to attain their maximum intensity. The word *förlorad* reached my ear again; then that thunderclap which had dragged me from my torpor.

'No, no. These voices are not reaching my ears through the solid rock. The walls are solid granite, and wouldn't allow the loudest bang to pass through. The sound must be coming along the gallery itself! There must be some peculiar acoustic effect here!'

I listened again; and this time, yes, this time I heard my name distinctly thrown through the air.

It was my uncle speaking. He was talking to the guide: *förlorad* was a Danish word!

Then everything became clear. To make myself heard, I too had to speak along the side of the gallery, which would carry the sound of my voice just as wires carry electricity.

But there was no time to lose. If my companions were only to move a few feet away from where they stood, the acoustic effect would be destroyed. So I moved again towards the wall, and said as distinctly as I could: 'Uncle John!'

I then waited for a reply with the greatest possible anxiety. Sound does not travel very quickly, and the density of the layers of air does not even add to its speed: it only increases its intensity. A few seconds, a few centuries elapsed, and finally these words reached my ears: 'Axel, Axel! Is it you?' ...

'Yes, yes!' ...

'Where are you, my boy?' ...

'Lost, in the dark!' ...

'And your lamp?' ...

'Out.' ...

'And the stream?' ...

'Lost!' ...

'Axel, my poor Axel, hold on.' ...

'I'm exhausted. I no longer have the strength to reply. But carry on speaking to me!' ...

'Courage', said my uncle. 'Do not speak; listen to me. We have searched for you both upwards and downwards in the tunnel, but we did not find you: I was devastated! Assumed that you were still following the Hans-Bach down, we went down again, firing our guns. Now, if our voices are in contact, this is only an acoustic effect! I cannot touch your hand yet. But do not despair, Axel. It is already a good thing to be able to hear each other.' ...

While he was speaking I had been thinking. A hope, still faint, was coming back to me. Before anything else, there was one thing I had to know. I therefore put my mouth close to the wall, and said: 'Uncle John?'...

'My boy' came back after a while. ...

'We must first of all find out how far apart we are.'...

'It's easy.'...

'Do you have your chronometer?'...

'Yes.'...

'Well, take it. Pronounce my name, noting exactly the second at which you speak. I will repeat it as soon as it gets to me, and you will also observe the exact moment when my reply reaches you.'...

'Well, and half the time between my call and your answer will be how long my voice takes to reach you.'...

'Exactly, Uncle John.'...

'Are you ready?'...

'Yes.'...

'Well, stand by, I am about to pronounce your name.'...

I applied my ear to the gallery, and as soon as the word 'Axel' reached me, I repeated the word, then waited. ...

'Forty seconds', said my uncle, 'forty seconds between the two words. Thus sound takes twenty seconds to go up. Now, at 1,020 feet per second, that makes 20,400 feet: a little more than a league and a half.'...

'A league and a half!', I whispered.

'It is not a lot, Axel!'...

'But must we go up or down?'...

'Down, and I will tell you why. We have reached a vast open space, where a large number of galleries culminate. The one you followed must necessarily take you to this point, for it appears that all these fissures, these fractures of the globe, radiate out from the vast cavern we are in. Get up, then, and start walking again. If necessary drag yourself along, slide on the steep slopes, and you will find our open arms at the end of your walk. Off you go my boy; off you go!'...

These words brought me back to life.

'Good bye, Uncle John", I cried, 'I am starting off. As soon as I leave here, our voices will not be able to communicate. Good bye then!'...

'Goodbye, Axel! Good bye!'...

These were the last words I heard.

This surprising conversation, transmitted through the vast mass of the Earth, exchanged over a little more than a league and a half, ended with these words of hope. I said a prayer in order to thank God, for he had led me through these dark and immense solitudes to perhaps the only point where my friends' voices could reach me.

This astounding acoustic effect can easily be explained by simple natural laws; it arose from the peculiar shape of the gallery and the conductibility of the rock. There are many examples of this propagation of sounds, not perceptible in intermediate spaces. I remembered that the phenomenon can be observed in various places, including the Whispering Gallery at St Paul's Cathedral in London, and especially some weird caverns in Sicily, those quarries near Syracuse, of which the most interesting is known as the Ear of Dionysus.

These memories came into my mind, and I realized that, since my uncle's voice reached my ears, no obstacle could exist between us. By following the path of the sound, logically I was able to reach him if my strength did not fail me.

I accordingly got up. I dragged myself along more than I walked. The slope was quite steep. I slid down.

Soon the speed of the descent began to increase alarmingly: it was about to look like a real fall. I no longer had the strength to stop me.

Suddenly the ground disappeared from under my feet. I felt myself rolling and hitting the walls of a vertical gallery: a real shaft.

My head struck a sharp rock, and I lost consciousness.

Chapter 29.

When I came to, I found myself in semi-darkness, lying on thick blankets. My uncle was watching over me, he was looking for any sign of life. At my first sigh he took hold of my hand, when I opened my eyes he uttered a loud cry of joy: 'he is alive, he is alive!'

'Yes, I am', I said in a weak voice.

'My boy', said my uncle, clasping me to his breast, 'you are saved!'

I was deeply touched by the tone in which these words were spoken, and even more by the feelings hidden behind. But such trials were necessary to produce a display of emotion like this in the professor.

At that moment Hans joined us. He saw my hand in my uncle's, and I venture to say that his eyes showed a great joy.

'*God dag,*' he said.

'Hi, Hans, hi,' I murmured. 'And now, Uncle John, tell me where we are.'

'Tomorrow, Axel, tomorrow. You're still too weak today. I've bandaged your head with compresses which mustn't be moved. Sleep, my boy: tomorrow you will know everything.'

'At least', I cried, 'tell me what time it is, what day it is.'

'Eleven p. m., Sunday, 9 August, and I forbid you to ask any more questions until the tenth of this month.'

Actually, I was very weak, and my eyes soon closed involuntarily. I did need a good night's rest, and slept with the idea that my isolation had lasted four long days.

When I woke up the next morning I looked around. My berth, composed of all our travelling rugs, was in a charming grotto, adorned with magnificent stalagmites, and with a floor covered in fine sand. There reigned a semi-darkness. No torch, no lamp was lighted, and yet a certain inexplicable light entered from the outside through a narrow opening in the grotto. I also heard a vague and indefinite murmur, like the moaning of waves breaking on a shore, and, occasionally, the whistling of the wind.

I began to wonder if I had woken up properly, if I wasn't still dreaming, if my brain, cracked by my fall, did not perceive purely imaginary noises. However, neither my eyes nor my ears could be mistaken to that extent.

'It's a ray of daylight', I thought, 'coming through that crack in the rocks. That's really the murmur of the waves! And that is the whistle of the wind! Am I wrong, or have we returned to the surface of the Earth? Has my uncle given up his expedition, or has he reached his goal?'

I was puzzling over these insoluble questions, when the professor came in.

'Good morning, Axel', he said happily. 'I think you are fine.'

'Yes, I am', I replied, sitting up in bed.

'Of course you are, for you slept calmly. Hans and I each took turns to watch over you, and we saw you recovering by leaps and bounds.'

'I really feel much better now; to prove it, I will do justice to the breakfast you are going to put before me!'

'You will eat, my boy! The fever has left you. Hans has been rubbing your wounds with some sort of ointment known only to Icelanders, and they have closed up marvelously. Our hunter is a very reliable man.'

While speaking, my uncle prepared some food, which I devoured, despite his advice. While I was eating I overwhelmed him with questions, to which he did not hesitate to respond.

I learned that my providential fall had brought me to the end of an almost perpendicular tunnel. As I had come down in the middle of a torrent of rocks, the smallest of which would have been enough to crush me, it followed that a section of the rock face must have slid down with me. This terrifying vehicle had carried me straight into my uncle's arms, where I had fallen, unconscious and covered with blood.

'It is truly incredible that you weren't killed a thousand times. But, good Lord, let's stay together from now on, otherwise we will be in danger of never seeing each other again.'

'Stay together from now on!' The journey wasn't over, then? I stared at him, which immediately prompted the question: 'what is the matter, Axel?'

'I want to ask you a question. You say that I'm safe and sound?'

'Yes I do.'

'I have all my limbs intact?'

'Yes you have.'

'And my head?'

'Your head, apart from one or two bruises, is exactly where it ought to be: on your shoulders.'

'Well, I think I have lost my mind!'

'Lost?'

'Yes. We haven't returned to the surface of the Earth, have we?'

'Most certainly not!'

'Then I must be mad, for I can see the daylight, I can hear the wind blowing and the sea breaking.'

'Oh! Is that all?'

'Will you please explain?'

'I will not explain anything, for it is inexplicable. But you will see and soon realise that geology has much more to say.'

'Let's go then', I cried, suddenly getting up.

'No, Axel, no! The open air might be bad for you.'

'Open air?'

'Yes, the wind is rather strong. I don't want you to put yourself in danger like that.'

'But I am fine.'

'Patience, my boy. A relapse would put us in a difficult position and we have no time to lose, as the crossing could take a long time.'

'The crossing?'

'Yes. Have another rest today, and tomorrow we will sail.'

'Sail?'

The word surprised me.

Sail! Did we have a river, a lake, or a sea at our disposal? Was there a ship anchored at some interior port?

I was very much intrigued. My uncle tried in vain to restrain me. When he realized that my impatience would do me more harm than the fulfilment of my longings, he gave in.

I dressed quickly. As an extra precaution, I wrapped myself in one of the blankets and went out of the grotto.

Chapter 30.

At first I saw nothing. My eyes, no longer used to the light, snapped shut. When I was able to open them again, I stood still, far more stupefied than delighted.

'The sea!', I cried.

'Yes. The Lidenbrock Sea, and I like to believe that no other navigator will contest the honour of having discovered it and the right to name it with my own name.'

A massive waterbody, the beginning of a lake or ocean, stretched away ahead of us. The shoreline, greatly indented, offered the lapping water a fine golden sand, dotted with those small shells that housed the first beings of the Creation. The waves broke over it with that sonorous murmur peculiar to vast enclosed spaces. A light foam was swept up by the breath of a moderate wind, and some of the spray was blowing into my face. On this gently sloping shore, about 210 yards from the edge of the waves, expired the last foothills of gigantic cliffs that soared, widening, to an immeasurable height. Some of them, piercing the shoreline with their sharp edges, formed capes and promontories nibbled by the teeth of the surf. Further on, the eye was drawn by their shapes clearly outlined against the hazy horizon in the distance.

It was a real ocean, with the capricious contours of the coastlines of the surface, but empty and atrociously wild.

If I was able to look so far across this sea, it was because of a special light which revealed the smallest details. It was not the light coming from the sun with its bright beams and the splendid irradiation of its rays, nor the pale and vague gleam of the moon, which is only a cold reflection. No, the luminous power of this light, its flickering diffusion, its bright and dry whiteness, its low temperature, its brilliance, superior even to the moon's, pointed to an electrical origin. It was like an aurora borealis, a continuous cosmic phenomenon, filling this cavern big enough to hold an ocean.

The vault suspended above my head and the sky seemed to be made of big clouds, moving and irresolute water vapours which, due to condensation, surely burst into torrential rain on certain days. I would have thought that under such extreme atmospheric pressure, evaporation could not take place. However, by some physical law which was beyond my understanding, there were great clouds filling the air. But at this moment 'it was a fine day'. The electric layers produced an astonishing play of light amongst the high clouds. Clear shadows stood out on their lower curves and often, between two separate strata, a ray of remarkable intensity slipped through to us. It was not the sun, for its light gave no heat. The effect was sad, completely depressing. Instead of a firmament bright with stars, I felt the granite vault above these clouds weighing down on me: this space, immense as it was, would not have been enough for the promenade of the least ambitious satellite.

I remembered then a theory of a British captain which compared the Earth to a vast hollow sphere, inside which the air was kept luminous by reason of the great pressure, while two heavenly bodies, Pluto and Proserpina, traced their mysterious orbits. Was he right?

In reality we were imprisoned in a vast excavation. It was impossible to say how wide it stretched, since the shore broadened until it was out of sight, nor how long, for the eye was soon restricted by a slightly uncertain horizon. As for its height, it must have been several leagues at the very least. It was impossible to make out where the vault rested on its granite buttresses, as there was a big cloud floating in the atmosphere, which had to be over two miles up, a height greater than on Earth. This was undoubtedly due to the considerable density of the air.

The word 'cavern' cannot describe this massive place. The words invented by man are inadequate for those who venture into the depths of the Earth.

I could not think what geological event might explain the existence of such a hollow. Could the cooling down of the globe have produced it? I was acquainted, through the tales of travellers, with several famous caverns, but none had such dimensions as this.

If the grotto of Guachara, in Colombia, visited by Lord Humboldt, did not divulge the secret of its depth to him, although he explored it for 2,500 feet, its extent could not in all plausibility have been much more than that. The vast Mammoth Cave in Kentucky was another example of gigantic proportions, since its ceiling rose five hundred feet above an unfathomable lake: travellers had explored more than ten leagues of it without ever reaching the end. But what were these holes compared to the one I was now admiring, with its vapory sky, its electric irradiations, and a vast ocean imprisoned in its wombs? My imagination felt powerless before such immensity.

I remained silent and gazed at these marvels. Words to describe my feelings failed me completely. I felt as if I were on some distant planet, observing Uranus or Neptune, phenomena which my terrestrial nature had no knowledge of. New words were needed for new sensations, and my imagination could not provide them. I looked, I thought, I admired, in a stupefaction mingled with a certain amount of fear.

The unexpectedness of this spectacle had restored the flush of health to my cheeks; I was in the process of treating myself by means of astonishment, bringing about my cure through this new therapy; besides, the vigour of the very dense air was reviving me, by providing more oxygen for my lungs.

It will not be difficult to understand that, after being confined in a narrow gallery for forty-seven days, it was infinite ecstasy to breathe in this breeze loaded with wet and salty emanations.

I could not possibly regret leaving my dark grotto. My uncle, already used to these marvels, was no longer astonished.

'Do you feel strong enough for a little walk?', he asked.

'Yes I do: nothing would give me greater pleasure.'

'Well then, take my arm, Axel, and we will follow the meanders of the shoreline.'

I accepted eagerly, and we began to discover this new ocean. On the left, abrupt rocks, stacked on top of each other, formed a sublime titanic pile. Innumerable cascades slipped over their sides and turned into transparent waterbodies. A few light vapours, springing from rock to rock, pointed to where hot springs lay; and streams flowed gently towards their shared lake, seeking the opportunity of the slopes to murmur more pleasantly.

Amongst these streams I recognised our faithful travelling companion, the Hans-Bach, which came to disappear peacefully into the sea as if it had never done anything else since the beginning of the world.

'We will miss it in future', I said with a sigh.

'Bah!', replied the professor. 'That or another one, what difference does it make?'

I found him quite ungrateful.

But at that moment my attention was distracted by an unexpected sight. Five hundred paces away, beyond a high promontory, appeared a tall, thick, dense forest. It consisted of trees of medium height, shaped like regular sunshades, with neat and geometric silhouettes; the air currents seemed to have no influence on their foliage, and in the midst of the breezes they stayed as still as a clump of petrified cedars.

I hurried forward. I could find no name for these singular varieties. Did they belong to one of the two hundred thousand known vegetable species, or would we have to give them a special place in the flora of water-based vegetation? No. When we arrived under their shade, my surprise turned into admiration.

I was in the presence of products of the Earth, but constructed on a gigantic scale. My uncle called them immediately by their name: 'it is just a forest of mushrooms.'

He was right. These plants that prefer a hot and humid environment had grown a lot. I knew that the *Lycoperdon giganteum* reached, according to Bulliard, eight or nine feet in circumference; but here we had white mushrooms thirty or forty feet high, with caps of the same width. There were thousands of them. No light could pierce their dense shade, and complete darkness reigned beneath those domes, crowded together like the round roofs of an African city.

I still wanted to push further in. A mortal chill seeped down from these fleshy vaults. We wandered about for half an hour in these damp shadows, and it was with a real feeling of well-being that I got back to the seashore.

But the vegetation of this subterranean land was not confined to mushrooms. Further arose in groups a great many other trees with faded leaves. They were easily recognizable; common shrubs of the Earth, of phenomenal size, lycopodia a hundred feet high, giant sigillarias, tree ferns as tall as pines from northern latitudes, lepidodendrons with cylindrical forked stalks ending in long leaves bristling with coarse hair like monstrous succulent plants.

'Astonishing, magnificent, splendid!', cried my uncle. 'Here we have the complete flora of the Second Era of the world, the Transition Era. Here we have those humble garden plants which became trees during the first centuries of the Earth. Look, Axel, and admire! No botanist has ever been so lucky!'

'You are right, Uncle John. Providence seems to have wanted to preserve in this enormous greenhouse all the antediluvian plants which have been reconstructed so successfully by scientists.'

'You are right there, my boy, it is a greenhouse; but you could add that it may be a menagerie too.'

'A menagerie?'

'Without a doubt. Look at this dust we are treading on, look at the bones scattered on the ground.'

'Bones, indeed! The bones of antediluvian animals!'

I swooped down on the age-old remains, made of some indestructible mineral substance. I unhesitatingly put a name to these gigantic bones which resembled dried-up tree trunks.

'Here is the lower jawbone of a mastodon', I said; 'here are the molars of a dinotherium; and here we have a thigh-bone which can only have belonged to the biggest of these animals, the megatherium. Yes, it really is a menagerie, for these bones were definitely not carried here by some cataclysm. The animals they belonged to lived on the shores of this subterranean sea, in the shade of these arborescent plants. Look, I can see whole skeletons. However...'

'However?'

'I cannot understand how such quadrupeds came to be in this granite cavern.'

'Why?'

'Because animal life only existed on Earth in the Secondary Period, when the sedimentary soil was formed by the alluvial deposits, replacing the red-hot rocks of the Primitive Era.'

'Well, Axel, there's a very simple answer to your objection; namely that this soil is sedimentary.'

'What! So far below the surface of the Earth!'

'Without a doubt, and it can be explained geologically. At a certain period, the Earth consisted only of an elastic crust, subjected to alternate upward and downward movements, by virtue of the laws of gravity. These probably gave rise to landslides, and a section of the sedimentary formations was carried down to the bottom of newly opened chasms.'

'That must be true. But if antediluvian animals lived in the subterranean regions, who is to say that one of those monsters is not still wandering around in the middle of these dark forests or behind these steep rocks?'

At the idea, I looked around with a certain dread; but no living creature appeared on the deserted shores.

I felt a little tired, and went and sat down right at the end of a promontory, at whose foot the waves were noisily breaking. From there I could see right round the bay, constituted by an indentation in the coast. At the end there had formed a little harbour enclosed by pyramid-shaped rocks. Its calm waters slept, sheltered from the wind. A brig and two or three schooners might have anchored there with room to spare. I almost expected to see some ship coming out, all sails set, making for the open sea on the southerly breeze.

But this illusion soon disappeared. We really were the only living creatures in this subterranean world. At times, when the wind dropped, a silence deeper than the silence of the desert fell upon these arid rocks and weighed upon the surface of the ocean. I tried, then, to see through the distant mists, to tear apart the curtain which had fallen over the mysterious depths of the horizon. I was confused! Where did this sea end? What could be found on the other side? Would we ever be able to sight the shores on the other side?

My uncle, personally, had no doubts about the matter. As for me, I both desired and feared it.

After an hour spent in contemplation of this marvelous scenery, we set off once more along the shore to return to the grotto. Thoughtful, I fell into a deep sleep.

Chapter 31.

I woke up the next day completely cured. I thought a bathe would do me a lot of good, and so I went and plunged for a few minutes in the waters of this Mediterranean Sea. Such a name, surely, suited the sea better than any other.

I returned and ate with a healthy appetite. Hans knew perfectly how to cook our limited menu. Equipped with fire and water, he could vary our usual fare a little. He gave us some coffee at the end of the meal, and never had this delicious beverage tasted better.

'Now', said my uncle, 'it's time for the tide, and we must not miss the opportunity to study this phenomenon.'

'What! A tide?'

'Yes, a tide!'

'Can the influence of the moon and the sun be felt down here then?'

'Why not? Are not all bodies subject to the force of gravity? This mass of water must therefore be subject to that universal law. So, despite the atmospheric pressure on the surface, you will see it rise like the Atlantic itself.'

During this time we were walking along the sand, and the waves were creeping slowly up the shore.

'Look, there's the tide beginning', I cried.

'Yes, Axel, and judging from the tidemark of foam, you can see that the water rises about ten feet.'

'That's fantastic!'

'No, it's natural.'

'Say what you like, Uncle John, this all seems extraordinary to me, and I can hardly believe my eyes. Who would ever have thought that there could be a real ocean inside the Earth's crust, with its own ebb and flow, its own sea breezes and storms!'

'And why not? Is there some physical reason to prevent it?'

'Not that I can see, if we abandoned the theory of heat at the centre.'

'So up to this point Davy's theory appears to be confirmed?'

'It looks like it, and if that is the case there is nothing to oppose the existence of seas or lands inside the Earth.'

'No doubt, but uninhabited.'

'But why shouldn't these waters shelter a few fish of some unknown species?'

'Well at any rate we haven't found a single one so far.'

'We could cast a line and see if a hook has the same success here as in the sublunary oceans.'

'We will try that, Axel, for we must unravel all the mysteries of these new territories.'

'But where are we, Uncle John? For I haven't yet asked you that question to which the instruments must have answered you.'

'Horizontally, 350 leagues from Iceland.'

'As much as that?'

'More or less.'

'And the compass is still pointing south-east?'

'Yes, with a deviation to the west of 19° 42 min, just like on the surface.

As for its lead angle, there is something strange which I have been observing most carefully.'

'What do you mean?'

'The needle, instead of dipping towards the Pole as it does in the northern hemisphere, is pointing upwards instead.'

'That means that the point of magnetic attraction lies somewhere between the surface of the Earth and the place we have reached?'

'Exactly, and it is quite probable that if we reached the polar regions, near the seventieth parallel where James Ross discovered the magnetic pole, we would see the needle point stand straight up. Therefore this mysterious centre of attraction is not located at any great depth.'

'And that's something that science has never even suspected.'

'Science, my boy, is composed of errors, but errors that it is right to make, for they lead step by step towards the truth.'

'How far down are we?'

'Thirty-five leagues.'

'So', I said, examining the map, 'the Scottish Highlands are above us, and up there the snow-covered peaks of the Grampians are rising to prodigious heights.'

'Yes', replied the professor with a laugh, 'it's a bit heavy to hold up, but the vault is solid; the great architect of the universe built it of good materials, and man would never have been able to give it such compressive strength! What are bridge arches and cathedral vaults next to this nave three leagues in diameter, beneath which an ocean and its storms can behave as they wish?'

'Oh, I'm not afraid of the sky falling on my head. Now, Uncle John, what are your plans? Don't you want to go back to the surface of the Earth?'

'Go back! What an idea. On the contrary, my intention is to continue our journey, since everything has gone so well to date.'

'But I can't see how we are going to find our path under this liquid plain.'

'I have no intention of diving in head first. But if, properly speaking, oceans are nothing but lakes, since they are surrounded by land, then all the more reason for this inner sea to be surrounded by granite banks.'

'There's no doubt about it.'

'Well then! I'm sure to find other exits on the opposite shore.'

'So, how long would you guess this ocean to be?'

'Thirty or forty leagues.'

'Ah', I said, thinking that this estimate could well be inaccurate.

'Consequently we have no time to lose, and will set sail tomorrow.'

I looked instinctively round for the ship which would carry us.

'So', I said, 'we're going to embark. Good! And which ship are we to travel on?'

'It won't be a ship, but a good solid raft.'

'A raft!', I cried. 'A raft is just as impossible to build as a ship, and I can't see…'

'You can't see, Axel, but if you were listening you would be able to hear!'

'Hear?'

'Yes, hammer blows, which would tell you that Hans is already at work.'

'Building a raft?'

'Indeed.'

'What! Has he already been chopping down trees?'

'The trees were already down. Come along, and you will see him at it.'

I walked for a quarter of an hour and then saw Hans at work on the other side of the promontory which enclosed the small natural harbour. After a few more steps I was beside him. To my astonishment, a half-finished raft lay on the sand; it was made from timbers of a distinctive wood, and a great number of beams, curved beams and frames were strewn over the ground. There was enough material to build an entire fleet.

'Uncle John', I cried, 'what wood is this?'

'Pine, fir, birch, all sorts of northern conifers, petrified by the sea water.'

'Is that possible?'

'It is what we call *surtarbrandur*, or fossilized wood.'

'In that case, like lignite, it must be as hard as stone, and unable to float.'

'Sometimes that is the case: some of the trunks have become true anthracite; but others, such as these, have only just begun to be transformed into fossils. Watch this', added my uncle, throwing one of these precious remains into the sea.

The piece of wood disappeared for a moment, then bobbed up again to the surface of the water to float up and down following its movements.

'Are you convinced?', said my uncle.

'Convinced that what I see is incredible!'

By the following evening, thanks to Hans's skill, the raft was finished; it was ten feet long by five feet wide; the beams of *surtarbrandur* bound together with stout ropes, formed a solid surface. Once it had been launched, the improvised vessel floated serenely on the waters of the Lidenbrock Sea.

Chapter 32.

On the 13th of August we woke up early. We were now going to inaugurate this new sort of transport, fast and not too tiring.

A mast made of two pieces of wood fastened together, a yard made from another, and a sail borrowed from our blankets made up the rigging of our raft. There was no lack of rope. The whole thing was solid.

At six o'clock the professor gave the signal to embark. Our provisions, luggage, instruments, and weapons, along with a good supply of fresh water collected among the rocks, were already on board.

Hans had fitted a rudder which allowed him to steer his floating construction. He took the helm. I unhitched the mooring line attaching us to shore. The sail was trimmed and we set off.

As we were leaving the little harbour, my uncle, who was very attached to his geographic nomenclature, decided to give it a name and proposed mine, amongst others.

'Well, I have another to suggest.'

'And what's that?'

'Gräuben's. Port Gräuben will look very good on the map.'

'Port Gräuben it is.'

And that was how the memory of my dear Vironian girl became linked to our adventurous expedition.

The wind was blowing from the north-east. We ran before the wind at a good speed. The very dense atmospheric layers had a great propulsive power and acted on the sail like a big electric fan.

After an hour, my uncle had been able to estimate our speed relatively precisely.

'If we continue to advance at the present rate,' he said, 'we will cover at thirty leagues every twenty-four hours, and it won't be too long before we reach the opposite shore.'

I did not reply, and made my way to the front of the raft. The northern coastline was already disappearing behind the horizon. The two limbs of the shore were spread wide apart, as if to assist our departure. An immense ocean stretched before my eyes. Massive clouds were twirling around, casting their grey shadows on the surface, shadows which seemed to weigh down upon that dismal water. The silvery rays of the electric light, reflected here and there by droplets, sprinkled the wake with scintillating points. Soon the shore disappeared in the distance: we did not have any point of reference anymore. Had it not been for the frothy wake of the raft, I could have believed that we were totally motionless.

At about midday, immense marine plants appeared, floating on the surface of the waves. I was aware of the extraordinarily prolific power of these plants, which creep along the bottom of the sea at a depth of more than twelve thousand feet, reproduce under pressures of four hundred atmospheres, and often form masses large enough to impede the progress of ships. But there can never, I believe, have existed algae as gigantic as those of the Lidenbrock Sea.

Our raft swept along beside wracks, whose length was three or four thousand feet. They were immense snakes growing in far-off abysses. I had fun gazing for hours along their infinite ribbon-like lengths, thinking each moment that I had reached the end: my patience was fooled, not my amazement.

What natural force could have produced such plants? What must the Earth have looked like during the first centuries of its formation when, acted upon by heat and humidity, the vegetable kingdom was developing solitarily on its surface?

Night came, but, as I had noticed the evening before, the luminosity of the atmosphere did not reduce at all. It was a consistent phenomenon whose permanence we could count on.

After supper, I stretched out at the foot of the mast, and soon fell asleep amongst indolent reveries.

Hans, motionless at the tiller, let the raft run. As the wind was aft, he did not even have to steer it.

On leaving Port Gräuben, Professor Lidenbrock had given me the job of keeping the 'ship's log', with instructions to put down even the most insignificant observations, to note interesting phenomena, the direction of the wind, our speed, the distance covered: in a word, every incident of this weird crossing.

I will confine myself, therefore, to reproducing here those daily notes, written, as it were, at the dictation of events, in order to give a more precise account of our crossing.

Friday, the 14th of August. Steady breeze from the NW. Raft progressing with extreme rapidity, going perfectly straight. Coast about eighty miles to leeward. Nothing on the horizon. The intensity of the light is constant. Weather fine: the clouds are very high, thin and floating in an atmosphere resembling molten silver.

Thermometer: 32°C.

At midday Hans ties a hook to the end of a line. He baits it with a small piece of meat and casts it into the sea. He doesn't catch anything for two hours. Are there no fish in this sea? But yes, there is a tug on the line. Hans draws it in, and then pulls out a fish, which is wriggling furiously.

'A fish!', cries my uncle.

'A sturgeon!', I shout in turn, 'a small sturgeon!'

The professor is examining the animal carefully, and he does not agree with me. This fish has a flattened, curved head, and the lower parts of its body are covered with bony plates; it has no teeth; quite well-developed pectoral fins are fitted to its tailless body. This animal certainly belongs to the order in which naturalists classify the sturgeon, but it differs from that fish in many quite basic details.

My uncle is not mistaken, after all. Following a short examination he says: 'this fish belongs to a family which has been extinct for centuries, and of which only fossil traces remain, in the Devonian strata.'

'What! Have we really captured alive an authentic inhabitant of the primitive seas?'

'Yes, we have', said the professor, continuing his observation, 'and you may notice that these fossil fish are distinct from any existing species. To hold a living specimen of the order in one's hand is a great joy for a naturalist.'

'But what family does it belong to?'

'To the order of ganoids, family of the Cephalaspis, genus... '

'Well?'

'Genus Pterychtis, I would swear to it. But this fish displays a peculiarity, which is apparently encountered in the fish of underground waters.'

'Which one?'

'It is blind.'

'Blind!'

'Not only blind, but without eyes.'

I look. It really is true. This, however, may be a one-of-a-kind creature. So the hook is baited again and thrown back into the water. The ocean must be well stocked with fish, for in two hours we take a large number of Pterychtis, as well as fish belonging to another extinct family, the Dipterides, though my uncle cannot classify them exactly. All are eyeless. This unexpected catch fortunately renews our stock of provisions.

It now seems very probable that this sea contains only fossil species, in which both fish and reptiles alike are more perfect the longer ago they were created.

Perhaps we are going to find some of the saurians that science has succeeded in recreating from bits of bone or cartilage? I take the telescope and examine the sea. It is deserted. We are still too close to the coast.

I look up. Why should not some of the birds reconstructed by the immortal Cuvier be flapping their wings in the heavy strata of the atmosphere? These fish would provide them with enough food. I search the space above, but the airs are as uninhabited as the shores.

Nevertheless, my imagination carries me away into the wonderful hypotheses of paleontology. It is a daydream. I fancy I can see on the surface of the water enormous Chersites, these antediluvian tortoises resembling floating islands. Along the darkened shores are passing the great mammals of the first days, the Leptotherium found in the caverns of Brazil, the Merycotherium, all the way from the glacial regions of Siberia. Further up, the pachydermatous Lophiodon, that gigantic tapir, is concealing itself behind the rocks, ready to do battle for its prey with the Anoplotherium, a singular animal taking after the rhinoceros, the horse, the hippopotamus, and the camel, as if the Creator, in too much of a hurry in the first hours of the world, had put together several animals in one. The giant Mastodon, twisting and turning its trunk, uses its tusks to break up the rocks on the shore, whereas the Megatherium, standing on its enormous legs, is excavating the earth for food, all the while awaking the sonorous echoes of the granite with its roaring. Higher up, the Protopithecus, the first monkey to appear on the face of the globe, is clambering up the steep slopes. Still higher, the Pterodactyl, with its winged claws, glides on the dense air like a huge bat. Above them all, in the topmost layers, are immense birds, more powerful than the cassowary, greater than the ostrich, spreading their vast wings, about to hit their heads against the roof of the granite vault.

This whole fossil world revives in my imagination. I am going back to the biblical ages of the Creation, long before man was born, when the incomplete Earth was not yet ready for him. My dream then goes ahead of the appearance of animate beings. The mammals disappear, then the birds, then the reptiles of the Secondary Period, and finally the fish, the crustaceans, the molluscs, and the animals with moving joints. The zoophytes of the Transition Period themselves return to nothingness. The whole of the world's life is summed up in me, and mine is the only heart that beats in this deserted world! There are no longer seasons; no longer climates; the internal heat of the globe is increasing unceasingly, cancelling out the effect of the radiant orb. The vegetation grows exaggeratedly. I pass like a shadow amongst arborescent ferns, walking cautiously on the iridescent marl formations and colorful sandstones; I lean against the trunks of giant conifers; I lie down in the shade of sphenophylla, asterophyllites, and lycopodia a hundred feet high.

The centuries are flowing past like days! I am working my way up the series of earthly transformations. The plants disappear; the granitic rocks lose their purity; the liquid state is about to replace the solid because of the action of a greater heat; the waters are flowing over the surface of the globe; they boil; they evaporate; the vapour is covering up the entire Earth, which stage by stage becomes nothing but a gaseous mass, heated to red-hot, as big as the sun and shining as bright!

In the centre of this nebula, one million four hundred thousand times as big as the globe it will one day form, I am carried off into outer space! My body changes its structure, it sublimes and mixes, like an imponderable atom, with these immense vapors, which draw in infinity their blazing orbit!

What a dream! Where is it taking me? My feverish hand jots down the strange details. I have forgotten everything: the professor, the guide, the raft. An hallucination has taken hold of my head...

'What is the matter?', said my uncle.

My eyes, wide open, are looking at my uncle but they don't see him.

'Take care, Axel, you're going to fall overboard!'

At the same time, I feel myself seized by Hans's firm hand. Had it not been for him, under the sway of my dream, I would have thrown myself into the waves.

'Is he going mad?', cries the professor.

'What is it?', I say at last, coming to.

'Are you ill?'

'No; I had an hallucination for a moment, but it has passed. Is all well on board?'

'Yes, there is a steady breeze and the sea is calm! We are going fast and unless my calculations are out, we will soon land.'

At these words, I rise and scan the horizon: the water and the clouds are still indistinguishable.

Chapter 33.

Saturday, the 15ᵗʰ of August. The sea keeps on moving monotonously. No land in sight. The horizon seems a very long way away.

My head is still dull from the violent effects of my dream.

My uncle, who has certainly not dreamed, is, however, in one of his moods. He is scanning every point in space with his telescope and crossing his arms disappointedly.

I notice that Professor Lidenbrock has a tendency to revert to his impatient character of before, and I note this fact in my logbook. It required my danger and sufferings to extract a spark of kindness from him; but now that I am better, his nature has resurfaced. And yet why get annoyed? Isn't the journey proceeding under the most favourable circumstances? Isn't the raft going amazingly fast?

'You look worried, Uncle John?', I say, seeing him often putting the telescope to his eye.

'Worried? No.'

'Impatient then?'

'The reaction can be understood!'

'And yet we are advancing at a rate…'

'I do not care! It is not our speed that is too small, but the sea that is too big!'

I remember then that the professor, before our departure, estimated the length of this subterranean ocean to be about thirty leagues. We have already done at least three times that distance, but haven't discovered the slightest sign of the southern shores.

'We are not going down', continued the professor. 'All this is lost time. I did not come so far for a boat trip on a pond!'

He calls this crossing a boat trip, and this ocean a pond!

'But', I say, 'since we have been following the route indicated by Saknussemm…'

'That is the question. Have we been following the route? Did Saknussemm ever encounter this great stretch of water? Did he cross it? Did the rivulet we took as a guide lead us astray?'

'In any case, we can't regret coming this far. The spectacle is magnificent, and…'

'Seeing is not the question. I have a goal and I want to achieve it. So don't talk to me about admiring!'

He doesn't need to say it again; and I leave the professor in his restlessness. At six in the evening, Hans asks for his wages, and the three dollars are counted out to him.

Sunday, the 16th of August. Nothing new. Same weather. The wind has a slight tendency to freshen. When I wake up, the first thing I do is observe the intensity of the light. I live in fear that the electric phenomenon might dim and then go out. Nothing of the sort happens. The shadow of the raft is clearly outlined on the surface of the water.

This sea is truly infinite. It must be as wide as the Mediterranean, or even the Atlantic. Why not?

My uncle tries sounding several times. He ties one of our heaviest picks to the end of a rope, and allows it to go down for two hundred fathoms. No bottom. We have great difficulty in pulling our sounding line in again.

When the pick has finally been dragged on board, Hans calls my attention to some deep marks on its surface. The piece of iron looks as though it has been firmly gripped between two hard objects.

I look at the hunter.

'*Tänder.*'

I do not understand. I turn to my uncle: he is lost in thought. I don't want to disturb him. I come back to the Icelander. He makes himself understood opening and closing his mouth several times.

'Teeth!', I cry with stupefaction, examining the iron bar more closely.

Yes, the indentations on the metal are the marks of teeth! The jaws on which they are fastened must have a prodigious strength! Is it some monster of a lost species swimming restlessly under the deep strata of the waters, hungrier than a shark, more dangerous than a whale? I am unable to detach my eyes from the half-gnawed bar. Is my dream of last night about to become a reality?

These thoughts upset me all day, and my imagination scarcely calms down in a sleep of a few hours.

Monday, the 17th of August. I have been trying to remember the particular instincts of the antediluvian animals from the Secondary Period, which, following on from the molluscs, the crustaceans, and the fish, emerged before the mammals appeared on the globe. Back then, the world belonged to the reptiles. These hideous monsters dominated the Jurassic seas. Nature endowed them with the most perfect body. What gigantic organisms! What exceptional strength! The present-day saurians, even the largest and most formidable crocodiles and alligators, are but feeble reductions of their fathers of the first ages.

I shudder at my own evocation of these monsters. No human eye has ever seen them alive. They appeared on the Earth a thousand centuries before man, but their fossil bones, discovered in the clayey limestone that the British call Lias, have allowed us to reconstruct them anatomically, and thus know about their colossal size.

In the Natural History Museum of Hamburg I have seen the skeleton of one of these saurians measuring thirty feet from head to tail. As an inhabitant of the Earth, am I going to find myself face to face with the representatives of an antediluvian family? No, it is impossible! And yet marks of powerful teeth are engraved on the iron bar! I notice that they are conical like the crocodile's.

My eyes stare with terror at the sea. I am afraid that one of these inhabitants of the submarine caverns will suddenly emerge.

I imagine that Professor Lidenbrock shares my ideas, if not my fears, for after an examination of the pick, he casts his eyes over the water.

What could have possessed him to sound the ocean? He has disturbed some creature in its retreat, and if we are not attacked on the way...

I glance at our firearms, and check that they are in working order. My uncle sees me doing this and nods approvingly.

Already wide disturbances on the surface of the water indicate suspicious movements in the greatest depths. Danger is near. We must keep our eyes peeled.

Tuesday, the 18ᵗʰ of August. Evening comes, or rather the hour when sleep closes our eyelids, for there is no night on this ocean, and the implacable light constantly tires our eyes, as if we were navigating in the sunlight of the Arctic seas. Hans is at the helm. During his watch I fall asleep.

Two hours later, I am awakened by an awful shock. The raft has been lifted right out of the water with indescribable force, and thrown down 128 feet away.

'Eh, what is it?', cries my uncle. 'Have we hit a rock?'

Hans points at a massive blackish object, about 426 yards away, which is moving steadily up and down. I look and cry: 'it's a colossal porpoise!'

'Yes, and over there is a sea lizard of a most unusual size.'

'And further on a prodigious crocodile. Look at its huge jaws, and its rows of aggressive teeth. Oh, it has disappeared!'

'A whale, a whale!', shouts the professor, 'I can see its enormous tail. Look, it is expelling air and water through its blowholes!'

Actually, two liquid columns rise to a considerable height above the waves. We remain surprised, stupefied, horrified at the sight of this herd of sea monsters. They have supernatural dimensions: the smallest of them could crush the raft with a single bite. Hans seizes the helm, so as to run before the wind and flee this danger zone, but he sees more dangerous enemies on the other side: a tortoise about forty feet across, and a serpent, about thirty, thrusting an enormous head above the waters.

Impossible to flee. These reptiles advance upon us; then move round the raft with a speed that could not be equaled by boats going very fast. They swim about it in concentric circles. I pick up my rifle. But what effect could a bullet have on the scales covering the bodies of these animals?

We remain speechless with horror. They are now coming at us, the crocodile on one side, the serpent on the other. The rest of the marine herd have disappeared. I am about to fire. Hans stops me with a sign. The two monsters pass within a hundred and six yards of the raft; then, they make a rush at each other: their fury prevents them from seeing us.

The combat starts 213 yards from the raft. We distinctly see the two monsters seizing hold of each other.

But now the other animals also seem to be taking part in the struggle, the porpoise, the whale, the lizard, and the tortoise. I catch sight of them at every moment. I point them out to the Icelander. But he shakes his head.

'*Tva*,' he says.

'What, two? He claims there are only two animals...'

'He is right', says my uncle, whose telescope has not left his eye.

'It's incredible!'

'The first of these monsters has the snout of a porpoise, the head of a lizard, and the teeth of a crocodile: hence our mistake. It is the most frightful of all the antediluvian reptiles: the Ichthyosaurus.'

'And the other?'

'A serpent, concealed under the hard shell of a turtle, and a mortal enemy of the first: the Plesiosaurus!'

Hans is quite right. Only two monsters are disturbing the surface of the sea. I have before me two reptiles from the primitive oceans. I can see the bloody eye of the Ichthyosaurus, as big as a man's head. Nature has given it an extremely powerful optical apparatus, able to resist the water pressure in the depths where it lives. It has been called the saurian whale, for it is just as big and just as quick as that animal. This one is not less than a hundred feet long, and I can get some idea of its girth when it lifts its vertical tailfins out of the water. Its jaws are enormous and according to the naturalists contain as many as 182 teeth.

The Plesiosaurus, a serpent with a cylindrical trunk and a short tail, has legs shaped into paddles. Its whole body is covered with a hard shell, and its neck, as flexible as a swan's, rises more than thirty feet above the waves.

These animals attack one another with indescribable fury. They raise mountains of water, which surge as far as the raft. Twenty times we are on the point of capsizing. Hisses of a frightening volume reach our ears. The two animals are tightly embraced. I cannot distinguish one from the other. Everything is to be feared from the rage of the victor.

One hour, two hours pass. The struggle continues with the same savagery. The two fighters now approach the raft, now move away from it. We remain motionless, ready to fire.

Suddenly the Ichthyosaurus and Plesiosaurus disappear, producing a real maelstrom in the open sea. Several minutes go by. Will this combat finish in the ocean depths?

Suddenly, an enormous head surges out: it is the head of the Plesiosaurus. The monster is mortally wounded. I can no longer see its enormous shell. Only its long neck stands up, beats down, rises, bends over again, lashes at the waters like a gigantic whip, writhes like a worm cut in two. The water spurts out to a great distance. It blinds us. But soon the reptile's agony comes to an end: its movements diminish, its contortions calm down, and finally a long section of snake stretches out like an inert mass on still water.

As for the Ichthyosaurus, has it gone back to its underwater cavern or will it reappear on the surface of the sea?

Chapter 34.

Wednesday, the 19ᵗʰ of August. Fortunately, the wind, blowing with force, has allowed us to flee the scene of the struggle. Hans is still at the helm. My uncle, drawn from his absorbing ideas by the incidents of the battle, now retreats again into his impatient contemplation of the sea.

Our journey becomes monotonous and uniform once more. I have no desire to see it change, if it is at the price of yesterday's dangers.

Thursday, the 20ᵗʰ of August. Light wind, NNE, quite variable. Temperature: high. We are moving at a rate of three leagues and a half per hour.

At about twelve o'clock a very distant sound is heard. I make a note here of the fact without being able to give an explanation for it. It is like a continuous roar.

'Far off', says the professor, 'is some rock or small island against which the sea is breaking.'

Hans hoists himself to the top of the mast, but does not signal a reef. The ocean is calm as far as the line of the horizon.

Three hours go by. The roaring seems to come from a distant waterfall.

I mention this to my uncle, who shakes his head. I, however, am convinced that I am right. Are we heading for some mighty waterfall which will drop us into the abyss? This method of travel will probably please the professor, as it approaches the vertical, but for my part...

In any case, not many leagues to windward there must be some very noisy phenomenon, for now the sound of the roaring is extremely loud. Is it coming from the sea or the sky?

I look up at the water vapour suspended in the atmosphere, and I try to penetrate its depths. But the sky is serene. The clouds, carried up to the very top of the vault, seem motionless, and are completely invisible in the intense glare of the light. We must therefore look elsewhere for the cause of the phenomenon.

I scrutinize the horizon, pure and free from all haze. Its appearance is unchanged. But if this noise is coming from a waterfall, from a cataract, if the ocean is being precipitated into a lower cavity, if these roars are being produced by masses of falling waters, there would be a current, and its increasing speed would show me the extent of the danger to which we are exposed. I check the current. There isn't any. An empty bottle I drop in the water simply remains to leeward.

At about four o'clock Hans stands up, takes hold of the mast, and climbs to the top. From there, his eye scans the arc of the ocean's circle before the raft and stops at a particular point. His face expresses no astonishment, but his eyes do not move.

'He has seen something', says my uncle.

'So it would seem.'

Hans climbs down, and stretches his arm out towards the south saying: '*der nere*!'

'Over there', says my uncle.

Seizing the telescope, he gazes with great attention for about a minute but it seems endless.

'Yes. Yes!'

'What can you see?'

'A tremendous column of water rising above the waves.'

'Another sea-monster?'

'Perhaps.'

'Then, let us head more to the west, for we know what to expect from the dangers of meeting up with these antediluvian monsters.'

'Faster', replies my uncle.

I turn towards Hans. He maintains course with an inflexible rigour.

Nevertheless, given the distance separating us from this creature, which cannot be less than twelve leagues, and given that the column of water from its blowhole is clearly visible, its dimensions must be extraordinary. To flee is therefore the course suggested by basic common sense. But we have not come here to be prudent.

We go straight ahead. The nearer we get, the taller the column of water becomes. What monster can fill itself with such volumes of water and shoot it out so continuously?

At 8 p.m., we are not more two leagues away. Its black, enormous, mountainous body lies on the water like an island. Is it an illusion or is it fear? It seems not less than a mile long. What, then, is this cetaceous monster which Cuvier and Blumenbach had not foreseen? It is motionless as if asleep. The sea seems unable to shift it; it is the waves instead that lap at its side. The water column, rising to a height of five hundred feet, breaks into spray with a deafening noise. We run like lunatics towards this mighty mass which a hundred whales could not feed for a single day.

I am terrified. I don't want to go any further. I will cut the halyard if necessary! I rebel against the professor who does not say anything to me.

Suddenly Hans gets up and points at the menacing spot:

'*Holme*.'

'An island!', cries my uncle.

'An island?', I reply, raising my shoulders.

'Of course!', exclaims my uncle, bursting into laughter.

'But what about the water column?'

'*Geyser*,' says Hans.

'Yes, obviously a geyser,' responds my uncle, 'like those in Iceland.'

At first I cannot admit that I am so totally wrong. To have taken an island for a sea monster! But the truth comes out and, finally, I have to accept my mistake. There is nothing here but a natural phenomenon.

As we get nearer, the dimensions of the column become truly colossal. It is difficult to tell the difference between the island and an enormous whale, with its head rising 62 feet above sea level. The geyser, a word the Icelanders pronounce 'geysir' and which means 'fury', emerges majestically at one end of the island. Dull detonations are heard every now and then, and the enormous jet, subject to violent rages, shakes off its plume of vapour and jumps up as far as the first stratum of cloud. It is alone. Neither exhalations nor hot springs surround it, and the whole volcanic power is concentrated in it. Rays of electric light come and mix with this dazzling column, with each drop taking on all the colours of the prism.

'Let's go alongside', says the professor.

However, we have to take precautions to avoid the water column, which would sink the raft in an instant. Hans, steering skillfully, takes us to the other end of the island.

I leap on to the rock. My uncle nimbly follows, while the hunter remains at his post, like a man beyond such surprises.

We walk over granite mixed with siliceous tuff; the hot soil shivers under our feet like the sides of a boiler with superheated steam whirling inside. We come in view of the little central hollow from which the geyser rises. I plunge a thermometer into the water bubbling from the centre: it registers a temperature of 163°!

This water comes from a burning source of heat. This is singularly in contradiction with Professor Lidenbrock's theories. I cannot resist pointing it out.

'Well', he says, 'what does that prove against my theory?'

'Nothing', I reply shortly, seeing that I am up against an implacable stubbornness.

Nevertheless, I am forced to confess that we have been remarkably fortunate up until now, and that, for a reason which still escapes me, our journey is taking place in unusual conditions of temperature. But it is certain that, sooner or later, we will reach one of those regions where the central heat reaches its utmost limits and goes far beyond the gradations on the thermometers.

We will see. That is now the professor's favourite phrase. Having baptized the volcanic island with the name of his nephew, he gives the signal to embark.

I stand still for a few minutes more, staring at the geyser. I notice that the jet of water is irregular in its outbursts: it diminishes in intensity, then regains new vigour, which I attribute to variations in the pressure of the vapour built up in its reservoir.

At last we leave, avoiding the steep rocks of the southern side. Hans has taken advantage of this brief halt to fix the raft.

Before we put off, I make a few observations to calculate the distance covered, and note them in my logbook. Since Port Gräuben, we have covered 270 leagues. We are now 620 leagues from Iceland, and underneath England.

Chapter 35.

Friday, the 21ˢᵗ of August. The following day the magnificent geyser has disappeared. The wind has freshened, and quickly takes us away from Axel Island. The roaring sound gradually dies down.

The weather, if such a term may be used here, is about to change. The atmosphere is gradually being loaded with water vapour, which carries with it the electricity generated when the salt waters evaporate. The clouds are lowering perceptibly and taking on a uniform olive color; the electric rays can scarcely pierce this opaque curtain which has fallen on a stage where a stormy drama is going to be performed.

I feel extremely overwhelmed, like all creatures on Earth when a catastrophe is about to happen. The cumuli, piled up in the south, present a sinister appearance: they have the 'pitiless' look I have often noticed at the beginning of a storm. The air is heavy, the sea calm.

In the distance, the clouds look like enormous bales of cotton, piled up in picturesque disorder. They gradually swell up, and gain in size what they lose in number: they are so heavy that they are unable to run from the horizon. But in the breath from the upper streams of the air, they gradually melt together, become darker and soon present a single layer of a threatening appearance; now and then a ball of misty cloud, still lit up, collides with the grey carpet, and is soon swallowed up by the impenetrable mass.

The entire atmosphere is saturated with fluid; I am impregnated with it; my hair stands on end as if beside an electric machine. It occurs to me that if one of my companions touched me now, he would probably get a violent shock.

At 10 a.m., the symptoms of the storm become more pronounced; the wind seems to soften in order to draw breath again; the cloud resembles a gigantic goatskin bottle inside which terrible storms are accumulating.

I do not want to accept the evidence of the sky's threatening signs, and yet I cannot stop myself saying: 'it looks as though we are going to have some bad weather.'

The professor does not answer. He is in a foul mood at the sight of the ocean stretching interminably before his eyes. At my words he shrugs his shoulders.

'We're going to have a storm', I continue, pointing towards the horizon. 'These clouds are lowering upon the sea, as if to crush it.'

Dead silence! The wind falls. Nature lies as if dead, ceasing to breathe. Upon the mast, where I can already see a slight St Elmo's fire, the sail hangs in loose, heavy folds. The raft is motionless in the midst of that sticky sea, without swell. But since we are not moving, what is the point of maintaining the sail, for it may be our downfall as soon as the tempest hits us?

'Let's flake the sail, let's bring down the mast! That would be the sensible thing to do.'

'No, for God's sake', cries my uncle, 'a hundred times, no. May the wind take hold of us, may the storm sweep us away. Let me finally see the rocks of some shore, even if the raft must break into a million pieces.'

These words are scarcely out of his mouth, than the appearance of the southern horizon is transformed. The accumulated vapors turns into water, and the air, violently sucked in to fill the vacuum produced by the condensation, becomes a hurricane. It comes from the most distant corners of the cavern. The darkness increases. I can only just take a few incomplete notes.

The raft rises, it jumps. My uncle is cast down. I drag myself over to him. He is holding on to the end of a rope with all his might, apparently gazing with pleasure at the spectacle of the infuriated elements.

Hans does not move. His long hair, pushed down over his motionless face by the tempest, gives him a strange appearance, for the end of each hair is illuminated by a tiny, feather-like radiation. His frightening mask is that of an antediluvian man, living at the time of the Ichthyosaurus and Megatherium.

The mast still holds. The sail stretches like a bubble about to burst. The raft hurtles at a velocity that I cannot estimate, but is still slower than the drops of water displaced beneath it, which the speed turns into clean straight lines.

'The sail, the sail!', I cry, gesturing that it should be brought down.

'No!', says my uncle.

'*Nej*', says Hans, gently shaking his head.

By now, the rain forms a roaring cataract in front of this horizon towards which we race: we are raving maniacs! But before it reaches us, the veil of cloud is torn apart, the sea begins to boil, and the electricity, produced by some great chemical action in the upper layers, is brought into play. Dazzling streaks of lightning combine with fearful claps of thunder; flashes without number crisscross amongst the crashes. The mass of water vapour becomes incandescent; the hailstones striking the metal of our tools and firearms become luminous; each of the waves surging up resembles a volcanic breast in which seethes an inner fire that vomits flames.

My eyes are dazzled by the intensity of the light, my ears deafened by the din of the thunder. I am forced to hold on to the mast, which bends like a reed before the violence of the storm! ...

(Here my travel notes became very incomplete. I have only found one or two fleeting observations, jotted down automatically so to speak. But even in their brevity, their incoherence, they are imprinted with the feelings which governed me and thus, better than my memory, they accurately describe the situation.) ...

Sunday, the 23rd of August. Where are we? Carried away at a considerable speed.

The night has been awful. The storm is not calming down. We are living in the midst of an uproar, a constant detonation. Our ears are bleeding. We are unable to exchange a single word.

The lightning never stops striking. I see backward zigzags flashing rapidly and then working their way back up to crash into the arch of the granite roof. What if it collapsed? Other flashes of lightning diverge or become globes of fire and explode like bombs. The general level of noise does not seem to be increased by this; it has already gone beyond the order of magnitude that the human ear can distinguish. If all the powder magazines in the world were to explode at the same time, 'it would not make any difference'.

There is a constant production of light from the surface of the clouds; their molecules incessantly give off electrical matter; the gaseous principles of the air have been changed; innumerable columns of water go straight up into the air and then fall down foaming.

Where are we going? My uncle is still flat out at the front of the raft.

The heat increases even further. I look at the thermometer, it reads: ... (the figure has been deleted.)

Monday, the 24th of August. Will this terrible storm ever end? Why should this state of hyper-dense atmosphere, once it has been modified, not remain as it is indefinitely?

We are exhausted. Hans the same as ever. The raft heads endlessly south-east. We have already done about two hundred leagues since Axel Island.

At noon the violence of the hurricane increases. We are forced to lash down every item in the cargo. Each of us ties himself down as well. The waves pass over our heads.

Impossible to say a single word to each other for the last three days. We open our mouths, we move our lips; no audible sound is produced. Even speaking directly into the ear does not work.

My uncle comes close. He pronounces some words. I think he says: 'We are lost.' I am not certain.

I make up my mind, and write a few words to him: 'Let's take the sail down.'

He nods to indicate his consent.

His head has not had time to resume its original position, when a disc of fire appears on the edge of the raft. The mast and sail are carried off in a single movement, and I see them fly away to a tremendous height like a Pterodactyl, that fantastic bird of the earliest centuries.

We are horrified. The ball is half white, half electric blue, of the size of a ten-inch bomb. It moves leisurely around, while turning with an astonishing speed under the omnipotence of the hurricane. It wanders about here and there; it clambers onto one of the cross-beams of the raft, jumps on the food bag, goes slightly down, jumps again, then lightly touches our powder keg. Horror, we are about to explode. But no, the blinding disc moves to one side, it goes up to Hans, who stares at it without blinking; then to my uncle, who throws himself on his knees to avoid it; it comes towards me, as I stand pale and shivering in the dazzling heat and light; it spins near my feet, which I try to pull back. I can't.

A smell of nitrous gas fills the air; it penetrates our throats and lungs. We suffocate.

Why can't I move my foot? Is it riveted to the raft? Then I understand: the arrival of the electric globe has magnetized all the iron on board. The instruments, the tools, the firearms are crashing together with a keen jangling noise; the nails in my boot are violently attracted to a plate of iron encrusted in the wood. I can't shift my foot.

At last, by a violent effort, I tear my foot away, just as the rotational movements of the ball are about to seize hold of it and drag me away too, if...

Oh what intense light! The globe explodes! We are being covered in torrents of flames! Then everything goes out. I just have time to see my uncle lying on the floor, Hans still at the helm, 'spitting fire' under the influence of the electricity that penetrates him.

Where will we end up, oh where? ...

Tuesday, the 25ᵗʰ of August. I have just come out of a very long faint. The storm is still continuing; the lightning rages like a swarm of snakes released into the air.

Are we still on the sea? Yes, being carried along with incalculable speed. We have passed under Britain, under the Channel, under France, possibly under the whole of Europe! ...

A new noise can be heard. Clearly the sea breaking on rocks. But then...

Chapter 36.

Here ends what I called the 'ship's log', fortunately saved from the shipwreck. I proceed with my narrative as before.

What happened when the raft hit the reefs on the shore, I cannot say. I felt myself being thrown into the waves, and if I escaped death, if my body was not torn to pieces by the sharp rocks, it was because Hans's strong arm pulled me from the abyss.

The fearless Icelander carried me out of reach of the waves and onto burning sand where I found myself lying side by side with my uncle.

Then he returned to the rocks, against which the furious waves were beating, in order to save a few things from the wreckage. I could not speak; I was shocked and exhausted; it took me more than an hour to recover.

A pouring rain continued to fall, but with that very violence which heralds the end of the storm. Some piled-up rocks gave us protection from the torrents from the skies. Hans prepared some food which I was unable to eat. Exhausted by the three nights keeping watch, we fell into a painful sleep.

The following day, the weather was magnificent. Sea and sky, as if by agreement, had calmed down. Every trace of the storm had disappeared. Cheerful words from the professor greeted me when I woke up. He was utterly happy.

'Well, my boy, did you sleep well?'

It seemed that we were in the old house in the Königstrasse, that I was quietly coming down for breakfast, and that my wedding with poor Gräuben was to take place that very day?

Alas, if only the tempest had driven the raft eastwards, we would have passed under Germany, under my beloved city of Hamburg, under that street which contained all I loved in the world. At that point, forty leagues would have separated me from her! But forty leagues of granite wall; in reality, more than one thousand leagues to cover!

All these unhappy ideas passed quickly through my mind before I answered my uncle's question.

'What?', he repeated, 'Can't you say how you slept?'

'I slept well; I am still tired but it's nothing.'

'Nothing, a little tired, and that's it!'

'You seem to be in very good humor this morning.'

'I am delighted, my boy; delighted! We have arrived.'

'At the end of our expedition?'

'No; at the edge of that sea which seemed endless. We will now resume our journey by land, and really plunge into the bowels of the Earth.'

'Uncle John, can I ask you a question?'

'Certainly, Axel.'

'How are we going to get back?'

'Get back? You are thinking about the return before we have even arrived!'

'Not really: all I want to know is how it will be done.'

'In the simplest way possible. Once we have reached the centre of our spheroid, either we will find a new path to climb up to the surface, or we will simply turn round and go back the way we came. I do not imagine that the route will close up behind us.'

'Then we will have to repair the raft.'

'Obviously.'

'But what about the food, have we got enough left to do all these great things?'

'Yes, of course. Hans is a clever fellow, and I am sure he has saved most of the cargo. But let's go and see for ourselves.'

We left this grotto, open to all the winds. I had a hope that was also a fear; it didn't seem possible to me that anything of what the raft had been carrying could have survived its terrible landing. I was wrong. When I reached the shore, I found Hans in the middle of a large number of objects, all laid out in order. My uncle wrung the hunter's hands with deep gratitude. This man, of a superhuman devotion, one that would perhaps never be equaled, had worked while we slept, saving the most precious articles at the risk of his life.

Nevertheless, we had experienced important losses: our firearms for example, but after all we could manage without them. The supply of powder had remained intact, after narrowly escaping being blown up in the storm.

'Well', said the professor, 'as we have no guns, we will simply have to give up hunting.'

'Yes, but what about the instruments?'

'Here is the manometer, the most useful of all, and for which I would have given the rest. With it I can calculate the depth and know when we have reached the centre. Without it, we might go too far and come out at the antipodes!'

His good mood was over the top.

'But the compass?'

'Here it is on this rock, safe and sound, as well as the chronometer and thermometers. The hunter is a valuable man!'

One had to agree. Amongst the instruments, nothing was missing. As for the tools and implements, I spotted ladders, cords, pickaxes, picks, etc., scattered over the sand.

There was still the question of provisions to sort out.

'And what about the food?'

'Let us see about it.'

The boxes were lined up along the shore in a perfect state of preservation; most of their contents were unharmed by the sea, and we could thus still count on a total of four months' supply of biscuits, salt meat, gin, and dried fish.

'Four months!', cried the professor. 'We have time to go there and come back, and with what is left I plan to give a huge dinner to my colleagues at the Johannaeum!'

By this time I should have been used to my uncle's character, and yet this man still amazed me.

'Now', he said, 'we must renew our stock of fresh water, using the rain that the storm has poured into the hollows in the granite. There is no danger of suffering from thirst. As for the raft, I will ask Hans to repair it as best as he can, although I do not believe we will use it again.'

'Why not?'

'Just one of my ideas, my boy. I do not believe we will go out the way we came in.'

I looked at my uncle with suspicion. I wondered whether he had gone mad. And yet 'his point was quite right indeed'.

'Let's have breakfast', he concluded.

I followed him onto a high promontory, after he had given instructions to the hunter. There, with dried meat, biscuits, and tea, we had an excellent meal: one of the best in my life, I must say. Necessity, the open air, the peace and quiet after the excitement, all combined to make me feel hungry.

During breakfast, I asked my uncle if he knew where we now were.

'It may be rather difficult to calculate', I added.

'To calculate exactly, yes, even impossible, for I could keep no account of the speed or direction of the raft during the three days of the tempest. Still, we can estimate our approximate position.'

'Well, our last observation was made at the island with the geyser.'

'At Axel Island, my boy! Do not decline the honour of giving your name to the first island discovered in the interior of the Earth.'

'All right. At Axel Island, we had done about 270 leagues by sea and were over 600 leagues from Iceland.'

'Fine. Let us start then from that point, and count four days of storm, during which our speed cannot have been less than eighty leagues every twenty-four hours.'

'It's very likely. That would make as much as three hundred leagues more.'

'Yes, and the Lidenbrock Sea would then be about 600 leagues across!

Do you realise, Axel, that it is as big as the Mediterranean?'

'Yes, especially if we have only crossed it and not gone its whole length!'

'Which is very likely.'

'And what is strange', I said, 'is that if our calculations are right, we have over our heads, at this very moment, the Mediterranean itself.'

'Do you think so?'

'Yes, for we are 900 leagues from Reykjavik.'

'My boy, we have travelled quite a good way, but whether we are under the Mediterranean, Turkey, or the Atlantic can only be determined if our direction has not changed.'

'The wind appears steady to me. My view is that this shore must be south-east of Port Gräuben.'

'Well, it is easy to check by consulting the compass. Let us therefore go and check this compass!'

The professor headed for the rock on which Hans had placed the instruments. My uncle was cheerful and high-spirited; he rubbed his hands and walked as if he were an opera singer. A young man in truth! I followed him, rather curious to know whether I was right in my estimation.

As soon as we had reached the rock, my uncle took the compass, laid it flat and looked at the needle, which oscillated, and then, under the magnetic influence, stopped in a fixed position.

My uncle looked, rubbed his eyes, then looked again. Finally he turned to me, surprised.

'But what's the matter?'

He pointed to the instrument. I examined it and a loud cry of surprise escaped from my lips. The needle marked north where we expected south! It pointed at the shore rather than out to sea!

I shook the compass, then examined it again. It was in perfect condition. Whatever position we made the needle take, it returned obstinately to the same surprising direction.

There could be no doubt about it: during the tempest, there had been a sudden change of wind, one we had not noticed, and which had brought the raft back to the shores my uncle thought he had left behind.

Chapter 37.

It would be altogether impossible for me to give any idea of the feelings that shook professor Lidenbrock: amazement, incredulity and, finally, rage. Never in my life had I seen someone so upset at first, and then so furious. The fatigues of our crossing, the dangers we had passed through, everything had to be started all over again. Instead of going forward, we had gone backwards.

But my uncle regained the upper hand rapidly.

'Fate plays me such tricks! The elements are conspiring against me. Air, fire, and water are joining forces to stop me getting through. Well, they are going to see what my willpower can do. I will not surrender, I will not retreat, and we'll see who wins: man or Nature!'

Standing on a rock, irritated, threatening, John Lidenbrock, like fierce Ajax, seemed to defy the gods. I judged it sensible to intervene and stop this mad eagerness.

'Listen to me', I said in a firm voice, 'there must be a limit to every ambition in this world. One must not fight against the impossible. We are ill-equipped for a sea voyage; one cannot cover 500 leagues on a poor construction of beams, with a blanket as a sail and a stick for a mast, against the unleashed winds. We cannot steer, we are the victims of the storms: it would be sheer folly to attempt this impossible crossing a second time.'

I was allowed to go through these irrefutable reasons for about ten minutes without interruption. But this was only because of the professor's inattention: he did not hear a single word of my arguments.

'To the raft!', he cried.

Such was his response. In vain did I implore him, did I lose my temper: I came up against a will harder than granite.

Hans was just finishing his repairs to the raft. It was almost as if this strange being had guessed my uncle's projects. By means of a few pieces of surtarbrandur, he had strengthened the vessel. A sail had already been hoisted, and the wind was playing over its floating folds.

The professor said a few words to the guide, who immediately loaded our luggage on board and prepared everything for departure. The atmosphere was quite pure and the north-west wind held steady.

What could I do? Resist, one against two? Impossible. If only Hans had supported me. But no, as far as I could see, the Icelander had set aside his free will and taken a vow of self-denial. I could get nothing out of this enslaved servant. I had to move forward!

I took my usual place on the raft, but my uncle stopped me with his hand.

'We will leave tomorrow', he said.

I made the gesture of a man resigned to everything.

'I mustn't neglect anything. Since fate has cast me upon this part of the coast, I won't leave it until I have explored it.'

In order to understand his remark, I need to explain that, though we had come back to the northern coastline, this was not at exactly the same spot as our starting point. Port Gräuben had to be to the west. Hence, nothing was more sensible than carefully explore this site.

'Let's explore!', I cried.

And we set off, leaving Hans to his activities. The area between the high-water tidemark and the foot of the cliffs was very large. It would take about half an hour to get to the rock wall. Our feet crushed innumerable seashells of every shape and size, once the houses of animals of the first ages. I also noticed enormous shells with a diameter of more than fifteen feet. They once belonged to those gigantic Glyptodonts of the Pliocene

Period, of which the modern tortoise is but a small-scale model. Besides, the soil was covered with a large amount of stony objects: pebbles rounded by the waves and arranged in successive rows. I came to the conclusion that in past ages the sea must have covered this area. The waves had indeed left evident signs of their passage on the scattered rocks, now lying beyond their reach.

This could to a certain extent explain the existence of such an ocean, 140 leagues below the surface of the Earth. In my opinion, this liquid mass must have been gradually lost into the bowels of the Earth: it clearly came from the water of the oceans, reaching its destination through some sort of fissure. Nevertheless, it had to be assumed that this fissure was now blocked up, for, if not, the cavern, or rather the immense reservoir, would have been completely filled in a relatively short period. Perhaps some of the water had even had to fight against subterranean fires, and so was vaporized. Hence an explanation for the clouds suspended above our heads and the emission of the electricity which created the storms inside the Earth's mass.

Such a theory of the phenomena we had witnessed struck me as satisfactory, for however great the marvels of Nature, they can always be explained with physical reasons.

We were thus walking over a kind of sedimentary soil formed by the water, like all the formations of that period on the surface of the globe. The professor carefully examined every crack in the rocks. If an opening existed, it became vital for him to evaluate its depth.

We had been following the shores of the Lidenbrock Sea for about a mile, when suddenly the ground changed appearance. It seemed to have been upset, turned upside down by a violent upheaval of the lower strata. In many places, hollows and hillocks proved there had been a great dislocation of the Earth's mass.

We were advancing with difficulty over the broken granite mixed with flint, quartz, and alluvial deposits, when a field, more than a field, a plain of bones, appeared before our eyes. It looked like an immense cemetery, where the generations of two thousand years mingled their eternal dust. Large bulges of remains stretched out in the distance. They undulated away to the limits of the horizon and disappeared in a wet mist. Within that area, of perhaps three square miles, was accumulated the whole history of animal life, hardly written in the inhabited world's too recent ground.

We were carried forward by an impatient curiosity. With a dry sound our feet crushed the remains of these prehistoric animals, whose rare and valuable fragments are fought over by the museums of the great cities. A thousand Cuviers would not have been enough to reconstruct the skeletons of all the once living creatures which now rested in that magnificent ossuary.

I was amazed. My uncle had raised his long arms towards the thick vault which was our sky. His wide-open mouth, his sparkling eyes behind the lenses of his glasses, his head moving up and down, to the left and right, his whole expression indicated utter astonishment. He was in front of a priceless collection of Leptotheria, Merycotheria, Lophiodons, Anoplotheres, Megatheria, Mastodons Protopitheci, Pterodactyls, of every monster from before the Flood, piled up there just for his personal satisfaction. Imagine a fanatical book-collector walking in the Royal Library of Alexandria burned by Omar, a long time ago, but suddenly and miraculously reborn from its ashes. That was my uncle, Professor Lidenbrock!

But he was even more dazzled when, racing across the organic dust, he seized a bare skull and screamed in a trembling voice: 'Axel, Axel, A human head!'

'A human head, Uncle John?', I replied, just as amazed.

'Yes, my dear nephew. O Milne-Edwards, O Quatrefages, why are you not there with Professor Lidenbrock?'

Chapter 38.

To explain this reference to the two distinguished French scientists, it should be recalled that a paleontological event of great importance had taken place some months before our departure.

On 28 March 1863, French workmen under the direction of M. Boucher de Perthes had unearthed a human jawbone at a depth of fourteen feet below the soil, in a quarry at Moulin-Quignon, near Abbeville (Somme). It was the first fossil of the sort ever to see the light of day. Near it were stone axes and worked flints, which time had covered with a uniform coloured patina.

This discovery had a huge impact, not only in France but in England and Germany. Many scholars from the Institut Français, including Messrs. Milne-Edwards and Quatrefages, took the affair very much to heart, demonstrated the incontestable authenticity of the bone, and hence became strong advocates of the skull during the 'jawbone affair', as it was called in Great Britain.

In addition to the United Kingdom geologists who considered the fact as certain (that is to say Messrs. Falconer, Busk, Carpenter, etc.), stood German scientists. The most enthusiastic, the most passionate was, of course, my uncle.

The authenticity of a human fossil from the Quaternary Era seemed therefore proved and approved beyond a shadow of a doubt.

Such a view, it is true, was vigorously challenged by M. Élie de Beaumont. This respected scientist maintained that the formation of Moulin-Quignon did not belong to the 'diluvium' but was more recent. In agreement with Cuvier on this point, he contended that the human race could not have existed at the same time as the animals of the Quaternary Era. But my uncle, in accordance with the great majority of geologists, had held his ground, had argued and discussed, and M. Élie de Beaumont had remained relatively isolated in his view.

My uncle and I were familiar with the successive ins and outs of this affair, but what we did not know was that, after we had left, it had undergone further developments. Additional jawbones of the same sort, although belonging to individuals of different types and different nations, were discovered in the loose grey soil of certain large caves in France, Switzerland, and Belgium, together with weapons, utensils, tools, and the bones of children, adolescents, adults, and old people. The existence of

Quaternary man became therefore more and more certain with each passing day.

And this was not all. New fragments excavated in Pliocene formations from the Tertiary Period had enabled daring scientists to attribute a much greater age to the human race. These fragments, it is true, were not human bones, but merely the products of his industry: tibias and femurs of fossil animals which were striated, carved so to speak, and which bared the signs of man's handiwork.

Thus, in a single move, man had leaped many centuries up the ladder of time. He now came before the Mastodon; he became a contemporary of the Elephas Meridionalis; his existence dated back a hundred thousand years, since that was when the most famous geologists said the Pliocene system was formed!

The above elements constituted the state of paleontological science at that time, and what we knew of them was sufficient to explain our reaction to this ossuary beside the Lidenbrock Sea. My uncle's stupefaction and joy are easy to understand, especially when, twenty yards further on, he found himself in the presence of, or rather face to face with, an authentic specimen of Quaternary man.

It was a perfectly recognizable human body. Had some particularity of the soil, as in the Saint-Michel Cemetery in Bordeaux, preserved it unchanged down through the centuries? It was difficult to say. But in any case this body was before our eyes exactly as it had lived, complete with stretched, parchment-like skin, limbs still fleshy and soft (apparently at least), teeth still preserved, a considerable head of hair, and fingernails, and toenails of a frightening length.

I was dumbstruck at this apparition from another age. My uncle, so talkative, so eager to make speeches about anything, fell silent as well. We propped the body up against a rock. He looked at us from his hollow eye sockets. We touched his sonorous chest.

After a few moments of silence, my uncle reverted to Professor John Lidenbrock, undoubtedly carried away by his personality and forgetting the circumstances of the journey, our immediate surroundings, and the titanic cavern holding us. He must have thought he was lecturing to his students at the Johannaeum, for he adopted a professorial tone and addressed an imaginary audience: 'gentlemen, I have the honor of showing you a man from the Quaternary Era. Some eminent scholars have argued that he does not exist, while others, no less eminent, have maintained that he does. The doubting Thomases of Paleontology, if they were here, would be able to touch him, and thus be forced to admit their error. I know full well that science must be careful about discoveries of this sort. I am not unaware of the exploitation of fossil men by the Barnums and other charlatans of this kind. I know the story of Ajax's kneecap, of the so-called body of Orestes found by the Spartans, of Asterius' ten-cubit-long body described by Pausanias. I have read the reports on the Trapani skeleton discovered in the fourteenth century, which people wished to believe was Polyphemus', as well as the accounts of the giant dug up in the sixteenth century near Palermo. You are as aware as I, gentlemen, of the analysis carried out at Lucerne in 1577 of the big bones claimed by the illustrious doctor Félix Plater to belong to a nineteen-feet-tall giant. I have devoured Cassanion's treatises, and all the monographs, brochures, presentations, and counter-presentations ever published on the skeleton of Teutobochus, who invaded Gaul, and who was excavated from a sandpit in the Dauphiné in 1613. In the eighteenth century, I would have combated Peter Camper's affirmations regarding the existence of Scheuchzer's pre-Adamites! I have held in my hands the publication entitled *Gigans...*'

Here re-emerged my uncle's inherent impediment of not being able to pronounce complicated words in public.

'The book entitled *Gigans...*'

He couldn't go any further.

'*Giganteo...*'

Impossible, the wretched word just would not come out! There would have been much laughter at the Johannaeum.

'*Gigantosteology*', Professor Lidenbrock said, between two oaths. Then, continuing all the better, and warming up: 'yes, gentlemen, I am aware of all these matters. I also know that Cuvier and Blumenbach have identified the bones as simply those of mammoths and other animals of the Quaternary Period. But to doubt in the present case would be to insult science! The corpse is there! You can see it; you can touch it. It is not a mere skeleton, it is an entire body, preserved for exclusively anthropological purposes!'

I did not contradict this assertion.

'If I could wash it in a solution of sulfuric acid, I would remove all the earth encrustations and splendid shells attached to it. But the precious solvent is unavailable at the moment. However, as it stands, this body will tell us its story.'

Here, the professor picked up the fossil corpse and adjusted it with all the dexterity of a peddler.

'As you can see, it is less than six feet tall, and we are a long way from the so-called giants. As for the race it belongs to, it is incontestably Caucasian. It is of the white race, it is of our own race! The skull of this fossil is oval-shaped and regular, without developed cheekbones, without a projecting jaw. It presents no sign of prognathism modifying the facial angle. Measure this angle, it is nearly ninety degrees. But I will proceed further along the path of deductions, and I will venture to say that this human specimen belongs to the Japhetic family, which extends from the Indian subcontinent to the far limits of western Europe. Pray do not smile, gentlemen!'

Nobody was smiling, but the professor was used to seeing people put a smile on their face during his lectures.

'Yes', he continued with renewed vigour, 'this is a fossil man, and a contemporary of the Mastodons whose bones fill this auditorium. But I cannot tell you by what route it arrived here and how the strata it was enclosed in slid down into this enormous cavity of the globe. Undoubtedly, in the Quaternary Period, considerable upheavals in the Earth's crust still occurred. The lengthy cooling of the globe produced fissures, cracks, and faults, into which part of the upper terrain must have dropped. I am not committing myself but, after all, this man is here, surrounded by the handiwork he produced, his axes and worked flints which define the Stone Age. Unless he came as a tourist, as a scientific pioneer, I cannot then question the authenticity of his ancient origin.'

The professor stopped speaking, and I broke into unanimous applause. My uncle was in fact right, and more learned people than his nephew would have found it very difficult to argue with him.

Another clue. This fossilized body was not the only one in the enormous ossuary. With each step we took in this dust, we came across other bodies: my uncle was able to pick out the most wonderful specimens that would have convinced the skeptics.

It was indeed an amazing sight, that of generations of men and animals mingling in this cemetery. But a puzzling mystery then arose, that we were not yet able to solve. Had these creatures slid down to the shores of the Lidenbrock Sea during some convulsion of the Earth, when they were already ashes? Or had they rather passed their lives down here, in this underworld, under this unnatural sky, being born and dying here, just like the inhabitants of the Earth? Until now, only monsters of the deep and fish had appeared before us in living form. Was some man of the abyss still wandering along these lonely shores?

Chapter 39.

For another half-hour we trampled over the layers of bones. We went straight ahead, forced on by a burning curiosity. What other wonders did this cavern hold, what treasures of science? My sight expected any surprise, my imagination any astonishment.

The seashore had long since disappeared behind the hills of the ossuary. The foolhardy professor, heedless of losing the way, led me further and further on. We walked in silence, bathed in the electric waves. By a phenomenon I cannot explain, the light was uniformly diffused, so that it lit up all the sides of objects equally. It no longer came from any definite point in space, and consequently there was not the slightest shadow. It was like being under the vertical rays of the midday sun in midsummer in the midst of the equatorial regions. All mist had disappeared. The rocks, the distant mountains, the blurry forms of a few faraway forests, all took on a strange appearance under the even distribution of the luminous fluid. We were like that fantastic character of Hoffmann's who lost his shadow.

After about a mile, we saw the edge of an immense forest, but not this time a grove of mushrooms like the one near Port Gräuben.

It displayed the vegetation of the Tertiary Period in all its splendour. Great palm trees of species no longer in existence, superb palmoxylons, pines, yews, cypress, and thujas represented the coniferous family, all joined together by an impenetrable network of lianas. The ground was carpeted with a springy covering of moss and hepaticas. Some rivulets murmured under the shade, if this term can be used, for there was no shadow. On the banks there were tree ferns, like those of the hothouses of the inhabited globe. Colours, however, were absent from all the trees, shrubs, and plants, deprived as they were of the life-giving heat of the sun. Everything was dissolved into a uniform hue, a faded brown. The leaves were not their usual green, and the very flowers, so numerous in the Tertiary Age when they first appeared, were at that time without colour or perfume, as if made of a paper that had been discolored by the effect of the atmosphere.

My uncle ventured into this gigantic thicket. I followed, not without a certain apprehension. Where nature had provided such vast stores of vegetable foodstuffs, might fearful mammals not be encountered? In the large clearings left by fallen trees, gnawed by time, I noticed leguminous plants, acerinae, rubiaceae, and a thousand edible shrubs, much appreciated by the ruminants of all periods. Then there appeared, all intermixed and intertwined, trees from highly different countries on the surface of the globe, the oak growing beside the palm tree, the Australian eucalyptus leaning on the Norwegian fir, the northern birch mingling its branches with the New Zealand kauri. It was enough to confuse the most ingenious classifiers of terrestrial botany.

Suddenly I stopped short. I held my uncle back.

The uniform light made it possible to see the smallest objects in the depths of the thicket. I thought I saw, no, I really did see, enormous shapes wandering around under the trees! They were in fact gigantic animals, a whole herd of Mastodons, no longer fossil, but fully alive, and resembling the ones whose remains were discovered in the wetlands of Ohio in 1801. I watched these great elephants with their trunks swarming about below the trees like a legion of snakes. I heard the sound of their great tusks as the ivory tore at the bark of the ancient tree-trunks. The branches cracked, and the leaves, torn off in great quantity, disappeared into the monsters' massive maws.

Hence, the dream where I had seen the rebirth of this complete world from prehistoric times, combining the Tertiary and Quaternary Periods, had finally become a reality! And we were there, alone in the bowels of the Earth, at the mercy of its fierce inhabitants!

My uncle was gazing.

Suddenly he seized me by the arm, crying: 'come on; forward, forward!'

'No, no, we are unarmed: what could we do amongst these giant quadrupeds? Come back, Uncle John, come back: No human creature can brave with impunity the anger of these monsters!'

'No human creature?', said my uncle, lowering his voice. 'You are wrong, Axel! Look, look over there! It seems to me that I can see a living creature, someone like us: a man!'

I looked, shrugging my shoulders, determined to push incredulity to its furthest limits. But struggle as I might, I had to give in to the evidence.

There, less than a quarter of a mile away, leaning against the trunk of an enormous kauri tree, was a human being, a Proteus of these underground territories, a new son of Neptune, shepherding that uncountable drove of Mastodons!

Immanis pecoris custos, immanior ipse.
(Guardian of a monstrous herd, and more monstrous himself)!

'*Immanior ipse*', indeed! This was no longer the fossil creature whose body we had propped up amongst the bones: this was a giant, able to command these monsters. He was more than twelve feet tall. His head, as big as a buffalo's, was covered with a mop of unruly hair, a real mane, like that of the elephants of the first ages. He held in his hand an enormous stick, an appropriate crook for this shepherd from before the Flood.

We remained motionless, in a daze. But we might be spotted. We had to run away.

'Follow me', I cried, dragging my uncle with me: for the first time in his life, he didn't resist.

A quarter of an hour later, we were out of sight of this redoubtable enemy.

And now, when I consider it calmly, now that peace has returned to my mind, now that months have gone by since this strange, this supernatural, encounter, what am I to think, what am I to believe? No, it's impossible! Our senses must have been mistaken, our eyes can't have seen what they saw! No human creature lives in that underground world. No race of men populates those deep caverns of the globe, oblivious of the inhabitants of the surface, not communicating with them in any way! It's insane, deeply insane!

I would rather believe in the existence of some animal with a humanoid structure, some ape from the first geological eras, some Protopithecus, some Mesopithecus like the one discovered by M. Lartet in the bone bed of Sansan! But this one was far bigger than all the measurements known to modern Paleontology. Never mind: however unlikely, it was an ape! But a man, a living man, and with him a whole generation buried in the bowels of the Earth: never!

Meanwhile we had left the clear, luminous forest, speechless with shock, weighed down by a stupefaction that came close to nervous exhaustion. We couldn't help running. It was a real escape, like those terrifying uncontrollable movements that one sometimes undergoes in nightmares. Instinctively we made our way towards the Lidenbrock Sea. I was on the verge of insanity but a particular worry brought me back to more practical considerations.

Although I was certain I was covering ground we hadn't been over before, I kept noticing groups of rocks whose shapes reminded me of Port Gräuben. This, in fact, confirmed what the compass had indicated, that we had unintentionally headed back to the north of the Lidenbrock Sea.

Sometimes it was puzzling. Hundreds of streams and cascades fell from the rocky outcrops. I thought I was back near the layer of surtarbrandur, near our faithful Hans-Bach and the grotto where I had come back to life. Then, a few yards further on, the shape of the cliffs, the appearance of a stream, the surprising outline of a rock made me start doubting again.

I mentioned my hesitation to my uncle. He was hesitating like me. He was unable to find his way through this uniform landscape.

'We obviously didn't come back to the exact point we left from', I said, 'but the storm must have brought us back to just below it, and by following the coast, we will reach Port Gräuben again.'

'If that is true, then there seems no point in carrying on with this exploration, and it is best to return to the raft. But are you absolutely sure, Axel?'

'It's difficult to be definite, Uncle John, for all the rocks look so similar. But I think I remember the promontory where Hans built the raft. We must be near the little harbour. And it may even be here,' I added, examining a creek I thought I recognised.

'It is impossible Axel, for we would at least have come across our own traces, and I see nothing…'

'But I do!', I cried, darting towards an object glimmering on the sand.

'What is it?'

'Look here!'

I showed my uncle the rust-covered knife I had picked up.

'Well', he said, 'you had brought this weapon with you?'

'No, I hadn't. But you…'

'Not that I know; I have never had this thing on me.'

'It's really strange.'

'It is quite simple. The Icelanders often carry weapons like this, and Hans must be its owner, and have dropped it…'

I shook my head. Hans had never had this knife on him.

'Is it then the weapon of some antediluvian warrior', I exclaimed, 'of a living human being, of a contemporary of that gigantic shepherd? But it can't be! It isn't from the Stone Age! Not even the Bronze Age! This blade is made of steel...'

My uncle stopped me dead on this track where a new diversion was leading me, saying in his cold tone: 'calm down, Axel, and come to your senses. This knife is from the sixteenth century: it is an authentic dagger, like the ones that gentlemen used to carry on their belts in order to give the coup de grâce. It is Spanish. It belongs neither to me, nor to you, nor to the hunter, nor even to the human beings that may live in the bowels of the Earth!'

'Do you mean that...'

'Look, this blade has not got chipped by sinking into people's throats; and it is covered in a layer of rust, more than a day thick, more than a year, more than a century even.'

The professor, as usual, was getting excited as his imagination ran away with him.

'Axel, we are on the path of a great discovery. This blade has been lying on the sand for one, two, three hundred years, and it got chipped because it was used on the rocks of this subterranean sea!'

'But it couldn't have just arrived on its own. It couldn't have got twisted by itself! Somebody must have got here before us!'

'Yes, a man.'

'Who?'

'The man who used this knife to engrave his name. His aim was, once more, to show the way to the centre with his own hand. Let's see if we can find it!'

We enthusiastically worked our way along the high cliffs, looking for the smallest clefts that might turn into a gallery.

We eventually came to a place where the shore got narrower. The sea came nearly to the foot of the cliffs, leaving us at most two yards to pass. Between two projecting rocks loomed the entrance of a dark tunnel.

There, on a slab of granite, two mysterious letters were carved, half worn away: the twin initials of the bold and fantastic traveller: A. S.

'A. S.!', cried my uncle, 'Arne Saknussemm! Always Arne Saknussemm!'

Chapter 40.

Since the beginning of our journey I had been astonished many times; I would have thought that I was immune to surprise and blasé to any new wonder. Nevertheless, at the sight of the two letters engraved on this spot three centuries previously, I felt an amazement which came close to stupor. Not only could the signature of the learned alchemist be read clearly on the rock, but I had in my hand the stylus with which he had traced it. Unless I was completely dishonest with myself, I could no longer doubt the existence of the traveller or the truth of his journey.

While these thoughts whirled through my brain, Professor Lidenbrock was indulging in a slightly excessive praise of Arne Saknussemm: 'O marvelous genius! You did everything to open up to other mortals the way through the crust of the Earth, and now your comrades can follow the traces your feet left in these dark underpasses three hundred years ago! You intended these marvels to be contemplated by eyes other than your own! Your name, engraved on the successive stages of the route, leads the traveller bold enough to follow you straight to his goal, and it will be found yet again at the very centre of our planet, once more carved by your own hand! Well, I too intend to sign my name on this, the last of the granite pages. But henceforth let this cape, first seen by you on this sea first discovered by you, be known as Cape Saknussemm!'

This is more or less what I heard, and I felt won over myself by the enthusiasm conveyed in such words. An inner fire rekindled in my breast. I forgot everything, even the dangers of the downward journey and the perils of the return. What another had done I wished to do too, and nothing that was human seemed impossible to me.

'Forward, forward!', I cried.

I was already heading towards the dark gallery, when I was stopped: the professor, the one who normally got carried away, was recommending calm and patience.

'Let's first go and find Hans, and then bring the raft over here.'

I was happy to obeyed and slipped back between the rocks on shore.

'You know, Uncle John?', I said as we walked, 'we've been very lucky so far, haven't we?'

'Oh, do you think so Axel?'

'Yes, even the storm helped put us on the right track again. God bless the hurricane! It brought us back to this coast, which wouldn't have happened if we had had fine weather. Imagine for a moment that our prow (in so far as a raft can be said to have a prow) had touched the southern coastline of the Lidenbrock Sea, what would have become of us? We wouldn't have seen Saknussemm's name, and we would now be washed up on a shore that offered no way out!'

'Yes, Axel, there is something providential in the fact that, sailing southwards, we should have come north and returned to Cape Saknussemm. Indeed it seems to me more than astonishing, and there is something I don't understand.'

'Well it doesn't really matter. What counts is to make use of the facts, not explain them!'

'No doubt, my boy, but...'

'But now we are about to head north again, passing under the countries of Northern Europe, under Sweden, even under Siberia and other places! We are not going to plunge under the deserts of Africa or the breakers of the ocean. That's all I need to know!'

'Yes, you are right. Everything is for the best, since we are going to leave this horizontal sea which was taking us nowhere. Now we will go down, then further down, and then down again! Do you realise that we have only 1,500 leagues to cover?'

'Bah, hardly worth mentioning! Off we go, come on!'

This insane conversation was still continuing as we joined up again with the hunter. Everything was ready for leaving immediately. All the packages were on board the raft. We embarked, hoisted the sail, and Hans steered us along the coast towards Cape Saknussemm.

The wind direction was not very favourable for a kind of vessel unable to tack against it. As a result, quite often we had to use the alpenstocks to move forward. The rocks, lurking under the surface, often forced us into long detours. Finally, after three hours' navigation, at about 6 p.m., we reached a suitable spot for landing.

I sprang ashore, followed by my uncle and the Icelander. The crossing had not calmed me down. I even suggested 'burning our boats' so as to cut off all possibility of retreat. But my uncle disagreed. I found him singularly half-hearted.

'At least let's set off without wasting a moment.'

'Yes, my boy, but first we should have a look at this new gallery, to decide whether we need to get the ladders ready.'

My uncle switched on his Ruhmkorff lamp. The raft, moored on the shore, was left to its own devices. The mouth of the gallery was less than twenty yards away, and our little expedition, with myself as leader, headed for it without delay.

The opening, more or less round, was about five feet in diameter; the dark tunnel was cut in the living rock, and had been carefully bored by the eruptive substance that had passed through it; its floor was at the same level as the ground, so that you could enter it without problem.

We were following an almost horizontal path when, after only about twenty feet, our way forward was blocked by an enormous obstruction.

'Blasted rock!', I cried, seeing myself abruptly stopped by an insuperable obstacle.

In vain did we search to left and right, above and below: there was no passage, no alternative path. I felt bitterly disappointed, and could not accept that the barrier existed. I stooped down, and looked under the massive block: not even a crack. On top of it: the same granite barrier. Hans shone the light from the lamp on every part of the rock face; the light was not continuous. Any hope of getting through had to be given up.

I sat on the bare ground. My uncle was pacing up and down with great strides.

'But what about Saknussemm?', I cried.

'Yes, was he stopped by a stone door?'

'No! This piece of rock must be there because of some earthquake or other, or one of those magnetic phenomena that shake the Earth's crust. The passage must have been suddenly closed off. A good many years passed between Saknussemm's return and the fall of the rock. Isn't it obvious that this gallery was formerly the route the lava took, and that the eruption flowed freely along it? Look, there are recent cracks running along this granite ceiling. The roof is made of pieces swept along, of enormous boulders, as if the hand of some giant had laboured to build it. But one day, the vertical pressure became too strong, and this block, like the keystone of a vault, fell to the ground and blocked off the whole passage. This is an unexpected obstacle that Saknussemm didn't meet, and if we can't bring it down, we don't deserve to get to the centre of the world!'

That was the way I spoke. The professor's entire soul had passed into me. The spirit of discovery was arousing me. I forgot about the past, I didn't care about the future. I had submerged myself in that spheroid, and nothing existed for me on its surface: not the towns or the countryside, not Hamburg or the Königstrasse, not even my poor Gräuben, who must have thought that I was lost forever in the bowels of the Earth!

'Come on', said my uncle, 'using the pickaxes and ice axes, let's force our route, let's knock down these walls!'

'It's too hard for the pickaxes.'

'The ice axes then.'

'It's too deep for an ice axe.'

'But...'

'Well then, the powder, an explosion! Let's put some guncotton under the obstacle and blow it up!'

'Blow it up?'

'Yes, it's only a piece of rock to break up!'

'Hans, to work!', shouted my uncle.

The Icelander went back to the raft, and soon returned with one of the pickaxes, which he used to hollow out a cavity for the explosive. It was not an easy task. He had to make a hole big enough to hold fifty pounds of guncotton, whose explosive force is four times as great as black powder's.

I was in an extreme state of excitement. While Hans worked, I devotedly helped my uncle to prepare a long fuse made of damp gunpowder wrapped in a canvas tube.

'We'll get through!'

'We'll get through,' repeated my uncle.

At midnight, our work as miners was complete; the guncotton charge was crammed into the hole in the rock, and the fuse unwound through the gallery to the outside.

A spark was now enough to set off this imposing device.

'Till tomorrow then', said the professor.

I had to resign myself to waiting for six long hours!

Chapter 41.

The following day, Thursday, 27 August, was an important one in our underground journey. Every time that I think about it now, terror makes my heart beat faster. From that moment on, our reason, our judgement, our ingenuity were to have no influence at all on the events: we were to become the mere victims of the Earth.

We were up by six. The time had come to use explosives to force a way through the granite crust.

I requested the honour of lighting the fuse. Afterwards, I would rejoin my companions on the raft, which had not yet been unloaded; then we would head out for the open sea, so as to reduce the danger from the explosion, which could easily affect an area well beyond the outcrop.

According to our calculations, the fuse would burn for ten minutes before setting off the powder chamber. So I had plenty of time to get back to the raft.

But it was not without a certain trepidation that I got ready to play my part.

After a hurried breakfast, my uncle and the hunter went on board the raft while I remained on shore. I was equipped with a lighted lantern for setting off the fuse.

'Go my boy', said my uncle, 'but do make sure you come straight back afterwards.'

'Don't worry, I'm not going to hang around.'

I made straight for the mouth. I opened the lantern and picked up the end of the fuse. The professor had his chronometer in his hand.

'Are you ready?', he shouted.

'Yes I am.'

'Well, fire away my boy!'

I pushed the fuse quickly into the flame; it started to crackle; I sprinted back to the shore.

'Get on', said my uncle, 'and we'll head out.'

With a forceful shove, Hans pushed us off. The raft moved forty-two yards out.

It was a thrilling moment. The professor was watching the hand of the chronometer.

'Five more minutes... Four... Three... '

My heartbeats went wild.

'Two... One... For dust thou art, and unto dust shalt thou return!'

What happened next? I don't think I actually heard the noise of the explosion. But the shapes of the rocks suddenly changed before my eyes: they swung away like curtains. I glimpsed a bottomless void hollowed out from the very shore. The sea, seized with dizziness, had become nothing but one immense wave, on whose back the raft rose perpendicularly.

The three of us were thrown down. Within a second, light had given way to the most utter darkness. Then I felt the solid support disappearing, not beneath my feet but under the raft itself. I thought for a moment that it was sinking. It was not the case. I wanted to speak to my uncle but the bellowing of the waters did not allow him to hear me.

Despite the darkness, the noise, the surprise, and the excitement, I soon understood what had happened.

On the other side of the blown-up outcrop was an abyss. The explosion had set off a sort of earthquake in the fractured rocks, a chasm had opened up, and the sea, transformed into a great river, had carried us down into it.

I thought I was lost.

One hour, two hours -I don't remember- went by in this way. We stood shoulder to shoulder: we held each other's hands so as not to be thrown off the raft. It jolted with great violence whenever it touched the side. Such collisions were infrequent, however, and hence I deduced that the gallery was getting considerably larger. There could be no doubt that this was Saknussemm's route; but instead of following it on our own, our carelessness had brought down an entire sea with us.

It will be understood that these ideas crossed my mind in a confused way. Any association of ideas was difficult during this dizzy descent that looked like a free fall. To tell from the air whipping past my face, the speed must have been greater than the fastest trains. Lighting a torch would have been impossible in such conditions, and our last electrical apparatus had been broken at the time of the explosion.

I was therefore quite surprised suddenly to see a light beside me. Hans's calm face appeared. The adroit hunter had managed to light the lantern and although the flame flickered and almost went out, it threw some rays into the awful darkness.

The gallery was a wide one. I knew it. The light was not strong enough to reveal both walls at the same time. The slope of the water bearing us on was greater than that of the most insurmountable rapids in America. Its surface was as if made up of a set of liquid arrows shot with great power. I cannot describe what I felt with any more precise comparison. When the raft got caught in eddies, it was swept on while turning slowly round. When it went near the walls of the gallery, I shone the lantern on them, and got some idea of our speed from seeing the projections of the rocks as continuous lines, so that we were enclosed by a network of moving figures. I estimated our speed to be as much as thirty leagues an hour.

My uncle and I looked at each other with wild eyes, leaning back on the stump of the mast, which had broken in half during the catastrophe. We faced away from the air so as to avoid being suffocated by the speed of a motion that no human power could influence.

But the hours went by. The basic situation remained the same; then an incident arose to complicate it.

While trying to put our cargo in some kind of order, I discovered that most of the possessions on board had disappeared when the sea had attacked us so violently at the time of the explosion. I wanted to know the exact position of our resources, so I began a search while holding up the lantern. Of our instruments only the compass and chronometer remained. The ladders and ropes consisted of a mere end of a cable coiled around the stump of the mast. Not a single pickaxe, not an ice axe, not a hammer and, worse still, food for only one more day!

I searched amongst the cracks in the raft, in the smallest gaps between the beams and the joints. Nothing! Our provisions amounted to one piece of dried meat and a few dried biscuits.

I looked at them blankly, not wanting to understand. And yet what was the danger I was worrying about? Even had the provisions been enough for months or years, how could we get back out of the chasm that this inexorable river was carrying us into? What was the point of worrying about hunger-pains, when death was possible in so many other ways? Would we not have plenty of time to die of inanition?

Nevertheless, by a mysterious trick of the mind, I forgot about the immediate danger and focused on our uncertain future. Perhaps we could escape the river's fury and get back to the globe's surface. But how? I did not know. And where? I didn't care. A chance in a thousand is still a chance, while death through starvation left us no possibility of hope.

I thought of telling my uncle everything, of showing him how few things we had left, of calculating exactly how much time we still had to live. But I had the strength to remain silent. I wanted him to retain all his self-control.

At this moment the lantern slowly dimmed, and then went out altogether. The wick had burned through. I was pitch-black. There was no point in trying to reduce this impenetrable darkness. We still had one torch left, but it wouldn't have stayed alight. So, like a child, I closed my eyes to shut out all the darkness.

After quite a long time, our speed got much faster, as I realized from the battering of air on my face. The angle of the water got worse. We no longer seemed to be sliding, but falling. I had the clear sensation of a near-vertical drop. My uncle's and Hans's hands, clamped on my arms, held firmly onto me.

After an indeterminate period, something like a sudden shock happened; the raft hadn't collided with a hard object, but it had abruptly stopped falling. A waterspout, a huge liquid column, crashed down over the raft. I was suffocating. I was drowning...

However, this flood did not last long. After a few seconds, I found myself gulping air down again. My uncle and Hans were gripping my arm as if to break it; and the raft was still bearing the three of us on.

Chapter 42.

It must have been about 10 p.m. The first of my senses to start working after the last attack was that of hearing. Almost straightaway I heard -it was a real perception- I heard silence falling in the gallery, replacing the roaring which had been filling my ears for so many hours. Words from my uncle finally reached me like a murmur: 'we're going up!'

'What do you mean?', I cried.

'We're climbing! Yes, we are climbing!'

I stretched out my arm; I touched the wall; my hand got blood on it. We were rising very fast.

'The torch, the torch!'

Hans finally managed to light it and the flame, burning upwards despite our movement, spread enough light to reveal the scene.

'Exactly as I thought. We are in a narrow shaft, about twenty-five feet wide. When the water reached the bottom of the chasm, it started coming back up, taking us with it.'

'Where to?'

'I don't know, but we will have to be ready for any eventuality. I estimate our speed to be thirteen feet per second, 780 feet per minute, or more than three leagues and a half per hour. At this rate, one can cover a lot of ground!'

'Yes, if nothing stops us and if the shaft has a way out. But if it is blocked, if the air gets more and more compressed by the pressure from the water column, we will be crushed!'

'Axel', replied the professor very calmly, 'the situation is virtually hopeless, but there exists a possibility of salvation, and it is that possibility which I am examining. If we may die at any moment, we may also at any moment be saved. Let us accordingly be ready to seize the slightest opportunity.'

'But what can we do?'

'Maintain our strength by eating.'

At these words I looked at my uncle distraught. I had not been able to confess before, but now it had to be done.

'Eating?', I repeated.

'Yes, without delay.'

The professor said a few words in Danish. Hans shook his head.

'What!', shouted my uncle, 'are our provisions lost?'

'Yes, this is what is left: one piece of dried meat for the three of us!'

My uncle looked at me in amazement.

'Well', I said, 'do you still think we will be saved?'

My question received no answer. An hour passed. I began to feel a violent hunger. My companions were suffering as well, but not one of us dared touch the pathetic remains of the food.

We were still rising very fast. Sometimes the air stopped us breathing properly, as it does with aeronauts who ascend too quickly. But while aeronauts are subject to cold proportional to their height amongst the layers of the atmosphere, we were undergoing the diametrically opposite effect. The temperature was rising worryingly and had easily reached 40°C.

What did such a change mean? Until now Lidenbrock and Davy's theory had been confirmed by the evidence; until now special conditions of refracting rocks, of electricity, or of magnetism had modified the general laws of nature, making the heat stay moderate. Given that the theory of a central fire remained in my view the only correct one, the only justifiable one, were we going to return to an environment where this phenomenon held true, where the heat completely melted the rocks? I was afraid so, and said to the professor: 'if we aren't drowned or torn to pieces, if we don't starve to death, there's still the chance we might be burned alive.'

He merely shrugged his shoulders and returned to his thoughts. An hour passed without anything happening apart from a slight increase in the temperature. At last my uncle said something.

'Look', he said, 'we must decide.'

'Decide?'

'Yes. We must keep up our strength. If we try to extend our lives for a few more hours by eking out what is left of the food, then we will remain weak until the end.'

'Yes, till the end, which isn't far off.'

'Well then! Should a chance of salvation occur, should action become necessary, where will we find the strength to act if we let ourselves be weakened by inanition?'

'But, Uncle John, when we have eaten this piece of meat, what will we have left?'

'Nothing, Axel, nothing. But will devouring it with your eyes give you any energy? Your arguments are those of a man with neither will nor strength!'

'Then you've still not given up?', I said petulantly.

'No!', he replied firmly.

'What! You still think we have a chance of being saved?'

'Yes, most certainly! And while his heart still beats, while his flesh still moves, I cannot accept that an individual endowed with will-power can give into despair.'

What words! The man who pronounced them in such circumstances was clearly of no ordinary mettle.

'But what do you suggest?'

'We eat every last scrap of food and get our strength back. All right, so this meal will be our last. But at least, instead of being exhausted, we will be men again.'

'Well, let's eat!'

My uncle took the piece of meat and the few biscuits that had survived the shipwreck, divided them into three equal parts, and handed them out. This produced about a pound of food each. The professor ate hungrily, with a sort of intense fury; myself without pleasure despite my hunger, almost with disgust; Hans quietly, moderately, soundlessly chewing small mouthfuls, savoring them with the calm of a man the problems of the future cannot worry. By looking everywhere, he had found half a flask of gin; he passed it over, and this beneficial liquid revived me slightly.

'*Förtrafflig!*', said Hans, drinking in turn.

'Excellent!', replied my uncle.

I had found some hope again. But we had just finished our last meal. It was five in the morning.

Man is made in such a way that his health has a purely negative effect; once his need to eat has been satisfied, he finds it difficult to imagine the horrors of hunger; to understand them he has to experience them. Consequently, after a long period without food, a few mouthfuls of meat and biscuit overcame our previous gloom.

Afterwards, each of us was lost in his thoughts. What was Hans dreaming about, this man from the extreme West, but ruled by the fatalistic resignation of the East? For my part, all my thoughts were only memories, bringing me back to that surface of the globe which I should never have left. The house in the Königstrasse, my poor Gräuben, Marthe the maid, passed before my eyes like visions; and in the sad rumblings coming through the rocks, I thought I could hear the towns of this Earth.

As for my uncle, always focused, he was holding up the torch and carefully studying the nature of the formations; he was trying to discover where we were from the successive strata. This calculation, or rather estimation, could at best be highly approximate; but a scientist remains a scientist when he manages to retain his self-control, and Professor

Lidenbrock certainly possessed this last quality to an extraordinary degree.

I heard him murmuring words from the science of geology; I understood them and could not help being interested in this final piece of work.

'Eruptive granite', he was saying. 'We're still in the Primitive Period; but we're climbing, we're climbing! Who knows?'

Who knows? He had not given up hope. He touched the walls and a few moments later continued: 'Gneiss, mica-schists. Good! We will soon be in the Transition Period, and then…'

What did the professor mean? Could he measure the thickness of the Earth's crust above our heads? Did he have a single justification for his calculation? No; he had no manometer and no estimation could take its place.

Meanwhile, the temperature was increasing tremendously and I could feel myself bathing in a burning atmosphere. I could only compare it to the heat given off by the furnaces of a foundry when the metal is being poured out. By degrees, Hans, my uncle, and I had taken off our jackets and waistcoats; the least garment caused us discomfort, even pain.

'Are we moving towards a fiery furnace?', I called out at a moment when the heat was getting much worse.

'No', replied my uncle, 'it is impossible! It is impossible!'

'However', I said testing the wall, 'it feels burning hot!'

As I said these words, my hand touched the surface of the water but I had to draw it back quickly.

'The water is boiling!', I exclaimed.

This time the professor replied only with an angry gesture.

An invincible terror then took hold of my mind and would not let go. I felt that a catastrophe was soon going to happen, one that the most daring of imaginations could not conceive. An idea that was at first vague and doubtful, slowly became a certainty in my mind. I rejected it, but it came obstinately back, again and again. I did not dare put it into words. But a number of involuntary observations convinced me. In the flickering light from the torch, I noticed convulsions in the granite strata; a phenomenon was clearly going to happen in which electricity had a role; but this terrible heat, the boiling water! ... I decided to look at the compass.

It had gone mad!

Chapter 43.

Yes, mad! The needle was jumping from one pole to the other with sharp jerks, working its way through every point of the compass, spinning as if completely dizzy.

I knew that, according to the generally accepted theories, the Earth's mineral crust is never in a complete state of rest. The changes caused by the decomposition of internal substances, the vibrations produced by the larger streams, and the actions of the magnetic forces all tend to shake it around constantly, although the creatures living on the surface have no idea that it is moving. This phenomenon on its own, therefore, would not specially have frightened me, or at least would not normally have produced a very unpleasant feeling.

But further phenomena, sending clues unlike any others, could no longer be ignored. Explosions were occurring with an increasing and alarming intensity. I could only compare them with the sound of dozens of carts being driven hard over cobblestones. Their thundering was continuous.

The compass, shaken madly around by the electrical phenomena, also helped me make up my mind. The mineral crust was threatening to break up, the granite masses to come together, the chasm to be plugged, the void to be filled in, and we, poor atoms, were going to be crushed in the titanic embrace that resulted!

'Uncle John! We've had it!'

'What is this new panic?', he answered surprisingly calmly. 'What is the matter with you?'

'The matter? Look at the walls moving, these rocks which are falling apart, this scorching heat, this boiling water, this thickening steam, this crazy needle: all signs of an impending earthquake!'

My uncle gently shook his head: 'an earthquake?'

'Yes.'

'I think, my boy, that you are mistaken.'

'What? Don't you recognize the symptoms…'

'Of an earthquake? No, I am expecting something better than that!'

'What do you mean?'

'I'm hoping for an eruption, Axel.'

'An eruption! We are in the vent of an active volcano!'

'I think so,' said the professor, smiling. 'It is the best thing that could have happened to us.'

The best thing? Had my uncle gone mad? What did his words mean? How could he be so calm and happy?

'What?', I cried, 'we are in the middle of an eruption! Fate has placed us in the path of red-hot lava, fiery rocks, boiling water, of all the substances that are thrown up in eruptions! We are to be expelled, thrown out, rejected, regurgitated, spat out into the air, in a whirlwind of flame, along with huge amounts of rock and showers of ash and scoria! And that's the best thing that could happen to us!'

'Yes', said the professor, peering at me over his glasses.

'For it is the only chance we have of getting back to the surface of the Earth!'

I will skip the countless ideas that crossed my mind in that single moment. My uncle was right, absolutely right; and never had he seemed more daring or more self-assured than at this moment, when calmly waiting, and speculating on the chances of an eruption.

Meanwhile, we had continued rising; the night went by following this upward movement; only the noise all around became louder and louder. I was almost suffocating, I thought my last hour had come, and yet, imagination being such a strange thing, I gave in to truly childish thoughts. But I couldn't help my ideas: I had no control over them!

It was clear that we were being pushed upwards by the force of an eruption; under the raft there was turbulent, boiling water, and under that a whole sticky mass of lava, a huge conglomeration of rocks. When they got to the top of the crater, they would be thrown out in all directions. We were undoubtedly in the vent of a volcano.

But this time, instead of the extinct Snaefell, we were dealing with a volcano in full activity. I was wondering therefore what mountain it could possibly be, and which part of the world we were going to be thrown out onto.

Some northern region, of course. Before it had gone insane, the compass had been consistently pointing in that direction. Since leaving Cape Saknussemm, we had been swept due north for hundreds and hundreds of leagues. Were we underneath Iceland once more? Were we to be ejected from the crater of Mount Hekla or one of the seven other volcanoes on the island? Otherwise, within a radius of 500 leagues and, at that latitude, I could only think of the little-known volcanoes on the north-west coast of America. To the east, there was only one at less than 80°N: Mount Beerenberg, in Jan Mayen, not far from Spitzbergen. On the other hand, there was no general lack of craters, and they all had plenty of room to spew out a whole army. I tried to guess which one would serve as our exit.

Towards morning our ascent accelerated. The heat was increasing rather than decreasing as we approached the surface of the globe: this had to be a local effect, due to the influence of some volcano. No longer could there be any doubt at all as to our means of transport. An enormous force, a pressure of several hundred atmospheres produced by the steam built up in the Earth's breast, was irresistibly thrusting up at us. But how many terrible dangers would it expose us to?

Soon wild glowing lights shone on the walls of the vertical chimney, which was now widening out. On either side I could see deep corridors, like immense tunnels, sending forth thick steam and smoke: crackling flames were licking the rock faces.

'Look, Uncle John!'

'Yes, sulphur flames. Nothing could be more normal during an eruption.'

'But what if they come and burn us?'

'They won't.'

'And what if we suffocate?'

'We won't. The shaft is getting wider. If necessary, we can get off the raft and take shelter in some fissure.'

'But the water, the water! Rising all the time!'

'There is no water left, Axel, just a viscous lava-stream which is lifting us up on its way to the mouth of the crater.'

It was true that the water had disappeared, replaced by relatively dense eruptive matter, which was boiling, however. The temperature was becoming unbearable. A thermometer would have indicated more than 70°. I was bathed in sweat. But for the speed of the climb, we would certainly have been suffocated.

The professor did not pursue his suggestion of leaving the raft, which was perhaps just as well. Those few beams, roughly joined together, gave us a solid base, which we wouldn't have had anywhere else.

Towards eight in the morning a new incident happened for the first time. The upward movement stopped all of a sudden, with the raft remaining absolutely motionless.

'What's happening?', I asked, shaken by this abrupt halt as if the raft had hit something.

'An intermission.'

'Is the eruption slowing down?'

'I sincerely hope not.'

I stood up. I tried to look around. Perhaps the raft had caught against a rock projection and was momentarily holding back the flow of the eruptive material. If so, it ought to be freed at once.

But this wasn't the case. The column of ashes, scoria, rocks, and debris had itself stopped rising.

'Is the eruption stopping?'

'Ah!', said my uncle through clenched teeth, 'that's what you are worrying about, my boy. But don't worry: this can only be a temporary lull. It has already lasted five minutes, and in a short while we will be heading towards the mouth of the crater once again.'

While speaking, the professor consulted his chronometer; and he was soon proved right in this prediction too. The raft was once more caught up in a rapid, disorderly flux, which lasted for about two minutes, then stopped again.

'Good', said my uncle, noting the time, 'it will restart in ten minutes.'

'Ten minutes?'

'Yes. We are dealing with a volcano whose eruption is periodic. It lets us breathe when it does.'

He was absolutely correct. At the allotted time we were shot upwards again with great speed: we had to cling onto the beams or we would have been thrown off the raft. Then the thrust stopped once more.

Since that time, I have often thought about this remarkable phenomenon, but without being able to find a satisfactory explanation for it. Nevertheless, it seems clear to me that we can't have been in the principal chimney of the volcano, but rather a side-passage, where there was some sort of counter-effect.

How many times the process took place, I cannot say. All I can be certain of is that, each time the movement was repeated, we were hurled forward with increasing force, as if lifted by an actual projectile. During the pauses, we suffocated; when we were moving, the burning air took my breath away. For a moment I thought of the ecstasy of suddenly finding myself in the polar regions, at a temperature of −30°. In my overstimulated imagination I wandered over the snowy plains of the Arctic icecap, and longed for the moment when I could roll on the frozen carpet of the Pole! Little by little, my head, shaken by the repeated shocks, gave up thinking. If it had not been for Hans's arms, my skull would have been flung against the granite wall on more than one occasion.

As a consequence I have no clear memory of what happened during the next few hours. I have a confused memory of endless blasts, of Earth movements, of a swirling motion which grabbed hold of the raft. It undulated on the waves of lava, amidst a rain of ashes. It was surrounded by roaring flames. A hurricane, as if coming from some immense ventilator, fanned the flames of the subterranean fires. One last time, Hans's face appeared to me in a blazing halo. My last thought was the horrifying tragedy of the criminal fastened to the mouth of a cannon, at the moment that the shot goes off and sends his arms and legs flying into the air.

Chapter 44.

When I opened my eyes again, I felt the strong hand of the guide clutching my belt. With the other he was holding on to my uncle. I was not seriously injured, just a bit stiff. I saw that I was lying on the slope of a mountain, only a few feet away from a precipice which I would have fallen into with the slightest movement. Hans had clearly saved me from certain death while I was rolling down the flanks of the crater.

'Where are we?', asked my uncle, who looked highly annoyed to be back on Earth again.

The guide shrugged his shoulders as if to show he didn't know.

'In Iceland,' I ventured.

'*Nej*,' answered Hans.

'No!', cried the professor.

'He must be wrong', I said, getting up.

After the many surprises of the journey, another was waiting for us. I expected to see a cone covered with eternal snows, in the midst of the arid deserts of the north, under the pale rays of the polar skies, beyond the furthest latitudes. But, contrary to what I had expected, my uncle, the Icelander, and I were stretched out halfway up a mountain baked by the heat of the sun, which was scorching us with its rays.

I wasn't prepared to believe my eyes; but the indisputable burning my body was receiving brooked no reply. We had come out of the crater half naked, and the radiant orb, of which we had asked nothing for two months, was now bestowing on us floods of heat and light: we were being irradiated.

When my eyes had adjusted to this unaccustomed dazzle, I used them to make up for the failure of my imagination. At the very least, I was determined to be in Spitzbergen, I was not in the mood for giving up easily.

The professor found his voice first: 'it certainly doesn't look very much like Iceland.'

'Doesn't it look like Jan Mayen?', I said.

'Not really, my boy. This is not a northern volcano with granite peaks and a snow cap.'

'And yet...'

'Look, Axel, look!'

Above our heads, not more than five hundred feet away, was the crater of the volcano. Every quarter of an hour there came flying from it a tall column of flames mixed with pumice stone, ashes, and lava, together with a deafening explosion. I felt quakes every time the mountain breathed, sending out, like a whale, fire and air through its enormous blowholes. Below, on a steep slope, layers of eruptive material could be seen stretching seven or eight hundred feet down, meaning that the volcano couldn't be more than three hundred leagues high. Its base was hidden by a real basket of green trees, amongst which I distinguished olive trees, fig trees, and vines with ruby red grapes.

It didn't look much like the Arctic, I had to admit.

When one's gaze passed beyond the ring of greenery, it soon went astray on the waters of an exquisite sea or lake, which made this enchanted land an island only a few leagues wide. On the eastern side appeared a small harbor, with a few houses before, and boats of an unusual type rocking on the azure ripples. Beyond, islets rose from the liquid plain, in such great numbers as to resemble a big ant-heap. In the west, rounded shores appeared on the distant horizon; on some lay blue mountains of harmonious contours, on others, still further away, appeared measureless cones, above whose high summits floated plumes of smoke. To the north, a broad expanse of water sparkled in the sun's rays, revealing here and there the top of a mast or a convex sail swelling in the wind.

The improbability of such a landscape made it infinitely more wonderful and beautiful.

'Where are we? Where are we?', I repeated softly.

Hans shut his eyes in indifference, and my uncle stared perplexedly.

'Whatever this mountain is', he said at last, 'it is rather hot. The explosions are still continuing, and it would really not be worth coming out of an eruption, only to have one's head crushed by a falling rock. So let's go down and discover what we're up against. Besides, I am dying of hunger and thirst.'

The professor was certainly not a contemplative. For my part, I could have stayed hours longer on that spot, forgetting all needs and fatigues, but I was obliged to follow my companions down.

The slopes of the volcano proved very steep; we slipped into channels of ashes, avoiding the lava-streams stretching out like fiery serpents. While we worked our way down, I talked a great deal, for my imagination was too full not to go off in words.

'We're in Asia, on the coast of India, in the Malay Archipelago, or in the middle of the South Seas! We have gone right across the Earth, and come out at the antipodes!'

'But the compass?', asked my uncle.

'Yes, the compass', I said with embarrassment. 'If we listened to what it said, we would think we had headed north all the time.'

'So it lied?'

'Lied!'

'It might be the North Pole!'

'The North Pole? No... but...'

There was something that was indeed difficult to explain. I no longer knew what to think.

Meanwhile we were getting near the greenery which had looked so inviting. I was tormented by thirst and hunger. Fortunately, after two hours' march, a beautiful countryside came into view, completely covered with olive trees, pomegranate trees, and vines which seemed to belong to everybody. Besides, in our terrible state, we weren't hard to please. What ecstasy we felt pressing these delicious fruits to our lips, and devouring bunches of grapes swinging on these ruby red vines! Not far off, amongst the grass under the refreshing shade of the trees, I found a spring of fresh water. It was bliss to plunge our hands and faces into it.

While we were still enjoying a well-earned rest, a boy appeared between two clumps of olives.

'Ah!', I cried, 'an inhabitant of this blessed country!'

He was a poor little boy, very badly clothed, rather sickly, and apparently much alarmed by our appearance. Actually, half-naked as we were, with our untidy beards, we must certainly have presented a bizarre spectacle: unless this was a country of robbers, we were likely to frighten the natives.

Just as the urchin was about to run away, Hans darted after him and brought him back, ignoring the kicks and screams.

My uncle began by calming him down as well as he could, and then enquired in good German: 'what is the name of this mountain, my little friend?'

The child did not answer.

'Good', said my uncle, 'we are not in Germany.'

He then asked the same question in English.

Still no answer. I was very much intrigued.

'Is he dumb?', cried the professor, who, very proud of his multilingualism, then tried the same question in French.

Same silence.

'Let's try Italian then. *Dove noi siamo*?'

'Yes, where are we?', I repeated, slightly impatiently.

The boy didn't say anything.

'Well, are you going to talk?', cried my uncle, who was getting annoyed and shaking the urchin by the ears. '*Come si noma questa isola*?'

'Stromboli', answered the little shepherd, escaping from Hans's grasp and running through the olive trees towards the plain.

We weren't bothered about him! Stromboli! What an effect this unforeseen name produced on my mind! We were in the middle of the

Mediterranean, surrounded by that Aeolian Archipelago of mythological memory, in that ancient Strongyle where Aeolus held the winds and tempests on a chain. Those rounded blue hills to the east were the mountains of Calabria! And that volcano on the southern horizon was Mount Etna, terrible Mount Etna itself!

'Stromboli, Stromboli!', I repeated.

My uncle accompanied me with words and gestures. We were like a choir singing in unison.

O what a journey, what an amazing journey! We had gone in by one volcano and out by another, and this other was nearly 1,200 leagues from Snaefell, from the barren shores of Iceland and the outermost limits of the world! The hazards of our expedition had brought us to the heart of the most fortunate country on the globe! We had exchanged the lands of eternal snows for those of infinite greenery; and the greyish fogs of the freezing wastes above our heads had become the azure skies of Sicily!

After a delicious meal of fruit and cool water, we set off again towards the port of Stromboli. It did not seem advisable to say how we had arrived on the island; with their superstitious mentality, the Italians would certainly have thought us devils thrown up by the fires of Hell. We accordingly resigned ourselves to being mere victims of shipwreck. It was less glorious, but safer.

On the way, I heard my uncle murmuring: 'but what about the compass: it did point north! What can the reason be?'

'Really', I said, with an air of great disdain. 'It's much simpler not to explain it!'

'What! A professor at the Johannaeum would be disgraced if unable to discover the reason for a phenomenon of the physical world!'

Thus speaking, my uncle, half-naked, with his leather purse around his waist and settling his glasses on his nose, became once more the terrible professor of mineralogy.

An hour after leaving the olive grove we arrived at the port of San Vincenzo, where Hans asked for his thirteenth week's wages. These were duly given him, together with heartfelt handshakes.

At that moment, even if he did not share our very natural feelings, he at least gave in to a most unusual display of emotion.

He touched our hands lightly with the tips of his fingers, and he smiled.

Chapter 45.

We have now come to the end of a tale which many people, however determined to be surprised at nothing, will refuse to believe. But I am armed in advance against human scepticism.

The Stromboli fishermen received us with the kindness due to those who have undergone shipwreck. They provided food and clothing. On 31 August, after a wait of forty-eight hours, we were conveyed by a little *speronare* to Messina, where a few days' rest helped us recover from our fatigue.

On Friday, 4 September, we boarded the Volturne, one of the French Imperial mail-boats, and landed three days later in Marseilles, our minds submerged in only one problem, that of the wretched compass.

This inexplicable fact continued to seriously bother me. On the evening of 9 September we arrived in Hamburg.

I will not attempt to describe Marthe's amazement and Gräuben's joy at our return.

'Now that you're a hero, Axel,' said my dear fiancée, 'you will never need to leave me again.'

I looked at her. She was weeping and smiling at the same time.

I leave to the imagination whether Professor Lidenbrock's homecoming produced a sensation in Hamburg. Thanks to Marthe's indiscretions, the news of his departure for the centre of the Earth had spread through the whole world. People had refused to believe it, and when he returned, they still refused.

However, the presence of Hans and a few items of news from Iceland slowly modified public opinion.

Eventually my uncle became a great man, and myself the nephew of a great man, already something to be. Hamburg gave a civic banquet in our honour. There was a public meeting held at the Johannaeum, where the professor told the story of our expedition, omitting only the episodes involving the compass. The same day, he deposited Saknussemm's document in the municipal archives, and expressed his deep regret that circumstances stronger than his will had not allowed him to follow the footsteps of the Icelandic explorer down to the very centre of the Earth. He was modest in his glory, and it did his reputation a great deal of good.

So many honors made people jealous, of course. The professor received his share of envy, and since his theories, based on facts that were certain, contradicted the scientific doctrines of fire in the centre, he engaged in some remarkable debates with scientists of every country, both in writing and in the flesh.

As for myself, I personally cannot accept the theory of the cooling of the Earth. Despite what I have seen, I believe, and always will, in heat at the centre. But I admit that circumstances which are still not properly explained can sometimes modify this law under the effect of certain natural phenomena.

At a moment when these questions were still being hotly discussed, my uncle experienced a real sadness. In spite of his entreaties, Hans decided to leave Hamburg; the man to whom we owed everything would not let us repay our debt. He was suffering from homesickness for Iceland.

'Farväl', he said one day, and with this simple goodbye, he left for Reykjavik, where he arrived safely.

We were singularly attached to the excellent eider hunter; although absent, he will never be forgotten by those whose lives he saved, and I will certainly see him one last time before I die.

As a conclusion, I should perhaps say that this *Journey to the Centre of the Earth* created a sensation in the whole world. It was translated and published in every language: the most important newspapers competed for the main episodes, which were reviewed, discussed, attacked, and defended with equal fervor in the camps of both followers and disbelievers. Unusually, my uncle enjoyed during his lifetime all the fame he had won, and everyone, up to and including Mr Barnum himself, offered to 'exhibit' him in the entire United States, at an exceptional price.

But a worry, which might almost be called a torment, slipped into this fame. A single fact remained unfathomable: that of the compass. For a scientist, an unexplained fact is a mental burden. But Heaven intended my uncle to be completely happy.

One day, while arranging a collection of minerals in his study, I noticed the much-discussed compass, and began to examine it again.

It had been sitting in a corner for six months, without suspecting the fuss it was causing.

Suddenly I was flabbergasted! I shouted out. The professor came running.

'What is it?'

'The compass...'

'Well?'

'The needle points south not north!'

'What are you trying to say?'

'See, the poles are reversed!'

'Reversed?'

My uncle took a look, did a quick comparison, and then made the whole house shake with a superb jump.

What light shone in his mind and in mine!

'So', he cried when he could speak again, 'when we arrived at Cape Saknussemm, the needle of this accursed compass showed south instead of north?'

'Obviously.'

'Then our mistake is explained. But what could have caused this reversal of the poles?'

'Nothing simpler.'

'Explain yourself clearly, my boy.'

'During the storm on the Lidenbrock Sea, the fireball magnetized the iron on the raft and so quite simply disorientated our compass!'

'Ah!', exclaimed the professor, bursting into laughter, 'so it was a trick done by electricity?'

From that day onwards, my uncle was the happiest of scientists. I was the happiest of men, for my pretty Vironian girl, giving up her position as ward, took on responsibilities in the house in the Königstrasse as both wife and niece. There is little need to add that her uncle was the illustrious Professor Otto Lidenbrock, a corresponding member of every scientific, geographical, and mineralogical society in the five continents.

Journey
To
Empycrist II.

Against barbarity.

Laurent Paul Sueur

Table of contents.

Think,

Understand,

Change.

Chapter 1:

Obviousness.

The universe, as far as we can judge from our poor knowledge and perception, is characterized by an absence of colour. Everything works as if black, or at least a very dark blue, were to be the dominant impression, sometimes contradicted by the platinum scintillation of the celestial bodies. In the Solar System, we are blessed since we have Mars, with its reddish reflection, our gorgeous gold sun and, of course, the aquamarine-like Earth. The Earth, so heavenly beautiful, so unbearably offended by the human vermin! Are you dying? It seems so! It is impossible: it is the Creator's chef d'oeuvre, the epitome of perfection. However, over the years, its empyreal blue has faded and air pollution has put a yellowish veil between the crystalline depths of its oceans and the mesosphere. It is unbelievable! The titanic collisions this planet experienced did not destroy it and, man, this minuscule creature, could achieve what the immense universe was unable to fulfil. Would collective unconsciousness be stronger than celestial geometry?

Planet Earth is suffocating, for mankind had no other choice but to burn fossil fuels and release the venom that will kill it. Bad luck! Another technology would have painted a better present. Bad luck? No, bad attitude of mind: they would have invented a lot of other problems just for the pleasure of devouring themselves. Ordinary people are ogres! Their doubtful normalcy is the tip of their mental iceberg. What can we find underneath? Barbarity! All the vices they have consciously chosen before reaching a state of pure madness, the madness of normalcy. Ah, where are you reason and grace? Elsewhere, undoubtedly: in the mind of an exceptional soul, on the surface of another planet, in the logic of humane human organizations...

Their air is polluted, they have no more energy resources, and, now, they also have water supply problems! It has to be said that the global warming was a two-faced birthday present. Of course, it brought some water where it has disappeared but, at the same time, it brought a lot of water where there was already too much. Hence, some deserts with low population densities became livable places while most of the overcrowded parts of the world were flooded. Henceforth, the crops as well as the fruit trees were destroyed, and stagnant water caused large epidemics, as usual. Very few places were spared: some drylands of the center of the United States, China and Africa. Sunny California, what do you prefer: pestilential waters or the hellish reality of your burning thirst?

With fewer people on the planet, the many mistakes of man would have never led to such a disaster. Actually, 350 million must be the appropriate number of inhabitants: 8 billion is absurd. There is not enough quantity of renewable energy for so many people, even though it is not completely impossible to produce a sufficient amount of food. Moreover, since barbarity is inscribed in human nature, it is very important to let them spread out. They must not gather together if their level of consciousness is to low, or they would endanger themselves and even try to kill one another. Barbarity must not be societies' fate.

*

*   *

*

The Invictus is about to lift off. The spaceship is massive. It looks like a gigantic albatross, shining under the imperious sun of Port Isabel. Today, the weather is fine and the sky is rather blue; no, it is rather... yellow! Captain Smith is nervous, not because of the danger of the liftoff but because he thinks that the die is cast. All his hopes have vanished: he is here today, for he must find another planet so that the human race may survive and, perhaps, start all over again. John, you are so sad. Your mourning and the bottomless abyss of your regrets are palpable. You can hardly breathe; you are quiet... Are you shivering?

Barbara is next to him. She is thinking of her chimpanzees: they are sedated. So, they won't see anything, shout or try to escape, like the last time. She really cares about them, for she is certain they will help her to understand, at last, why they are so different from humans although they carry almost the same genetic material and physical characteristics. She has been working with them for the last 5 years and has taught them how to speak! Well, it is obvious they understand some words but I would not say they really communicate with her, nor with one another. Were the first hominins like them? When did they start to speak? Why? And what was the first word ever spoken? God, sun, water, earth? Oh, no! It was I... am!

Peter is also a biologist: he studies the plant kingdom. You should see what he has done in the greenhouse of the Invictus: it is the Garden of Eden. It is even better since there are no snakes, no Adam, no Eve, no fallen angels. But the Tree of the knowledge of good and evil must be there: he has planted so many different species. Couldn't he rather look for the Tree of the knowledge of the place of man in the universe? Everything has a place, a function and, therefore, a meaning. However, it seems that the place of man fluctuates or, at least, is not really understandable. Indeed, he is an element of the gigantic motion. The wasps once made him understand he was someone really special. Actually, these small creatures always eat the fruits of his trees before him: they make a little hole, what attracts other insects like the ants. In next to no time the fruit is eaten by them. Last year, for the very first time, they did not touch the peaches. Why? He does not know. What he knows is that, without him, animals and humans would starve and disappear...

The brunette on the other side of the cockpit is Jenny. She is a linguist. She understands and even speaks many different languages, what could be useful if they find intelligent beings on Empycrist II. She is not really convinced by that, because it is almost certain they will not speak Chinese, nor... Latin! It is strange: the very same object, or idea, always produces many different idiomatic results. It is strange because, from a physical point of view, all humans have the same larynx and brain, so, why don't they use the same sounds to call that object? Matter does not explain everything: matter explains nothing, indeed!

As for Paul, who is seated next to her, he is an astrophysicist, or a poet; well, it is the same! He is the most intelligent one of them all, a wise man who is mesmerized by the existence of everything, including himself. He would like to know the starting point of the universe and the reason for its existence. Nothingness does not exist: this overcrowded Creation comes from "something". He thinks that before the beginning of this "something", there was a thought, with its own logic, that created the universal motion. The planetary motion is, therefore, the reflection of the motion of the primordial will. This heavenly geometry reveals its essence, which is perfection. This cyclopean symmetry leads to man, the only creature that does not always reach its nature. It can also denature other creatures, like Barbara's apes. Man, with his imperfections, can consciously choose his destiny, refuse to follow the logic of perfection and remain in a state of pure barbarity...

*
*   *
*

Test director.
-How do you feel John?

John.
-... Bad, really bad.

Test director.
-... 20 minutes before liftoff.

John.
-... Everything seems OK.

Test director.
-You know how important your mission is?

John.
-Unfortunately! And I still think it is a stupid idea to go to this planet and organize a great migration. The problem is not the planet, it is the people who live on it. Give them another one and they will destroy it.

Barbara.
-John, if I may be so bold, it is not our responsibility to decide whether it is a good or a bad idea. We must obey: that's it!

John.
-Whom must I obey, what must I follow?

Test director.
-I have a little message from the president...

Jenny, Peter and Paul.
-Oh no...

John.
-Move on, and thank him for all he has not done!

Test director.
-... 9 minutes before liftoff.

John.
-Flight recorders on.

Paul.
-John, you are not the only person upset. Here, we all leave regrets behind us. Things could have been different but the reason and humanity of a few can nothing against the unconsciousness of the majority.

Peter.
-Consciousness can always escape.

Jenny.
-That's what we are doing.

Test director.
-5 minutes before liftoff. Connections removed.

Barbara.
-What will we find? We know what we leave behind, but what will we find?

Peter.
-The Garden of Eden. I hope so.

Jenny.
-Something better. Look at the Earth. It is unbearable here.

Paul.
-Solitude, obviously.

Jenny.
-What do you mean by that?

Paul.
-Man is the only intelligent creature in the endless universe.

Jenny.
-Empycrist II is Earth's twin sister, why wouldn't we find intelligent beings on its surface?

Paul.
-Because man is the aim of the Creation. He is the result of a decision, not of the implementation of material factors.

Test director.
-2 minutes before takeoff. Main engine on.

Barbara.

-... Will we find almond trees on Empycrist?

Peter.
-No, I don't think so.

Barbara.
-I like to see them bloom in February, while nature is still asleep.

Paul, Jenny and John.
-So do I.

Paul.
-But the sun will be brighter where we go...

Test director.

-6 seconds... main engine: maximum power.

Paul.
-Farewell Hell!

Test director.
-Liftoff.

John.
-Hello, Heaven!

Chapter 2:

The Invictus.

The Invictus is a modern cathedral: massive, dark, silent. The real captain is the computer for the engineers did not trust man's emotionally-influenced intelligence. Hence, artificial intelligence handles everything. One would even wonder whether there are not too many people in this expedition! Well, since the journey will last one year, five people, it is not too much to break the monotony of an endless odyssey. Each day might look like the day before. Some of them will be more busy than the others. It is obvious that Jenny, Paul and John won't have a lot of things to do, Peter will take care of the greenhouse, even though everything is automated, Barbara will keep on working on her apes. The rhythm of the days will follow the beat of their stomachs! At the moment, everybody is going to their cabin without thinking of their forthcoming boredom.

Barbara's cabin is really pretty. It looks like an 18th century boudoir, but where is Madame de Pompadour? It might be her! She is fifty and still attractive: cosmetic surgery can easily erase the traces of time while philosophy, or psychoanalysis, is not as efficient to make old little girls grow up. She is lying on her bed, wearing a blue negligee. She is thinking.

Everything is confused in her mind: the monkeys, the almond trees, her husband, Empycrist, her solitude, the absence of children. She would have liked to have children; she tried... She failed! Life was not so nice to her. She would have liked to be a mum. You could have become a woman... Unfruitful flowers turn into fragile old little girls sometimes. It is not your fault Barbara, but it is your Greek tragedy. This way, you would have understood what humanity means. You would have understood that what resembles you is not you. You would have experienced the passing of time which tells you that you must hurry up, define what the goal of human's life is, follow your human nature, accomplish what you have to do, and turn the ugly worm into a beautiful butterfly before you die. With a child, you would have created. Matter is not everything: it is what you see, it is not what you feel. Barbara, can you create? The love two individuals share must lead them to confirm the union of their willpower. When a woman mothers a child, she gives birth to a soul. Matters disappears, the mind imposes the brightness of its truth. Barbara, you cannot think yet!

She is facing a mirror. She does not see herself. Her empty gaze is diving into her empty life. Her eyes are wide open. She is parting her blond curly hair. She must pretty herself up for tonight's meeting. She is sighing.

Don't put too much mascara on your eyelashes, nor too much rouge on your cheeks and lips: you are not the Evil Queen, for you know you are not the fairest one of all. There is no need to take your daughter-in-law's heart: you don't hate her! You are crying. Do you know why? Humans' distress always turns them into less unpleasant beings, but it never turns them into more compassionate creatures. Do you understand yourself? No, you cannot because you first need to become a grownup and stop believing you are the center of the universe. If you want to see you as you are, you need to move away from yourself. Don't put too much perfume, you could inconvenience the captain. Moreover, there is no man to seduce. Put this little grey uniform on. It is decent, convenient, and not too feminine. You don't need to look like a femme fatale: don't try to pretend you are someone you are not. You will only fool yourself. They will immediately understand who you are by the way you talk. The look, the semblance of truth, are revealed by the emptiness of the words. Don't pretend you are a woman Barbara, for you are still a little girl, and they know it.

*

*   *

*

John.
-We must talk seriously about the nature of this mission.

Paul.
-Is it really necessary? We know the reason and the destination.

John.
-We know the reason and destination but we don't know whether it is a good idea to go there and organize a mass migration.

Paul.
-What do you mean by that?

Jenny.
-John is planning a kind of mutiny! We have just left the Earth and you are already questioning the mission!

Peter.
-But John is right: we are not obliged to follow an idea when it is a stupid idea. We are not obedient slaves. Port Isabel control team rarely speaks the word of truth.

Barbara.
-You, plotters!

Paul.

-Barbara is right, we must help mankind to survive.

Barbara.
-We are too weak, too small: we must obey their orders.

John.
-It is not a question of being big or small, obedient or disobedient, it is a matter of logic. It is completely absurd to give another planet to humans: they will also destroy it. The problem is not geography but mankind. Honestly, you should find another one each millennium. There are not so many viable planets in the universe. So, man must learn to deal with what he has received, and nothing else. Temperance should be the first virtue of societies.

Jenny.
So, we go there, fake our own death in a so-called crash, and hope they won't send another mission, not to rescue us but achieve what they have planned? It is not realistic.

Peter.
-We should already figure out what we are going to find on Empycrist. We are not certain we will be able to live on it.

John.
-We know for sure there is enough oxygen and water. So, life is possible.

Paul.
-Life is possible but does it mean the plants will provide the food we need? Will we be poisoned? Will we find fishes and animals we will be able to eat?

Peter.
-We are not obliged to eat meat; vegetables will do the trick.

Jenny.
-We could multiply Barbara's apes…

Barbara.
-Are you…

Jenny.
-I am joking Barbara. I am certain Peter will find a suitable substitute made out of vegetable proteins.

Barbara.
-Are there oceans and rivers on Empycrist II.

Peter.
-Yes there are. Moreover, the temperatures, I mean the climates, seem to resemble ours. That's why we are almost certain we will find a natural environment that will suit us.

Jenny.
-Do you really think we will find a superior life form?

Peter.
-I hope so… However… we might be compelled to schedule their own death if we implement Port Isabel's plan.

John.
-In that case, I assure you that we will not implement it. I don't want to repeat American history. No nation can afford to build itself from a manslaughter. Murder cannot be the foundation stone of a nation. Romulus cannot kill Remus or you inscribe barbarity in the collective unconsciousness and plan the downfall of your country. The Greeks and the Romans disappeared because of their primordial vices. I promise you that will not happen again. I will be proud to be the dangerous plotter

who will create a new society based on virtue, not crime. The meeting is closed.

*
* *
*

Peter is in the greenhouse: he wants to think about the mission. Everything is so artificial here, but his own garden on Earth was already a man-made realisation. I don't know why gardeners persist in aligning what they grow. Sometimes, I believe they would also like to align weeds in order to remove them easily. I understand the productivity logic of the farmers who increase their production that way, and allow their dreadful machines to steal the work, the hopes, the graceful life of a great many people. I don't really understand why they line up daffodils, tulips or rose bushes in their ornamental gardens. It is not really pretty. I would even say it is quite sad, for it reminds me of idiosyncrasies shared by many people: aren't human beings straight lines that will never meet? I might be slightly pessimistic but, even when people live together, some of them are even married, they are still parallel lines. They pretend to live together; however, there are no real mental interactions between them.

They remain their whole life in a bottomless solitude. There is nothing worse than this crowded loneliness.

Peter's greenhouse is much more impressive than his garden, and I know why: there is less symmetry here! It is not a French formal garden with its obsessive geometry; it rather looks like an English garden. No, it is an oasis in the very middle of these interstellar solitudes. It is insane: all the climates have been recreated and the most tropical species almost touch plants you could find on the top of the mountains or in very cold places. For instance, he has put a bilberry bush next to a mango tree, and they both grow very well! The result is… improbable.

Peter is seated on the moss, in front of the marble fountain. The sound of pouring water seems to help him think. What is he thinking? The scent of the orange blossoms is intoxicating. Is it April yet? No, it is January. Time is meaningless! The orange trees have all decided to bloom at the same time because they want to fructify. Peter thinks it will be easy to put all the plants on Empycrist. He will find a suitable location, give them a little help so that they may stand the weather. The main problem is pollination because, if they are all self-fertile, they need the help of insects, especially honey bees. He has a colony here. These small creatures are really helpful. Regardless of the hour, or the day, they work! Thanks to them, the intoxicating blossoms of the citrus trees will soon turn into tiny little fruits. On Empycrist, since the planet is huge, he will have to find a solution to keep them together, for they are not faithful and like to gather all types of pollen from many different flowers. He might have to limit the growth of the native plants. Please Peter, don't make the same mistakes… don't destroy everything; let nature act, for she might be more intelligent than you! Besides, you could have a good surprise: nature could even feed you on Empycrist II.

Chapter 3:

The gaze of the monkey.

Barbara's laboratory is very quiet today. The apes are sleeping. The night light, with its blue reflections, is painting shivering shadows that will soon wake up, shout and even try to speak. The five chimpanzees are still sleeping but Adam, Dr. Frankenstein's little protégé, is stretching his limbs. The cages are so small: how can they stand that? Oh, they are not mistreated, nevertheless, it is not a normal life, nor a pleasant one for a big wild animal. Is plenty of food every day worth the pain? Freedom is not only a human claim, it is an animal necessity. Wild animals have a function in the universe and they must act freely, according to their animal nature, in order to fulfil what nature has ordered. Don't put them in cages: they will lose their nature. Don't imprison them: they are not guilty. It is so beautiful to see a bird fly in the morning breeze, and so sad to see it bite the bars of its prison.

Barbara.
-Wake up Adam.

Adam.
-Rrrr…

Barbara.
-We have a lot of work today. We are going to learn some new words; we are going to try to pronounce them well and, maybe, we are going to write, aren't we?

Adam.
-Rrrr…

Barbara to herself while making a cup of coffee.
-They are so close to us. We almost share the same genetic material. They are our first cousins. Ad their brain is not that small: 410 grams, the weight of a human child's brain! I can teach them how to speak. I am sure

they think, so, they can speak, even if their larynx is not as effectual as ours. They seem so human. They are more intelligent than dogs!

Adam.
-Rrrr…

Barbara.
-What are you saying Adam?

Adam.
-Rrrr…

Barbara.
-You are so intelligent. 410 grams: it is not a lot but I will teach you how to become… human. Let's start with the name of the fruits: banana! Repeat after me: BANANA.

Adam.
-Hiii, hiii, hiii.

Barbara.
-Not bad, the diction is not impeccable but we almost understand what you are saying. Well, let's try with pineapple. Adam, say PINE APPLE.

Adam.
-Hiii… hiii, hiii.

Barbara.
-The rhythm is good… I know you understand me. Just say APPLE.

Adam.
-Hiii, hiii.

Barbara.

-Good, good boy Adam. Take this pen and draw it now.

The monkey takes the pen and draws what is neither a pineapple nor an apple. Nevertheless, there is something on his piece of paper. Does he understand her after all?

Barbara.
-It is beautiful, and so realistic! You are an artist, Adam... more gifted than Rimisky. You are as talented as the Magdalenian hominids in their caves: they left the outline of their hands, some impressive paintings of animals, and you are doing the same. Please, draw me a sheep... No, it is too difficult; draw me a chicken.

Adam.
-Rrrr... rrrr....

Barbara.
-Let me see... Well, I don't understand... It does not look like a chicken. Pronounce CHICKEN.

Adam.
-Hiii, hiii.

Barbara.
-No, it's not that. I should teach you first to pronounce "chicken", then you would be able to draw what you can name and, therefore, understand. Well, let's try something else. We are going to walk. Just imitate me. Walk, slide... head up... elegance... grace... humanity...

Adam jumping and happy to be outside of his cage.
-Haaa, haaa, haaa.

Barbara.

-No, it's not that. You are aping me! Stand up and walk... Do not put your hands on the floor. Raise your hands... Slide... You are not really elegant. Nature has not been good to you. Man has received more than you. You are quite ugly Adam. Don't jump! Don't be a bad boy: behave yourself. And stop talking! You, little brain!

*

*   *

*

Jenny.
-I am interrupting anything important?

Barbara.
-Not really: Adam is a naughty boy, he does not want to work today.

Jenny.
-Barbara, it is an ape, not a human: it usually eats black plums or African pears, it neither writes philosophy essays, nor laugh when the other inmates make fun of themselves.

Barbara.
-They do laugh.

Jenny.
-No, they don't: they just shout! Laughter is a human privilege. Man is the only creature that laughs. Laughter is the path towards the discovery of one's own opposition between man's behavior and reality. It compels him to perceive madness and flee it. As a matter of fact, you laugh at yourself or someone like you, you don't laugh at others. If you do so, you just express a wild hatred aiming at destroying all the others. The smile you see on their faces is a rictus, the devilish grimace of madness. Your monkeys don't smile, they grimace.

Barbara.

-These monkeys are not what you want to see in them: they are neither the apostles of Satan, nor the reflection of your hatred of... mankind. They are rather like children, very young children. They have a little brain: 410 grams. With a larger skull, their brain would have been able to grow... I should try surgery... do something on their skulls. The first hominids were really like them: small brains in small skulls. Something happened and the skull of the monkeys grew, then the brain of the hominids reached the fantastic weight of one thousand grams and, then, **one thousand AND four hundred grrramzzzzzz**... Mankind was born that way: **something** enabled his skull to grow. I want to find this **something**.

Jenny.
-Man is not an animal and you won't turn Adam into a human being. Man's ancestors were not monkeys but humans: human nature comes from human nature, and simian nature from simian nature. The parietal painters looked like their hominid ancestors who skillfully made knives out of stones: they had a human soul. You deduce the nature of something from flesh and bones. It does not work like that, for the essence of everything comes from something matter cannot explain.

Barbara.
-Humans are animals: mammals without fur! We share the same feelings; we are the same!

Jenny.
-We are not since your nature is unique. Man is the only creature that does not reach its own nature automatically. Your ape is an ape by nature: it knows what to do, how to behave and live in perfect harmony with the rest of the Creation, if you don't alter its nature! Man never reaches his nature without the combination of some factors. Of course, nature stubbornly orders him to pass through different stages that lead him from childhood to adulthood, from the eventuality of barbarity to the

eventuality of wisdom, but it's he who consciously chooses to be a humane human or not. You are so… you are so… Darwinian!

Barbara.
-Matter explains a lot of things. The body of the animals at least explains why the fittest survive and the weakest perish.

Jenny.
-The strongest do not survive: look at the dinosaurs.

Barbara.
-You are being specious Jenny.

Jenny.
-Well… maybe. Man is not that strong…

Barbara.
-His brain is!

Jenny.
-I know, look at the Capnodis Tenebrionis, this poor little thing.

Barbara.
-It is not what I call a poor little thing. It is a very resistant organism, highly adapted, and adaptable since it normally eats the peduncle of the leaves of the apricot tree but can change its diet when this food is not available. I have seen some, in the South of Spain, that ate the avocado trees' leathery leaves! It is a very good example of the domination of the fittest.

Jenny.

- It's quite the opposite! This beetle is not relevant but its food is meaningful. It always attacks the strongest trees, which means that the weakest ones survive! So?

Barbara.
-Darwin was not a plant biologist!

Jenny.
-Spit it out: the facts don't fit the theory!

Barbara.
-By the way, what are you doing here?

Jenny.
-... I don't remember!

```
        *
  *         *
        *
```

Barbara.
-Let's continue, Adam. Take your building blocks. No! We are going to do something new now. I am going to teach you the American Sign Language.

Adam.
-Rrrr...

Barbara.
-What? Is there anything wrong?
Adam.
-Rrrr... rrrr....

Barbara.

-I prefer that. How stubborn you can be sometimes! Show me your hands... They are beautiful... so strong... Show me your arms... Move them a little bit, not too much... You are not flexible. You are not elegant... You are an ape!... It is not your fault, it's mine... I should have studied bigger brains. Do you know that gorillas' brain weighs 500 grams? It is a great quantity of grey matter! My colleagues, at the University of Edelpic, have tried to make them speak. They have failed. It is strange, yours is smaller but you seem quite smart... Anyway, I should have studied the dolphins: 1700 grams of pure intelligence! Their larynx, their mouth cannot produce the sounds I need... Flesh is everything... isn't it?

Adam.

-....

Barbara.

-You are not saying anything.

Adam.

-....

Barbara.

-You could say something.

Adam.

-....

Barbara.

-After all I have done for you. You are so... ungrateful. Do not forget that I am the one who turned your obtuse intelligence into what you are today. I have created you! What have you got to say for yourself?

Adam.

-....

Barbara.
-Speak!

What a strange couple: the blond talkative Dr. Frankenstein and the brown-eyed silent chimpanzee. There are too many Dr. Frankensteins in the universities, and too many enslaved apes. The ones are not smart enough to understand their research is pointless, while the existence of the others cannot increase the level of awareness of these stupid doctors. He is looking, with his big black eyes, in the frantic pale blue eyes of Barbara. Both are salt statues gazing at the bottomless emptiness of the other. What do you want to tell her, Adam? I am not her, you can answer me! Adam... can you think?...

Chapter 4:

It cannot be the end.

The computer that controls the Invictus is a work of art. The engineers who conceived it wanted to create a machine that would be able to think instead of the crew. Man is not always driven by rational thoughts: a reliable apparatus can give him accurate data but, for mysterious reasons, he will not understand the unquestionable facts, take a bad decision and, sometimes, crash a plane, or a spaceship. The mission was too important to run such a risk. We must not underestimate the stress produced by these long missions and its mental consequences. One year in a tin can drive rats, monkeys and human beings crazy! Therefore, the computer scientists put their heart and soul into the making of this artificial intelligence. However, I know it does not think! Actually, it combines pieces of information and try to produce a logical conclusion, but it only deals with technical things: vectors, algorithms, square roots of highly foreseeable numbers. If you feed it with life and human feelings you will always bring disaster. There is no such thing as artificial intelligence because computers are the slaves of other people's will. There is no intelligence in slavery. It is something that comes from the acceptance of one's own bottomless ignorance. It does not follow the omnipotence of other people's illusion of technical grandeur. The awareness of one's own limitations is the key to the holy garden of wit. Besides, I don't like its voice and manners. It behaves as if it were a human being but it only apes its creators: parrots also speak but they don't pretend they are more than birds.

Computer.
-John, may I have a word with you?

John.
-You may.

Computer.
-According to the data, we may get into trouble when we reach the vicinity of Militus.

John.
-What kind of trouble?

Computer.
-Meteorites.

John.
-Don't we have an efficient deflector shield against that?

Computer.
-Yes, we have, of course.

John.
-Have you turned it on?

Computer.
-Yes, I have.

John.
-So, what's the problem, indeed?

Computer.
-A miscalculation may occur.

John.
-A miscalculation! Can you miscalculate computer?

Computer.
-Of course not! I am perfect.

John.
-I hope so. When do we reach Militus?

Computer.
-In ten minutes.

John.
-Already!

Computer.
-Yes, John… May I say anything else?

John.
-You may.

Computer.
-We have just been hit by small debris, but there is no damage…

John.
-Is the deflector shield at its maximum power?

Computer.
-No, the pieces of information I have allege the danger zone will be reached in five minutes.

John.
-Raise the level of protection right now.

Computer.
-It is not necessary.

John.
-Raise it.

Computer.

-We have been hit by a meteorite. There is some damage. Deflector shield: full power.

John.
-Describe all the damage.

Computer.
-There are holes in the structure. There is at least one in the water tank. Level of water supply: 3.12 %! There is one hole in the shuttle garage. The shuttles are OK. There is an unidentified problem in the power plant. Nuclear reactor shut down... the emergency power generator is operating.

John.
-Do we have enough power to continue the journey?

Computer.
-No.

John.
-How much power do we have?

Computer.
-12% of your needs.

John.
-Can we return to Earth?

Computer.
-... I don't know.

John.
-Is it a joke?

Computer.
-No.

John.
-Why don't you know?

Computer.
-... Because there are random factors.

John.
-Explain yourself.

Computer.
-We may hit another meteorite on our way back.

John.
-Why?

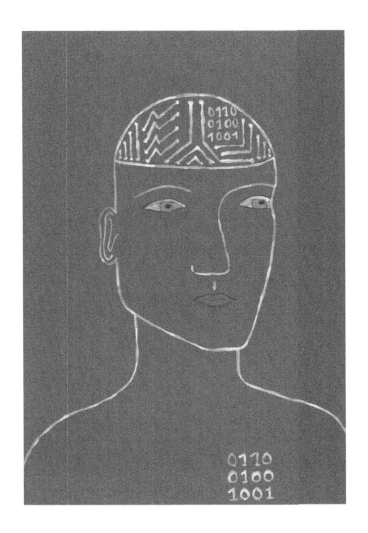

Computer.
-Why not?

John.
-Your hypothesis must be corroborated by facts.

Computer.
-… John, may I…

John.
-Shut up, computer!

I guess John is upset. He has turned off the computer's voice. The infallibility of things is an illusion. Ideas are, sometimes, infallible, not things. Well, I only know one: the poetical movement of heavenly geometry.

*
*　　*
*

Paul.
-I have felt a small vibration, John.

Barbara.
-The electricity has gone off in my laboratory.

Jenny.
-There is no running water in my cabin.

Peter.
- John, I don't understand: the heater, in the greenhouse, has stopped blowing warm air.

John.
-We have been hit by a meteorite. We have some problems...

Barbara.
-How is it possible? Don't we have a deflector shield?

John.
-A miscalculation from the computer.

Paul.
-It is impossible: computers do not miscalculate, they just misinterpret.

Jenny.
-You mean they misjudge.

Peter.
-I would rather say they misunderstand.

John.
-It messed up everything!

Paul, Jenny, Peter and Barbara.
-Oh!

Paul.
-So, what are we supposed to do?

John.
-Fix the problem without the help of this stupid machine.

Barbara.
-Beware, John, he can hear you: he might be offended. Have you noticed?
He is not talking.

John.
-**It** is a thing; **it** cannot be offended; and I have disabled the speakers.

Paul.
-Is there much damage?

John.
-We have lost a lot of water and the power plant is not functioning. I don't
really know what is wrong inside but if we don't find it, we are not certain
we will be able to continue the journey. Water is not a real problem since
we are next to Militus.

Paul.
-Do we have enough power to go back?

John.
-I don't know.

Barbara.
-Are we going to die?

John.
-It is not impossible.

Paul.
-We cannot die. If we die, mankind will disappear. They won't be able to survive very long.

Peter.
- Humanity cannot end like that.

Paul.
-It is not humanity that would end, it is barbarity. Actually, the history of mankind has not started yet. What you read in books is a tedious description of manslaughters.

Peter.
-It is even worse.

Paul.
-Why?

Peter.
-Because dawn does not sound the trumpet of the Apocalypse. It is a beginning, the moment when the feeble light of the sun makes visible the roads myriads of conscious minds will have to follow in order to build a graceful future together. The beginning has not started! It cannot be the end. I must go to the power plant.

Paul.
-I will go with you.

Jenny, Barbara, John.
-So will I.

*

*   *

*

      The power plant is located at the bottom of the spacecraft. At the end of an endless corridor, the heavy security door exhibits a radiation warning sign that makes them uncomfortable. Did they really want to ignore the fantastic quantity of electricity they need came from this source of energy? They open the door. In the airlock, they put on their personal protective equipment and their helmet. A soft blue light wraps them in an unreal iridescent outfit. Their breathing accelerates. Their angst is palpable. John faces the control panel in search of the causes of the breakdown. The others snoop around in order to check whether there is a mechanical problem. It is strange: there are no holes in the walls, nor deformations.

Paul.
-I don't see anything.

Jenny.
-Neither do I.

Peter.
-Everything is OK here.

Barbara.

-John, I am scared!

John.
-What's wrong Barbara? What have you seen?

Barbara.
-... I must see my husband!

Peter.
-John, she has not seen anything.

Jenny walking towards her.
-Barbara, there is no reason for panicking: you are not alone. We are here, with you.

Barbara.
-Our wedding was so beautiful. I remember my dress... I was like a princess, a princess without a crown but with an exquisite rhinestone tiara... Jenny, do you miss your husband?

Jenny.
-... I would like to say yes...

Paul.
-I miss my wife!

Barbara.
-We are alone here... I have chosen my husband, I have not chosen to be with you.

Paul.
-You never choose all the people with whom you live, but you always choose to build a present together and a brighter future.

Barbara.
-... Maybe. The same kind of people must build their future together.

Paul.
-Not the same people; different, I should say very dissimilar people must define where they want to go. Sameness leads to nowhere since it kills the possibility of choosing and, with it, any kind of movement. Sameness is the negation of life and, at the same time, the embodiment of the fear of life.

Barbara.
-How could very different people go in the same direction?

Paul.
-Because, in spite of their different opinions, they share one essential quality: goodness. Goodness has different faces but one essence. Once established, it would reproduce the conditions of its propagation and eternally remain the owner of a humanized universe.

Barbara, Jenny and Peter.
-...

John.
-I think I have found what is going wrong.

Peter.
-Evilness is the owner of our world!

John.
-... The computer has switched off the power plant without reason!... Barbara, I think you will see your husband again! Jenny, check whether there is a leak in the cooling system.

Jenny.
-There is nothing, John...

John.
-Let's turn the power on.

Paul.
-Wow... light, again.

Jenny.
-You are luminous, John.

Peter.
-You mean brilliant!

Barbara.
-I would rather say bright!

John.
-No, I am not; Paul is!

Chapter 5:

Water.

Militus is a yellowish planet, a kind of gigantic Sahara desert, a dusty mineral reality. It is not appealing unless you like geology. Actually, there are lots of strange stony structures once carved by water. The hills look like immobile giants waiting for an improbable David. The wind carries sand in its furious arms. Sometimes, it sprinkles this powdery silicon over the canyons and the missing oceans. It is a scintillating snowfall that covers our giants with a suffocating dust. Where has the water gone? Geomorphology does not lie: it is water that has created these shapes, not the wind. Is it below the surface? Yes, but where exactly? There is no time to waste: they need water and must find some. The wordless computer has given them a map with the sites where they could find the precious liquid. Will it be fresh water? It is very unlikely but salt water will be easily turned into drinking water, in the Invictus. As for the pleasure of diving into the turquoise tumultuous mountain streams, they can just forget it, but it is not important since they will soon reach Empycrist II. There, they will rediscover the infancy of planet Earth. They will enjoy the wonders of what they have lost and will regain.

John.
-Paul, what is your opinion of the maps?

Paul.
-Pretty: there are many beautiful colours but I am not convinced there is water on this planet. There is no trace of plant life. Everything is so dry!

John.
-Militus is not Mars: there is an atmosphere, which provides evidence that water has not escaped into space.

Paul.
-Where are we going to land?

John.
-In the canyon you see over there.

Paul.
-Beware, it is a riverbed.

John.
-Paul, there is no water on the surface of this planet.

Paul.
-... Of course... How will we be able to find a spot where there is ground water?

John.
-It is elementary, Paul: find limestone and you will also find water underneath.

Paul.
-Do you think we will see traces of moisture on the ground?

John.
-Don't worry; your detector will help you! I know you are a physicist, not
a geologist.

Paul.
-John, I think I don't like stones. Everything is so mineral on this planet.
Even a fennec would ask for shade, flowers and water. I hate deserts; it is
not only the heat that I don't like, it is this unbearable silence.

John.
-I have visited the Sahara desert... in summer. I remember... the sky: so
blue! Azure, like my grandmother's eyes. A beautiful colour for a woman's
eyes... a bewitching colour.

Paul.
-The bluest blue needs grey. I visited Scotland in August 3057. I
remember the tormented clouds, the sound of the raindrops on the roofs,
at night, the scent of the air, in the morning, the greyish lakes that are
never thirsty. I love the rain.

John.
-We are going to land.

Paul.
-We must find a lake, in a cave.

John.
-I am not very optimistic, Paul.

*
*   *
*

John.

-Does your localizer work?

Paul.

-Yes, it does. So does my radio.

John.

-It's best to separate in order to cover a lot of ground. Go this way; I am going that way. Never switch off your radio.

Paul.

-I won't.

...

Paul.

-I have been walking for an hour and I haven't seen any trace of moisture.

John.

-What is the nature of the soil?

Paul.

-It is limestone. I can see the sediment layers on the sides of the canyon. It is such a long history. It is hard to believe there was a river here, before. What happened to this planet?

John.

-Its orbit changed, what modified the composition of its atmosphere. It was so close to its sun that a portion of the water evaporated. I guess the other portion is underneath the ground.

Paul.

-John, where you are, do you have these strange hills that look like giants?

John.

-Yes, and I feel like a Lilliputian. It is strange, I don't see you on my detector. Is it working?

Paul.

-It does not seem to be working, but it is not a problem: since I am following the riverbed, I can't get lost.

John.

-There is a lot of wind here, and so much sand.

Paul.

-I am covered with dust. What an unpleasant place. The Earth is not like that.

John.

-Oh, no, it was not like that.

Paul.

-What's this noise?

John.

-Some stones are falling.

Paul.
-It is an earthquake! I...

John.
-Could you say that again?

Paul.
-...

John.
-Paul, do you copy?

Paul.
-...

John.
-**PAUL**, are you OK?

Paul.
-Yes, John; I am just thinking... How did we get here?

John.
-I don't know.

Paul.
-You don't know or you don't want to know?

John.
-I don't want to know it.

Paul.

-But, if you don't, and if we don't, we will never learn from our mistakes. We condemn our species to an endless agony. John, I am asking you again!

John.
-Because... they are insane! They are unable to understand they are not God!

Paul.
-They are not insane: insane people know they are not God. Actually, they believe He is about to slash them to pieces, which is wrong: that is why they are mad!

John.
-Because... they are simpleminded.

Paul.
-Have you noticed? They seem so normal but, at the same time, intellectually limited and desperately... childish. Most of them are five-year-old boys and girls sharing the same immature daydreams, selfishness and whims.

John.
-Maturity, is the goal of a human's life.

Paul.
-No, it is the beginning.

John.
-What is the goal in that case, and what is the purpose of the universe?

Paul.
-You know the answer! Man is the ultimate goal: you may not understand it but you do feel it!

John.
-I have found water; I can smell it.

Paul.
-I am coming, John.

*

*   *

*

Paul.
-Where is it?

John.
-In that direction. Look here, there is some water, not a lot, but it seems there is a stream, which means we could find some more.

Paul.
-You are right: there is a stream. Let's follow this tunnel.

John.
-There is a strange smell.

Paul.
-Yes, it smells like mildew or... fungus!

John.
-But my detector says there is no life here!

Paul.
-The eternal life of fungi is not considered life by your detector!

John.
-Look at the drips on the walls.

Paul.
-Don't walk that fast, I can hardly breathe.

John.
-Hurry up, I am sure I am going to find water. Look over there: a pool.

Paul.
-Did you hear that?

John.
-What?

Paul.
-Drops. Keep quiet!... Yes, drops.

John.
-Of course, the sound of water drops falling in a...

They suddenly entered a huge cave where they found... a lake. Paul looked at the water as if it were the Holy Grail. He touched it with his right hand and put it feverishly on his right cheek: the salt almost burned his skin! John kneeled down and touched it. The light of his torch turned the opaque salty lake into a transparent aquamarine. Then, they slowly stood up and went back to the shuttle, in order to bring back a pipe. They put the end of the pipe in the very middle of the lake and sat down. It started to suck up the liquid. They remained silent. The noise of the pump covered the sound of the water drops. They looked like two grateful believers, in a deserted cathedral, thanking God for this extraordinary gift. There were no prayers, no songs, no demented organs, no inspired sermons; just faith and eternity. Sometimes, words are meaningless. Thoughts are truer than words, they are cathedrals, palpitating in the thirstiest deserts. Man does not need to speak; he must feel, understand and act. He is his own cathedral.

Chapter 6:

Bad news from the Earth.

Dizziness! A child is born; he grows up in inhumanity and remains all his life in barbarity, but he fathers a child. Dizziness! His daughter follows the same path and gives birth to the grandchild of the first monster. The history of mankind is an everlasting inferno, for man has decided to eat his own liver forever. I am falling: the idea of endless tragedy tortures me.

They got the news this morning, and it is not good. The Statue of liberty has decided to burn its bronze toga! The Creator cannot destroy his creature because it does not belong to him anymore. He has blessed it with the eventuality of consciousness. Therefore, it belongs to the logic of the one who conceives and inspires. Individual consciousness prevents man from disappearing. What happens if he does not reach this stage? He turns gold into lead. This morning, the sun woke up a world of lead; the Statue of Liberty opened its mouth in order to pronounce the unspeakable word: WAR!

Can you hear this sound? They are blowing the trumpets, for they want to destroy Masada. They have put their shining suit of armour on, in order to hide their vices. On the crowns of their leaders there are scintillating rubies that will soon be stained with the blood they do not want to see. Eve of the battle: the quixotic murderers murmur, the walls of Masada shiver, I am in pain. In the midst of a glade, a drummer boy awakens the beasts. Is it Dresden or Gettysburg? All the battles are the same. Sinners, please, don't do this! You cannot be that bad. Don't you know that red is the colour of sorrow? Sinners, do you really think you are going to become gods? Destruction is not a celestial attribute but a chthonic subterfuge. Fools, you are about to become the conscious embodiment of the Devil. Please, say no to yourself!

Can you hear this noise? Is it the roar of the drums? No, it is the sound of the heartbeats of the crucifiers and their victims, it is the echo of the bombs falling on Dresden, Tokyo and me. Planet Earth is burning: the skies are furious. It's noon, vapors of savagery are infecting the air: they can hardly breathe but they can kill. The Trevi Fountain is crying: the past of Rome is shaking and trembling. The giant sequoias of California are burning: the present of mankind is running away. Hell! Hell on Earth! The Hermes of Praxiteles won't be able to protect the little Dionysus he is holding in his arms. It is a sad sunny day and the statues, in the archeological museum of Delphi, are bleeding. Apollo is in mourning: the center of the world is hiccupping. Perched on the top of the Tholos, a falcon is gazing at the world. On one side there is mankind and its unbearable cruelty, on the other side there is nature and its peaceful beauty. He cannot look at the first without thinking about the other. His head turns in the direction of the sea. Time stops. In front of him there is a sea of olive trees, and an ocean of orange trees. Green, everything is so green. He breathes and jumps into the lightness of the breeze. The sun carries him to the empyreal blue of the sky. Blue, I want you blue: blue the Gulf of Corinth, blue the skies over Delphi, blue the eyes of the silent charioteer in the sanctuary. You cannot kill the bird: he does belong to eternal nature. You cannot kill the falcon: I am sure he will escape. White falcon, fly high, higher than their inhumane nature.

*

*   *

*

Test director.
-John, can you hear me?

John.
-Yes, I can.

Test director.
-How are you?

John.
-I miss the Earth, especially the daily cycle.

Test director.
-And the others?

John.
-They are fine. There is so much space here that we barely see one another. Each one of us is lost in his own solitude.

Test director.
-So, they won't hear me.

John.
-Oh no, I haven't seen them in two days and I can assure you that I am alone.

Test director.
-Have you watched the news?

John.
-I haven't since it is always the same thing: a terrorist attack here, a revolution there, and a war over there. There is nothing new under the sun: four Romans and five Carthaginians are lying on the ground!

Test director.
-You should have watched the news.

John.
-What's the matter?

Test director.
-There is a war going on here.

John.
-You mean the United States are involved in a conflict somewhere in the world!

Test director.
-I mean there is a full-scale war.

John.
-Many Romans and Carthaginians involved?

Test director.
-The whole planet. It is World War III here!

John.
-Are you joking?

Test director.
-I am not and that's why I want to talk to you.

John.
-I guess you want me to go faster but, you know, if there are no plants on Empycrist II, we will not be unable to feed the people you are planning to send here.

Test director.
-You are missing the point. We must cancel the mission.

John.
-You may give up your stupid idea of mass migration but I am telling you that I am going to Empycrist.

Test director.
-I am asking you to come back.

John.
-You must be joking. If there is a war, Earth is not a safe place to be! So, why should we come back? To be immolated on the altar of your insanity?

Test director.
-You must come back.

John.
-I won't: why should I obey you?

Test director.
-We pay: you obey!

John.
-In your raging world, money does not mean anything anymore. So, I don't care.

Test director.
-We have the power...

John.
-Which power? What does it mean? You have the power to kill yourself: that's it. You don't have the power to give the orders. Reason commands, not madness. Answer me: are you sane?

Test director.
-... Ye...

John.
-You are not! You are mad... all of you!

Test director.
-... We are your employer!

John.
-Not any more: I quit!

Test director.
-You cannot do that. This has never happened before... and why would you do that?

John.
-Because my reason compels me to follow my free will, not your ravings.

Test director.
-But…

John.
-Shut up! The conversation is over.

*

*　　*

*

John.
-Jenny, the flight director upsets me very much.

Jenny.
-Why?

John.
-He wants us to come back.

Jenny.
-Why should we come back? Have these people changed their mind about the migration?

John.
-Well, yes… Have you watched the news?

Jenny.
-Of course not… Planet Earth is so far away already… I think that is the least of my worries.

John.
-They are in trouble.

Jenny.

-This is not a surprise.

John.

-It is worse this time.

Jenny.

-Worse than what? Worse than Spartacus' ordeal on the Appian Way? Worse than World War II? How can it be worse? It can't! Don't you remember? History books are still bleeding!

John.

-It is worse because I think they have already destroyed a huge part of mankind and… nobody told me but… I think they have used nuclear weapons. You can easily imagine the consequences.

Jenny.

-They don't need atomic bombs to kill themselves. Give them a knife and they will kill all the people in their neighborhood. Don't give them anything and they will strangle their brothers and sisters. Even with their hands roped together, they could nuke the whole universe in their mind. John, what do you really know about this war?

John.

-I don't know a lot of things; I am just guessing.

Jenny.

-I would prefer facts because, if I start guessing, I will imagine the worst-case scenario. I will remember that man doesn't always bury the dead. I will understand his history led him from the charming painted caves of Lascaux to this burning present.

John.

-Decadence was not the only option… Call them!

Jenny.
-Port Isabel, Jenny's speaking. Can you hear me?

Test director.
-...

Jenny.
-Is there a connection problem?

John.
-No, everything works fine.

Jenny.
-Can you hear me?

Test director.
-...

John.
-If you want information, I can show you the records the computer has received. I guess you will get to know what has been bombed.

Jenny.
-I need something more accurate. They work for the U. S. Army: every day they receive the military reports.

John.
-Port Isabel, do you copy?

Test director.
-...

John.

-Well, we have lost contact with them.

Jenny.
-We are alone now.

John.
-We have always been alone! We are just without them, but with ourselves!

Jenny.
-I am scared!

John.
-Oh please, Jenny, you are starting to look like Barbara!

Jenny.
-What are we going to do?

John.
-Go to Empycrist: there is no other option. I have decided to go there!

Jenny.
-You can decide for yourself, not for the others. Our lives are also at stake.

Jenny to herself.
-What am I going to do?

John.
-Get some rest; we will decide tomorrow.

Chapter 7:

What must we do?

John.

-Thank you for being here on such short notice. Jenny has told you that we have lost contact with Port Isabel and that there is a war on Planet Earth. So, we need to talk about what we are going to do. Actually, there are two possibilities: reach Empycrist II, settle down and live, or go back to Earth, get killed, or starve, or whatever!

Barbara.

-You are not really objective, John.

Paul.

-John is right: if we go back, we won't survive.

Barbara.

-This is your point of view, not mine.

Jenny.

-It is not a point of view, it is the truth.

Barbara.

-Truth does not exist, there are only opinions.

Paul.

-The universe is not an opinion; it is a fact.

Jenny.

-Or a cumbersome opinion!

Barbara.

-I mean…

Paul.

-Poor Barbara, you don't mean anything! There is no meaning in your life: only illusions!

Barbara.
-I want to see my husband...

Paul.
-He is dead!

Peter.
-Paul, you could be more tactful.

John.
-Anyway... we must vote.

Jenny.
-We? Could you define "we"?

John.
-I mean the five of us.

Jenny.
-You mean the four of us.

John speaking to Jenny.
-What's the matter with you?

Jenny.
-What's the matter with Barbara! We cannot recognize the validity of an election if the voters are not perfectly sane.

Paul.
-It is not enough. They should also be intelligent and wise. Thus, I am not certain there are four voters here... I would say: three!

Jenny.
-What are you hinting at?

Paul.
-You are not what some people call a genius! You spend your time learning languages but what do you do with all this knowledge? Nothing! You can say "hello" and "could you pass me the salt please" in 27 different languages but we never hear you say intelligent things, especially in English! I suppose you only speak words of wisdom in Coptic!

Jenny.
-At least I speak; I am not dumb like Peter.

Peter.
-I am not dumb: I have nothing to say to you. You are neither pretty nor intelligent. You are so unpleasant and ordinary.

Jenny.
-...

Paul.
-Well, we are not here to love one another. We must vote; that's it.

Jenny.
-I don't want Barbara to vote.

Peter.
-I don't want Jenny to vote.

John.
-I know; we won't vote: I will decide. Democracy is a dangerous regime; it always leads to dictatorship, massacres and so on.

Paul.
-You are right John; and as a smart guy, a smart captain, you would make a good dictator. I've got a better idea: we should be evaluated on our mental abilities. Tests do not lie, even though some of them are questionable.

Peter.
-That's the understatement of the year! A schizophrenic can have an IQ of 125, which is more than the IQ of a well-balanced person!

Paul.
-The IQ test is, of course, not reliable. I dare say it is always illogical. Hermann Goring, a smart guy with an intelligence quotient of 138, is responsible for the death of almost 60 million people. It is not why I call a sign of intelligence! But don't worry: I have other tests dealing with interpersonal skills and general knowledge. I can assure you that they give a good idea of the level of intelligence of people.

John.
-Well, let's try your tests.

Jenny.
-I don't want to take these tests.

John.
-Barbara will be evaluated and you don't want to follow this procedure?

Jenny.
-The problem is not me but her!

John.
-You will follow the rules, my rules. Tomorrow, like all of us, you will take the test. Jenny, the conversation is over!

*

   *   *

   *

John.

-I have the results, and they make sense. Paul achieved the best results: 97% of the answers are right. It is not a surprise. Paul is very clever and knowledgeable; isn't he? Peter scored 90%; I scored 87%. As for Jenny, 38 % of the answers are... wrong, which is a lot.

Barbara.

-Did I get a good grade?

John.

-You scored 49%.

Barbara.

-I don't understand: the questions were so easy.

John.

-Apparently not: you had many problems with the interpersonal items!

Barbara.

-What does it mean?

John.

-It means that your perception of others is almost psychotic. It is obvious you do not understand people's elementary behavior.

Paul.

-Give her an example so that she may understand more easily.

John.

-You are right, Paul. Well, let's take item 37: "what do you fell when someone you don't know looks at you, in the street"? You answered, without hesitation: "I feel important: when men look at me, it's because I am pretty. Men always fall in love with me at first sight".

Paul.
-A very interesting item.

Peter.
-A very interesting answer too.

Barbara.
-It is true: men adore me!

John.
-The problem is that a person is not a man: a person is a person! It could have been a woman.

Jenny.
-It could have been a monkey!

John.
-Stop making fun of people, Jenny: your results do not allow such behavior! So, Barbara, what is your reaction when a woman looks at you, in the street?

Barbara.
-I hate that. It is always for the same reason: jealousy. Women are mean: they think I am going to steal their husband because I am prettier than them! Look at Jenny; she is rude towards me because she is jealous. But it's insane! I am not going to steal your husband: he is on Planet Earth, not here! You should see a psychiatrist!

Paul.

-It is not completely wrong.

John.
-No, it is not completely wrong but it is completely stupid. Barbara, you won't vote.

Barbara.
-I...

John.
-Barbara, don't make me lose my temper.

Barbara sighing.
-I won't, John...

Jenny.
-Fine, the four of us will vote.

John.
-No!

Jenny.
-No?

John.
-You won't vote!

Jenny.
-Why?

John.
-The items dealing with interpersonal skills are OK, even though they show us your true personality.

Peter.

-She is so unpleasant.

Paul.

-And ill-mannered. The kind of person you don't introduce to your mother!

Peter.

-The kind of person you are happy not to know!

John.

-Actually, this test reveals your abysmal lack of general knowledge, and this is a problem. Sane people can decide for themselves and others thanks to knowledge. They are sane, what enables them to perceive what is real or not; that's fine! However, without knowledge, they cannot fully understand the consequences of their deeds and are also condemned to ignore the essence of everything.

Peter.

-Give us an example of her lack of education.

John.

-Item 79: "who wrote Romeo and Juliet"? Your dismaying answer is, drum roll please, …: "Tchaikovsky"!

Peter and Paul.

-Gosh!

John.

-Isn't it a crime against humanity?

Peter.
-Too many ballet classes maybe!

John.
-It gets worse; listen to that: "who sculpted the Hermes of Praxiteles"? Her answer: "Phidias"!

Barbara.
-She must be crazy.

John.

-You might be right Barbara. Jenny, you won't vote!

Jenny.
-But...

John.
-Don't make me lose my temper!

Jenny sighing.
-Of course not, John...

*
*   *
*

John.
-Here are the issues on which we have to decide. Do you want to go to Empycrist II? Do you want to go back to Planet Earth? Do you want to choose another planet?

Paul.
-Isn't it a little bit biased John? It is clear you want to go to Empycrist, and this is the first question. You are trying to influence the voters this way, aren't you?

John.
-I am not trying anything, but it is obvious this is the only reasonable option!

Peter.
-I have a question John; what will happen if we answer "no" each time?

John.
-There is an easy answer: in this case, I will decide!

Peter.

-What if we answer "yes"?

John.

-Don't be ridiculous, we are intelligent: we have opinions, at least I have. If you do so, my vote will break the tie.

Paul.

-How will we vote?

John.

-By a show of hands.

Peter.

-Personally, I would prefer a secret ballot.

John.

-It doesn't make any sense. If you have an idea and regard it as fair, you explain it and fight for it.

Paul.

-John is right; you don't have anything to hide: we will not stone you to death!

John.

-Fine, if we all agree on everything, let's vote.

That is what they did, and the result was not a surprise: they all agreed to continue their journey to Empycrist. Was this vote a good idea? I am not so sure: when reason reigns, whatever the parameters, the result is always the same. Hence, in the different systems of government, if the people who decide are sane and knowledgeable, they always follow the diktat of reason! It is not the same if some of them are ignorant, immature or completely crazy. In this case, you must cross your fingers and hope the leaders will not implement a demagogic policy, and follow the voters' ravings. Most of the time, unfortunately, they are as crazy as the citizens since they emanate from this wild logic. Don't forget that Hitler came to power thanks to democratic elections; and look at what they did to Planet Earth: they voted in order to destroy it! Immature, unbalanced, insane, or ignorant people are unable to understand. If you allow them to take political actions, they will nuke the planet. The mind rabble must not vote!

They went back to their cabins and started to think about Empycrist. Actually, nobody has ever walked on its surface. What will they find? Is it the Promised Land they see in their dreams? The Garden of Eden is a place you build with your own hands; it is not given to you, for you don't deserve it. When you plant each tree, each little flower, and wait a long time to see the result, your dreams are rewarded with the relevance of your work. When you take care of a plant, something so different from you, you can feel you are trying to create a kind of paradise on Earth. Hush! At the moment, they are watering their dreams...

Chapter 8:

The Promised Land.

Empycrist, at last! Anxious, they are pressed against their seats. They are about to leave the planet's orbit. Behind them, there is the terrifying darkness of outer space; in front of them, there is the empyreal blue of Empycrit's oceans. They are about to start all over again. The human adventure is not over. Five people are going to breathe, walk, sing, paint and sow. In the greenhouse, the orange trees are blooming. There is water on Empycrist: you will drink soon. Everything is quiet; everyone is silent. Bang, bang: their hearts are beating. There will be no drums, no arrows, no war dances. Jenny is looking at the clouds. Bang, bang: this is the music of your hopes. Peter, how do you imagine the Promised Land? Green? It will be green, and blue! Paul can hardly breathe. The ground is close now. They can see grass... trees, and flowers too. Barbara is sighing. John is crying. It should have been different...

The door opens. Can you smell this? It is indescribable. It is the smell of peace. The butterflies welcome them. It is the dawn of felicity. The honey bees sing; the sun shines; time stops. They walk in the Garden of Eden. Millions of daffodils wave; billions of peonies bow. The pine trees shiver. Can you hear this sound? Birds! There are birds and they sing for you. A deer jumps into a river. Two squirrels play with a pine cone. The hinds look at them. Where are the cavemen? There is none. Where are the serpent and its apple? Here there are no apple trees, no serpents, no human beings. This is a gift from the universe to you. The sky is so blue! The grass is so green! Gaze, don't destroy! Use, don't adulterate! They sit down. They touch the water. The silent frogs look at them. So many miles, so much pain. I am ageless; I was born billions of years ago, and I remember... everything... Time, don't move! Let me feel this absence of pain...

Bang, bang: my heart is beating; time is moving again and the honey bees are starting to dance. The colours are exploding: Nature is blooming. Today is a good day to start to live in peace. Don't forget your past, for this original sin is the sleeping pain that will prevent you from repeating the same mistakes. Man, listen to her: she is about to teach you how to become yourself. You have reached Empycrist, at last: your odyssey is over. Reef the sails in, cast the anchor and **BE**!

*
*   *
*

Peter.
-I did not expect that.

John.
-I am speechless.

Paul.
-So am I.

Barbara.
-It is so…

Jenny.
-So unexpected and beautiful…

John.
-It is strange: it looks like the Earth.

Peter.
-No, it looks like the past of the Earth!

Barbara.
-Was it so…

Peter.
-Yes, it was so amazing.

John.
-But we have travelled through space not time!

Paul.
-We are not on Earth, for sure. This sun is not ours, and the planets of this planetary system are... different!

John.
-Different but so familiar!

Barbara.
-It doesn't make any sense.

Peter.
-It does make sense but we don't see it.

Paul.
-What is the meaning of the universe?

Jenny.
-Us!

Paul.
-I don't understand you.

Jenny.
-All this exists because we exist.

John.
-Is it a creation of our minds, the hallucination of poor thirsty fellows looking for an oasis of peace in the very middle of the desert of their sorrows?

Jenny.
-No, the exquisite and perfect mechanism works like a perpetual-motion clock. Everything is automatic, even the plants and the animals follow a kind of automatic existence. And inside the everlasting mechanism there is man. Man does not dance like the other things.

Paul.
-Man cannot dance because he is not an automaton: he thinks.

Jenny.
-Therefore, he is different from all the rest!

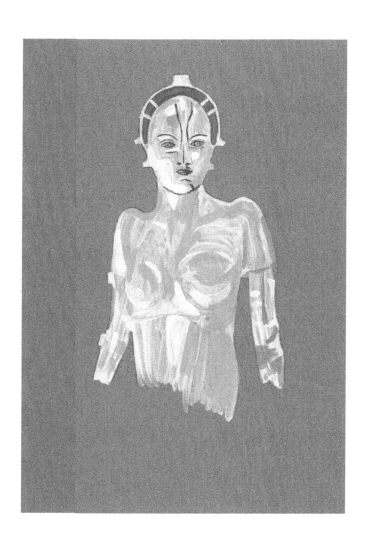

Paul.
-You are right Jenny: man has a special position. The will that created this unimaginable motion has given a part of itself, I mean its will, thinking skills and humanity, to one creature: man!

Jenny.
-The mind has given a mind to man, so that he may understand everything after a titanic war against himself. If he loses this war, he fails to become a man and falls into barbarity.

Paul.
-If he wins, he becomes a human being, understands his duties and takes the lead: he starts to create... Consciousness creates, barbarity exterminates...

John.
-But what must he create?

Jenny.
-He must create what we are going to create: a humanized universe.

Peter.
-He must create a civilization.

Barbara.
-Are we going to do this here?

John.
-We are five!

Peter.
-We are not here for that.

Barbara.

-Why are we here?

Peter.
-To find ourselves. We have reached the garden of consciousness and we have found the tree of the knowledge of... the truth!

*

*   *

*

Barbara.
-What are we going to do?

John.
-Go back!

Barbara crying.
-Everything is so much... larger than life here. Everything is perfect and... we will be happy! I don't want to go back: my husband is dead, your relatives and friends are dead... there's nothing left.

Peter.
-Man's life is a tragedy. The birds you see, the flower you touch don't suffer like us.

Paul.
-They don't suffer like us but it seems they are expecting something of us. They are looking at us as if we were going to tell them something extraordinary important, as if we were their creator.

John.
-What will we find on Earth?

Jenny.

-Very few people.

Barbara.
-We could bring them here, hasn't it been planned this way?

Paul.
-They must not come here. This divine perfection is not for them; it was for us.

John.
-What will we create on Earth?

Peter.
-A kind of paradise.

John.
-What kind of paradise?

Peter.
-Something that will not look like the past.

Jenny.
-Something that could last forever.

John.
-What kind of society?

Paul.
-I don't know yet.

Barbara.
-Are there still enough people to start all over again? ... I cannot have children: I am too old.

Jenny.
-I would have liked to have children.

Peter.
-I prefer other people's children. When I look at them, I don't see myself; I don't see their parents either. I just see life and the eventuality of wisdom.

Barbara.
-They will have children, and I won't love them: I will raise them. I'll love them when they become human beings.

Paul.
-We will educate them; old age will saw the seeds of consciousness.

They look at one another and don't speak anymore. The honey bees fly; the birds sing. Time, once again, seems to stop. Empycrist shines. I am hypnotized by this ethereal reality. Like the shadow puppets of an improbable pantomime, they stand up slowly and walk towards the spaceship. Barbara's blue eyes dive into the impertinent blue of the sky. Jenny sighs. Peter picks up a flower; Paul touches the water again. John cries: I don't know why

Chapter 9:

The return trip.

In the greenhouse of the Invictus, it's always spring. It is not as beautiful as Empycrist but it is more real, even though everything is artificial. Actually, there are more imperfections here, what makes it more credible. Perfection is rare and, thus, almost unreal. Peter is watering the plants while Barbara is reading a book. She has left her apes alone, for I think she is starting to understand that her research leads to nowhere.

Peter.
-Good morning Barbara.

Barbara.
-Hi, Peter.

Peter.
-You are not with your chimpanzees: what's going on?

Barbara.
-I am fed up. My work doesn't serve any purpose anymore. Since everything has been destroyed on Earth, I won't go back to the University of Edelpic; I won't pretend I have discovered something extraordinary; I won't get promoted; I won't terrorize ignorant students, and I... Well what can I do with these monkeys?

Peter.
-Honestly? Nothing! When I was a biology student, I remember that I did not like to study mammals. These big animals that are, most of the time, at the top of the food chain, are quite useless. Of course, some monkeys disseminate the seeds of some plant species but when you compare them with insects, you understand that without these tiny little things, life would not exist.

Barbara.
-I realize that I should have studied something else. Materialism is a dead end!

Peter.
-I am happy to hear you say so; I am happy and surprised...

Barbara.

-By the way, I am reading a book that I have never read. It is *Alice's Adventures in Wonderland.*

Peter.
-I read it when I was a child and I did not understand anything. Then, I read it again in 11th grade and I understood it dealt with something essential: the eternal fight between madness and reason.

Barbara.
-I am quite surprised. The childish creatures you find inside seem so wild. It is not a children's book.

Peter.
-In think it was first written for an adult: the author himself. Then, it was turned into a children's book, a book millions of children have read and misunderstood!

Barbara.
-The world described is terrifying.

Peter.
-It is the world underneath your reason. It is darkness and fear.

Barbara.
-What does the rabbit represent?

Peter.
-The time you must tame, if you want to understand your live is not eternal. It is the noise of the clock which reminds you that you must hurry up, become a sane adult before you die, or…

Barbara.
-Or?

Peter.
-You die but you stay alive! You consciously enter the Hades of madness. You become the Queen of Hearts. You roar, you vociferate, for you suffer. Your suffering is abysmal because you know it is your fault. And your fault compels you to behead.

Barbara.
-Why?

Peter.
-Because, this way, you try to gouge out the eyes that condemn you, these small mirrors in which you see your own savagery.

Barbara.
-She is the devil.

Peter.
-Yes, she is.

Barbara.
-And Alice?

Peter.
-She escapes. Little Alices always grow up because they want to grow up.
Don't you think so... Alice?

Barbara.
-... Yes... I want to grow up!

Peter.
-You have changed a lot... Barbara.

Barbara.
-Maybe, I don't know.

Peter.
-You don't know but you feel it, don't you?

Barbara.
-... Yes... I do!

*
*　　　*
*

John.

-I saw Barbara this morning and she is not the same person.

Peter.
-It is true that she has changed a lot. She is more mature, more intelligent, more civilized. You see John, when there is reason, people can move mountains.

John.
-Does it mean that you have moved this mountain?

Peter.
-Mountains move by themselves. What you can do is show a good example but, in the end, it is the individual who chooses to learn or not.

John.
-What happens if people don't want to learn?

Peter.
-Society must find them an appropriate place so that they may help it to survive and prosper. At the same time, they must be guided towards what they have once rejected.

John.
-I am quite pessimistic about education. I remember my young years: it was such a mess that I think I learned nothing in what they used to call "high schools".

Peter.
-High schools! John, it's already too late! You learn when you are six, not fifteen!

John.
-I remember when I was six. Everything was new and appealing.

Peter.
-Were you afraid by what you did not know?

John.
-Oh no, I wanted to see the world.

Peter.
-When you were fifteen, were you still in a hurry to see the world?

John.
-I was more self-centered, I would say.

Peter.

-Didn't you want to be with people like you?

John.
-Maybe… But what can you teach to a child of six? Can you teach him reason and humanity?

Peter.
-Of course, you can, and it is not really difficult. When you teach them reading and writing, you must already emphasize the meaning of the words and grammatical structures. In a language, everything is meaningful. When people understand what they write or say, it is obvious they do not react to senseless impulses. Words and tenses are ideas; combine them and look at the result: you lead your pupils to a heaven of meaning.

John.
-But drawing, or Fine Arts in general, can serve the same purpose.

Peter.
-You are right, and it is even more obvious. When a child draws the piece of reality he has in front of him, he learns to accept it as it is. When you copy, you obey the truth.

John.
-But what if he transforms it?

Peter.
-It depends, but if he makes it more beautiful, it means that he has understood who he is; he has understood that goodness is the daughter of beauty.

*

*   *

*

Paul.
-I have just seen Barbara, she… there is… I don't know… she has changed!

John.
-Isn't she more mature?

Paul.
-You are right: more mature. It is a miracle!

John.
-I guess Peter has something to do with this miracle.

Paul.
-Peter, you must be a genius because the intelligence of people always deteriorates as they get older.

Peter.
-This is true if they live alone. Loneliness is the enemy of improvement. Man is not an island, for his strange nature compels him to learn how to become a human being thanks to other human beings. You won't achieve that by yourself. Actually, when a child looks at the grownups' behavior, he slowly understands who he is and who he will become. He first perceives he is not an outgrowth of his mother when his father tells her he is also his son. Later, when his teachers teach him how to spell his name, he understands the subtle difference between him and his image. At last, many years later, he becomes the father of his own father and becomes a humane man.

Paul.
-And you achieved that with Barbara in such a short period of time!

Peter.

-The problem with Barbara is that she was alone with herself. When people are really isolated, even though they seem to live in society, one person can make the difference. But I haven't changed Barbara: we have changed her.

Paul.
-It is obvious that during this journey we have talked a lot to her.

Peter.
-Our reasonable minds have shown her the way towards her reasonable humanity.

John.
-If I understand you correctly, if we had left her alone in her laboratory, she would have remained an old little girl!

Peter.
-It is even worse than that: she could have gone completely crazy. Pets, even when they look like human beings, are dangerous false brothers.

Paul.
-People can even feel lonelier when they hear the lament of the birds they have put in a cage.

John.
-In our new society, there will be no more imprisoned birds.

Paul.
-Peter, I will free your orange trees...

John.
-You will do so but the most important thing will be to build a society where there will be no more lonely people.

Chapter 10:

This is our home.

Two years have passed and the Earth is still there. The spinning top rotates on its axis; it dances with the sun describing vertiginous ellipses. It is blue but this blue is not as beautiful as the colour they saw on Empycrist II... Empycrist was like a dream and here it is a rather sad reality. They are in the cockpit. They have fastened their seatbelt. They are looking at the blue sphere. They do not really want to know what they are going to find, for they already know it!

John.
-Back home!

The four of them sighing and looking at one another.
-Yes...

John.
-Before we land, I want to tell you that whatever we find, I will do everything possible to make it work.

Barbara.
-It will be difficult for us to cope with our memories.

Jenny.
-If life conditions are unbearable, we can take the survivors with us and go back to Empycrist.

Barbara.
-We don't want to go back there.

John.
-No we don't.

Barbara.
-We don't want to flee from ourselves. We must face our nature. It is time to gather stones together and build something that will last forever.

Paul.
-But the faithful have died.

Barbara.
-No, we are the faithful.

Paul.
-Anyway, the Romans have died.

Barbara.
-No, the Romans are still alive.

John.
-Paul, we are also the Romans: we can't help it!

Peter.
-I hope the level of radiation will not be too high.

Jenny.
-I hope the water won't be polluted.

Barbara.
-I hope we will find people, good people.

Jenny.

-I guess they will understand that what they did was not the solution. After a war, there is always less madness in the souls of the survivors.

Peter.
-What's this?

John.
-I don't know but... the temperature is rising!

Jenny.
-What does the computer say?

John.
-Jenny, I have disabled the speakers!

Jenny.
-Well, what does it indicate?

John.
-Who cares? We don't need artificial intelligence anymore. I am in manual mode. I'm going to land this can.

Barbara.
-What's that?

John.
-A big noise.

Paul.
-And a violent impact too! Don't tell me it's a meteorite again!

John.
-I am not telling you Paul!

Paul.
-Is it a meteorite?

John.
-A kind of! I am afraid the landing is going to be quite difficult.

Peter.
-John, we are going too fast.

John.
-I haven't got enough power to decrease the velocity sufficiently. **Emergency landing. Heads down!**

Paul.
-Not that again!

Barbara.
-Life always repeats itself!

Peter.
-My trees!

Barbara.
-I believe in you John!

John.
-Thank you Barbara. **Touchdown!**

...

John.
-Welcome home!

Barbara.
-Thank you John!

<pre>
        *
   *   *
        *
</pre>

   The spacecraft has landed next to a lake. Everything is quiet. They undo their seatbelt. Nobody is wounded and there is no major damage. The orange trees, in the greenhouse, have lost their white blossoms. John opens the door. They walk towards the lake. The Geiger counter doesn't show high levels of radiation. They remove their helmet. There is an intoxicating fragrance in the air. It is the scent of millions of daffodils and billions of peonies! The honeybees fly; the birds sing. Some frogs, two squirrels and a deer look at them. It's impossible! They seat down. John touches the water, and a frog too: it jumps into the lake. Everything is real. He smiles; the others cry. John, it belongs to you; do you know that? Look over there: there is a tree that shivers.

John.
-Man, come here.

Man.

-Who are you?

John.
-I am John. And you, who are you?

Man.
-I am me.

John.
-Where are we?

Man.
-In a place where it is possible to live.

John.
-What happened?

Man.
-They killed one another.

John.
-Why?

Man.
-Because they didn't know themselves; therefore, they were afraid of the others and devoured what was the reflection of their ignorance.

John.
-Are they all dead?

Man.
-Yes, for ignorance exterminates.

John.

-Man, does it mean that mankind has disappeared? Does it mean I am dead? Was it the aim of the universe?

Man.
-It wasn't. The aim of the universe was you. With your willpower you were able to choose your own destiny.

John.
-And I have chosen to die!

Man.
-Not you: the monsters have chosen to die.

John.
-Man…

Man.
-Yes John.

John.
-Who am I?

Man.
-You are the best part of the universe. You are the chef d'oeuvre of the mind that has created everything. John, you are a human being.

John speaking to himself.
-What must I do?

Man.
-Be yourself, John, and think.

Paul.
-What can we do if everybody is dead?

Jenny speaking to herself.
-What a waste!

Peter.
-Are you sure there are no other survivors?

Barbara.
-There are other survivors. The people who died were the monsters. The wise men and women survived.

Peter.
-Man, who are you actually?

Barbara.
-The best part of the universe: a man blessed with reason and humanity. He is the aim of everything, for he is the measure of nothing. He is the one who can only be compared to himself and, in the end, he makes his essence visible through his completeness. Man, let me take your hand and take you to the land of my human geometry.

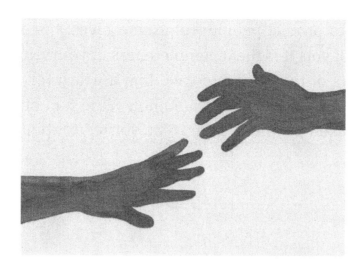

                *

     *   *

        *

On that day, the sun was shining and the sky was bluer than the bluest blue. Barbara held the hand of this man. He took them to a village where there were quite a few inhabitants. Peter planted all his trees on the shore of the lake. Barbara freed the chimpanzees; John burned the spaceship; Jenny deleted the memories of her computer; Paul tried to forget the past: people of good will don't need history books to tell them what to do, for their future relies on their nature.

Then, came the spring of a year I will remember forever. They all took the seeds Peter had preciously kept in hundreds of small boxes, and they sowed... Nature is a brilliant painter... Some months later, the seeds gave birth to a gigantic mosaic of colours, a sea of flowers. I remember the poppies; I love poppies. I remember the sweet peas. People of good will can turn the driest deserts into promised lands. The year after, Peter's fruits trees bloomed and fructified: they ate apricots and tangerines. Wise people always plant trees even though they are not certain they will taste the fruits of their labor. Little by little, they gathered stones together and they built. They built dams, canals, roads, bridges and houses. They rebuilt Jericho! However, this time, they forgot the high walls around.

They preferred to protect people from themselves: the enemy is not the human in front of you, it is the incompleteness of yourself. Therefore, they clipped the claws of the tiger and gave him a heart, for they gave him a mind. How did they achieve what a million years had not achieved? It is simple, they enabled people to think. Man started to think, and he started to create.

In the beginning, unique and eternal, there was the mind that conceives. Then, came the Age of Lead, a time of darkness, cruelty and sorrow; but man decided to become a creature that thinks...

By the way, can you

think?

92245397R00168